A NIGHT
OF ERRORS

A NIGHT
OF ERRORS

Michael Innes

PERENNIAL LIBRARY

Harper & Row, Publishers, New York
Cambridge, Grand Rapids, Philadelphia, St. Louis,
San Francisco, London, Singapore, Sydney, Tokyo

A hardcover edition of this book was published in 1947 by Dodd, Mead and Company. It is reprinted by arrangement with Dodd, Mead and Company.

First PERENNIAL LIBRARY edition published 1989.

Library of Congress Cataloging-in-Publication Data

Innes, Michael, 1906–
  A night of errors.

  I. Title.
PR6037.T466N5   1989   823'.912   88-45963
ISBN 0-06-080877-2

89 90 91 92 93 WB/OPM 10 9 8 7 6 5 4 3 2 1

Prologue

The Dromios came to England at the end of the sixteenth century, the precise date being probably 1592. There is no certainty on where they came from—Ephesus and Syracuse have both been suggested—but historians of the family admit that they seem to have been persons somewhat below the middle station of life, if not of actually servile condition. In England, however, they prospered, and already in the reign of James I were importing wines in a large way. On the strength of this they married first into the London citizenry—the Frugals, the Hoards and the Moneytraps—then into the landed gentry—the Mammons, the Overreaches, the Clumseys and the Greedys—and finally into the fringes of the aristocracy itself—the Nolands, the Littleworths, the Rakes, the Foppingtons and the Whorehounds.

In thus uniting to Levantine subtlety and enterprise so many of the solid English virtues the Dromio family gave itself an excellent start. But its ability to do something more than keep its head above water during the succeeding centuries it owed to another hereditary factor. Women who married Dromios found themselves more than commonly likely to have twins—and this not at the end of the child-bearing period but at its beginning. Here was a great political convenience. During the Civil Wars there was a Dromio Roundhead and a Dromio Cavalier of virtually indistinguishable presence and authority. And when party government was established the reigning Dromio and his twin would commonly be found eyeing each other with severity or even bellicosity across the Treasury and Opposition front benches. To be presented at one birth with both a little Liberal and a little Conservative is a blessing for which any man of property may give Lucina, goddess of labor, thanks. Whatever party ruled, there was generally a Dromio in some modest corner of the Ministry, ready to make interest for the family.

Towards the close of the eighteenth century the Dromios added to their trade in wine an equally lucrative traffic in Oriental rugs. On the strength of this, and some thirty years later, the then reigning Dromio was able to donate and subscribe himself into a baronetcy—a transaction prompting a wit of the time to remark that although carpet-knights were common enough carpet-baronets were something new.

But this Dromio, Sir Ferdinand, achieved another innovation, and one which proved disastrous in its results.

By now the Dromios were immemorially English. If the strongly marked features of the men folk were still discernibly those that looked out of family portraits painted in the time of the Commonwealth yet centuries of English weather and generations of English brides had bred into the family a dominant complexion which was Saxon enough. Sir Ferdinand, as if assured of the adequacy which this protective coloring had achieved, allowed himself the indulgence of marrying after a different fashion. His bride was the daughter of a Mr Eugenides, a Smyrna merchant who had made a fortune out of currants—and a fortune amply sufficient (so Sir Ferdinand thought) to compensate for any lack of breeding that the family might show. But breeding (in the more substantial sense) proved to be Lady Dromio's strong point. Some ten months after her marriage she presented Sir Ferdinand not with the traditional Dromio twins but with Dromio triplets. So contrary to all precedent did this odd performance seem that her husband was at first incredulous and sternly bade the nurse go back and count again. But no mistake had been made. It was almost as if Nature, prescient in the political as well as biological sphere, was determined that the Dromios should now have not a little Liberal and a little Conservative only but a little Socialist as well.

And Nature is much given to forming habits; if it were otherwise scientists would not be able to deal in what they call Natural Laws. With the Dromios the triplet habit supplanted the twin habit, and this, far from being beneficent, had calamitous results.

Whereas the twins had always worked together hand-in-glove the triplets invariably quarrelled. They quarrelled over bibs and tuckers, peg-tops and puppies, ponies, cronies and the less virtuous of the village girls. They quarrelled over chloroform and the

Corn Laws and the Chamberlains, over the Derby and the Grand National and the Disestablishing of the Church of Wales. But above all they quarrelled over carpets and wines, pitching at one another in venomous dispute the great names of Yquem and Lafite, Peyraguey and Rauzan-Gassies, Sehna and Tabriz, Bokhara, Savast and Kashmir.

The scandal of all this gradually spread abroad and both the commercial and the social world began to view the Dromios somewhat askance. As the prosaic number *Two* had seen the family fortune rise so now the mystical number *Three* bade fair to preside over its fall. Despite the spread of whisky and the ubiquity of beer the English drank as much wine as before, despite the horrid invention of linoleum and the vogue of parquetry they trod as heavily as ever on the products of Benares and Turquestan. But it seemed that nothing of this could save the Dromios from the decline which waits upon a divided house. And when round about the beginning of the twentieth century Sir Romeo Dromio married he prayed for nothing more devoutly than an end to all family tradition and the gift of an only son followed by a quiet nurseyful of girls. But the legacy of Miss Eugenides was with the family still and some hours after Lady Dromio was taken in labor the now customary news was brought to Sir Romeo in his study. Whereupon Sir Romeo, whose temper had suffered much through thirty years of association with intolerable triplet brothers, ran upstairs in a distraction—so family legend had it—and fell to tossing his three newly born sons about the room like tennis-balls. But the infants were none the worse, having inherited from their remoter ancestors a virtual invulnerability to drubbing. And their father, being presently persuaded of the impropriety of his proceeding, retired again to his study to consider the situation with whatever calm he could command.

This was the study in which was to take place the fatality which made the Dromios notorious. Had Sir Romeo, hard upon becoming so abundantly a father, not thus sat down to brood and to plan, had he accepted a position in the creating of which he had played if a brief yet a decidedly seminal part, then those shocking events which must still linger in the public mind would not have taken place, and the necessity of the present painful and candid narrative would have been obviated. And this should serve as a warning to merchants when closeted in their studies to confine themselves to calculating percentages and casting accounts, since their education has seldom equipped them to deal skilfully in intricate emotional problems. And particularly should they eschew trafficking in futures—unless indeed it be those of corn and cotton upon an Exchange.

To Sir Romeo it appeared evident that his forebears, from the rash Sir Ferdinand onwards, had merely tinkered with the disruptive legacy of Miss Eugenides. If his own remaining years were to pass in moderate tranquillity, if his heir was to be unharassed by fraternal cares, if the bouquet of the Dromio wines and the pile of the Dromio carpets were to regain that excellence which would come only from the superintendence of a eupeptic palate and untroubled eye, then it was essential that the late decisive action of Lady Dromio should be met by countermeasures of a like decisiveness.

To take two of the triplets and expose them upon the rooftop, although legitimate in both Syracuse and Ephesus a long time ago, would not be consonant with the domestic manners of the country in which the Dromios had now sojourned for some centuries. To give the younger boys their breeding at a distance would be reasonable and assuredly not criminal, but to Sir Romeo in his present excited state this in itself seemed a measure insufficiently permanent in its effects. For even if (what would come uncommonly expensive) an adequate provision were made for establishing the growing lads in whatever counts as a respectable station of life in Oregon or New South Wales it was almost certain that sooner or later they would come home to roost beneath the ancestral rooftree of Sherris Hall. And the thought of this Sir Romeo could by no means abide. Very possibly he himself would be gone. But this consideration, which would surely have afforded solace to a man not under the influence of a fixed idea, only agitated Sir Romeo the more. That the eldest of the three sons now born to him might so far modify recent family history as adequately to cope with such a family reunion never entered his head. For his thought now based itself upon a single irrational postulate: the disastrous triplet situation must not continue through another generation.

Increasingly in the grip of this persuasion, Sir Romeo paced his study, taking occasional swipes at any breakable object within reach. But no inspiration came—nothing in fact was wafted to him but a faint wailing from the nursery wing. Sir Romeo seized a stick, strode through a French window, gave himself the mild satisfaction of knocking down the gardener's boy on the terrace, and strode across the park, occasionally cursing the browsing sheep and cattle in a manner altogether unusual among the landed gentry. It was only when he reached the boundary of his demesne that the gardener's boy (who had followed in the inchoate hope of retaliating with some sudden privy injury to his employer's person) perceived him to grow suddenly composed. Sir Romeo returned to the house meditatively and without giving so much as a single thwack to the lowing kine. His bearing was that of a man to whom some great conception has come—a conception however which must be filled in with much meticulous detail.

Two days later the inhabitants of Sherris Magna were horrified to hear that a disastrous fire had broken out at Sherris Hall. The nursery wing was totally destroyed. Thanks to the courage of his father (who was early on the scene) the eldest of the triplets, Oliver, had been saved, but his brothers, Jaques and Orlando, had both perished. Such a calamity evoked the widest sympathy, and when they buried them the little port had seldom seen a costlier funeral.

It was otherwise with the funeral of Sir Romeo Dromio himself three months later. Unobtrusiveness is the right note to strike in the obsequies of a baronet who has died mad.

1

"Lucy," said Lady Dromio, "can you see the little silver bell?"

There was a lot of silver on the tea-table; nevertheless Lucy did not trouble to survey it, or to take her eyes from the single fleecy cloud sailing past almost directly overhead.

"No, mama. Swindle has fogotten it."

"How very vexatious." Lady Dromio, who had been peering despondently into an empty hot-water jug, glanced with equal despondence over the spreading lawns by which she was surrounded. The grass, she was thinking, was in something worse than indifferent order, and the motor-mower with which a sulky youth struggled in a distant corner must be some twenty years out of date. "How very vexing," Lady Dromio repeated.

"Yes, mama. But the situation is a familiar one."

"Familiar, child?" From under her white hair the

faded blue eyes of Lady Dromio expressed a large, vague surprise.

"Swindle, I think, has a horror of the ringing bell. He avoids it. One day he will undoubtedly try to avoid the clangor of the angel's trumpet too."

"Lucy, dear, what odd, clever things you say." Lady Dromio's tone was placid, but there was a remorselessness in the way she flicked open and shut the lid of the hot-water jug. The sound had no power over the absent Swindle, gently respiring in a summer day's slumber in his distant pantry. But it brought Lucy to her feet—a tall, dark girl in her early thirties, at once lackadaisical and restless. Her movement was received by Lady Dromio as if it was something entirely unexpected.

"Well, dear, if you would like to fetch some that will be very nice."

Lucy compressed her lips, held out her hand for the hot-water jug and departed across the lawn. Lady Dromio watched her go, turned to scrutinise her tea-table, watched again. Across the hot lawn Lucy was almost out of earshot. Lady Dromio called; she picked up and waved an empty cream-jug.

Lucy turned obediently back.

Lucy Dromio (for she was called that) was Lady Dromio's experiment, an experiment made some thirty years before. The Reverend Mr Greengrave, now advancing up the drive to pay a call, and observing the girl as she trailed towards the house, reflected that she was an abandoned experiment. Most experiments were that, of course, after thirty years. Was she an abandoned girl? Mr Greengrave, who was professionally obliged to weigh questions of this sort, shook his head doubtfully. He knew very little about Lucy despite an acquaintance stretching back over a considerable period. She was secretive. But then, for that matter, so was Lady Dromio, despite her open, amiable air. After all, was not Lucy perhaps Lady Dromio's experiment still—or rather a sort of private laboratory for the carrying out of tiny, daily vivisections? This was an uncharitable thought. But Mr Greengrave was aware that one has to do a lot of uncharitable thinking if one is to get people clear. And until one does that how can one help them?

What sort of a woman had Lady Dromio been before Mr Greengrave's time as incumbent of Sherris Parva? Pausing by a tulip tree and mopping his brow (for he was a shy man who had often thus to brace himself before plunging into parochial duties), the vicar reviewed what he knew of that early time. The lady now waiting placidly for her cream and hot water was the widow of Sir Romeo Dromio. Her married life had early ended in tragedy. Two of her children had died in a horrible disaster and not long afterwards her husband had died also—mad, it was said, and talking strangely. Sir Romeo, it seemed, had been a wayward and violent man, brooding over sundry reverses and misfortunes which the family had suffered over several generations. Through half a dozen parishes queer tales were still told of him. If some of these were true it must be judged that Lady Dromio had got off lightly, even at the cost of widowhood and the difficult care of a single surviving son. But these legendary tales were already hopelessly confused with popular memories of other and earlier Dromios noted for this or that sultry eccentricity. Not a comfortable family, had been Mr Greengrave's summary. He had never been prompted to sift or analyse chronicles so patently barren of edification.

But he knew that Lady Dromio had to all seeming taken everything quietly. The tablet she had erected to her husband's memory in Mr Greengrave's church was quiet. Any reference she ever made to him was quiet to the extent of, as it were, a metaphorical inaudibility. And she had done nothing in haste. When her son was eight years old, and having maturely rejected, maybe, any thought of second marriage, Lady Dromio had adopted the infant girl who was now Lucy Dromio. Perhaps she judged that a sister might ameliorate the manners of her son; perhaps she merely obeyed an inadequately satisfied maternal instinct. But all that was long ago. And, whatever the bill, Mr Greengrave doubted whether Lucy had filled it. Of necessity she must have been a pig in a poke, her virtues and vices unfolding from an unknown stock. And almost certainly she abundantly if covertly possessed something that had not been desired. Was it passion, or intelligence, or independence? Mr Greengrave did not know. Such ignorance about a parishioner disturbed him. Could the girl, he wondered, be drawn out? Perhaps now was a favourable time to gain her confidence, since her foster-brother was abroad and the atmosphere at Sherris Hall something less oppressive as a result.

Not, Mr Greengrave reflected, that Sir Oliver could be called a dominant personality. Weak, vain, sensitive, easily depressed: the master of Sherris was not one to a brief view of whom distance lent any enchantment. Yet (and this the confidential annals of the parish abundantly attested) he was markedly at-

11

tractive to women. How frequently do concrete human relationships run counter to expectation and rule! Mr Greengrave, to whom musings of this sort came more easily than that blending of tea-table talk with faint overtones of spiritual advice which is the parish priest's task, turned left and took a procrastinating route round the lily pond.

"One wonders," said Lucy, setting down the jugs, "if something might be done about Swindle."

"Done, dear?"

"He was actually asleep. It's like living at Dingley Dell with the Fat Boy."

"But Swindle is extremely thin."

"He certainly has a lean and hungry look. And possibly Dickens was wrong. If fat men sleep at night there may be inference that it is thin ones who are inclined to sleep during the day. But it would be curious if Shakespeare threw any light on Swindle."

Lady Dromio put down the teapot. "Shakespeare-" she said. "Well, that reminds me. I seem to have mislaid my novel. Such an interesting and unusual novel, Lucy, about a lot of people in a big hotel. Do you know, I think I must have left it in the drawing-room?"

"It is no matter, mama. For Mr Greengrave is about to call. Were he a resolute man he would be with us now. Look beyond the lily pond."

"Well, that is very nice. He will bring us a breath of the great world."

"That's doubtless."

Lady Dromio patted her well-ordered hair. "But it will mean more sandwiches, dear. And surely there must be another cake?"

Lucy rose. "This time," she said with resolution, "I shall waken Swindle."

"I think it will be better to wait until Oliver gets home."

"But that my be months. We can't have Swindle turned into a Rip van Winkle."

"No, dear—certainly not. I merely mean that about things in general we had better wait until Oliver gets home."

"Which, I hope, will be soon." Mr Greengrave, who usually made his eventual entry with a plunge, spoke heartily as he took Lady Dromio's hand. "It will be a pleasure to hear him read the lessons again."

Lady Dromio produced a welcoming smile and a non-committal noise. Very possibly she doubted the propriety of describing as a pleasure anything that transacted itself within the walls of a church. "Lucy," she said, "if you could just ask Cook—"

"Yes, mama. Sandwiches and a caraway cake and a cup and saucer."

Lady Dromio watched her adopted daughter trail across the lawn once more. "Dear, dutiful girl," she said.

"Yes, indeed." But because this had been insincere Mr Greengrave in penance resolutely added: "It is to be hoped that she will marry."

"So it is!" Lady Dromio spoke as if concurring in a novel and surprising thought. "But it is to be feared that she will not."

It occurred to Mr Greengrave that sometimes, and with an odd effect, the elder lady fell into the clipped and mannered speech of the younger. He felt that this pointed to Lucy's possessing the stronger will. Of

13

course a stranger would take Lady Dromio to possess no will at all—but that would be a mistake. Aloud Mr Greengrave conventionally said: "But so attractive a girl—and so advantageously placed in the county."

Lady Dromio received this old-world civility with a bow and at the same time turned in her garden chair. Perhaps she was looking for Lucy and the sandwiches, but the motion enabled her to make a critical inspection of Sherris Hall. The house was imposing enough and doubtless estimable among surrounding seats. Equally evidently it was in a state of some disrepair. Mr Greengrave, who had turned also, felt himself awkwardly involved with his hostess in a joint contemplation of this disagreeable fact. It was an attempt to suggest that he was aware only of the more permanent aspects of the building that prompted his next remark.

"How sure they were of their proportions in those days! The whole effect has always seemed to me a delight to the eye. And yet I have sometimes wondered about that wing where the billiard-room and gun-room are. Had they carried it up another storey—"

"But they did. I got the trustees to take it down. Those were the nurseries, you know, that were destroyed by fire. I am so sorry that Lucy is being rather a long time with your cup. You will be thirsty, dear Mr Greengrave, after walking across on this warm afternoon."

Mr Greengrave coughed. Having unwittingly led the conversation to painful memories he felt it incumbent upon him not to retreat upon small talk. "Your great sorrow," he said, "was before my time here. But I have often thought of it."

"So have I. I have been puzzled over it for years."

Mr Greengrave considered this doubtfully. "Yes," he said with caution; "the ways of Providence are often inscrutable indeed."

"Not over what happened, for that was always fairly clear to me. But over what I should have done. I was very young and I ended by doing nothing, apart from having that wing rebuilt as you see it now. I waited for Oliver to grow up." Lady Dromio sighed heavily. "But has he grown up? It is hard to say."

Mr Greengrave felt somewhat out of his depth. The afternoon was drowsy; the effect of his visitation was perhaps soporific; Lady Dromio seemed almost like one speaking in sleep. "I am sure," he said politely, "that Sir Oliver must be a great support."

"Things should be settled when they turn up. Otherwise there is uncertainty and suspense, and new problems arise before one has at all made up one's mind about the old. Oliver has a great many problems now—business problems for which he is not perhaps very fitted by temperament. Of course my brother-in-law is a help."

"Mr Sebastian Dromio?"

"Yes. My father-in-law had three sons, of whom Sebastian is the only survivor. He did not get on at all well with my husband, I am sorry to say, but after —but subsequently he was very helpful indeed. Perhaps you have never met him? He is coming down to visit us this evening. But here is Lucy with the supplies we have been waiting for." Lady Dromio reached out a hand for the caraway cake. "Lucy, have they remembered about Sebastian's room?"

"Yes, mama. Everything is being done to placate him and assuage."

Mr Greengrave felt that this called for a jolly laugh. "And is your uncle," he asked, "so formidable a man?"

"He will be very cross because Oliver is not yet back. His absence was to have been for not nearly so long."

"Then let us trust that Sir Oliver is enjoying himself." And Mr Greengrave turned to Lady Dromio. "Your latest news of him is good, I hope?"

With some deliberation Lady Dromio cut the cake. "Oliver," she said, "always enjoys himself abroad."

"Even on a business trip?"

Lucy advanced the plate of sandwiches. "We cannot positively say that it is that."

"Oliver's trip to America is certainly prompted by business considerations." Lady Dromio spoke as if this were a sort of moral extenuation for visiting so doubtful a country. "Although he is, of course, at the same time staying with friends."

"Or so we believe." Lucy took a sandwich herself. "Actually, we haven't heard for nearly—"

"Lucy, dear, do you know that there is neither salt nor pepper in these? How careless everybody has become."

"It is the influence of Swindle's slumbers, mama. But Oliver, at least, is not being careless. Indeed, he is being very prudent, is he not?"

"I hope he will always be that."

There was an awkward pause. Mr Greengrave, although hardened to hovering on the edge of family enigmas, began to wonder when he could take his leave. Between these two ladies not much had passed—but, in what had, more was meant than met the ear. And why did the protracted absence of Sir Oliver abroad mean that he was being very prudent? Was he keeping out of the way of something? What was the difference between a business trip and a trip prompted by business considerations? Why must Sebastian Dromio be placated and assuaged? And why had Lady Dromio, commonly so reticent, allowed herself those mysterious rambling sentences about the past? Why should she have been puzzled for years?

On all these questions, thought Mr Greengrave, the oracles are dumb. And as for the project of drawing out Miss Dromio—well, that had got nowhere. A blameless and pastoral project, while being at the same time humanly intriguing. Perhaps it might yet be possible...

Mr Greengrave rose. "How unfortunate," he said, "that I have calls yet to make in the village. But since the afternoon is so fine perhaps Miss Dromio..?"

"Yes, indeed." Lucy spoke with decision. "I will take the letters. That lawn-mower has made William so sulky that he would be quite certain to forget on purpose. Have you anything more to post, mama?"

"No!" Lady Dromio uttered the word with unexpected vigour. "I think the post is really a dangerous institution. It invites one to rash communications. I have sometimes written letters that I very much wanted to recall."

There was no doubt that the old lady was behaving a trifle oddly. Mr Greengrave could see that Lucy, who knew her well, was looking perplexed.

"Yes, to be sure." The vicar found himself making random conversation while Lucy departed for the letters. "Or at least the penny or twopenny-halfpenny post has destroyed one of the most delightful English literary forms. For who will treat seriously as a work of art something that one simply drops into a red box at the end of a lane? And consider, too, the speed of transmission. In the days of mail-coaches and packet-boats a letter had time to acquire patina on its journey. When Horace Walpole wrote to his friend Mann in Florence—"

"Of course—how very interesting." Lady Dromio, as she made this scarcely civil interruption, once more fell to flicking the lid of the hot-water jug. "But tell me—how long does the air-mail take to America?"

"From here in the village? I am afraid I scarcely know. Not more, I should imagine, than two or three days."

"I wish—" Lady Dromio checked herself. "But here is Lucy and she will be the better of a walk. Recently she has been rather restless, dear child."

To Mr Greengrave's ear the tone of this was not affectionate. At present the two ladies must be living rather a solitary life. Ought he to recommend prayer, some serious and improving book, a tennis party? Might he even venture to suggest an informal dance? And was he justified in making off with Lucy, who was attractive, after rather a perfunctory call upon Lady Dromio, who was difficult? With these questions unresolved, he found himself walking down the drive. And Lucy spoke. "This," she said, "is a really ghastly hole."

Mr Greengrave was shocked. "Good gracious," he said lightly, "we all feel like that about Sherris Parva!

There should be a law giving us a long holiday at least twice a year."

"I mean Sherris Hall. Home."

"I think young people often feel like that about home from time to time."

"I'm not young. I'm over thirty." She turned her head and regarded him soberly. "Intellectually my life is completely futile. Artistically it is null. I do not subserve even the simplest biological purposes."

A large part of Mr Greengrave wished that this walk had not taken place. But another part of him was encouraged. For here, at least, was a job—a hitherto elusive sheep suddenly revealed as in decidedly poor fleece. The vicar, as an honest shepherd, decided that a thoroughly drastic dipping was needed at once. "Of course," he said, "we all get out of spirits from time to time. But if you set up in a settled discontented way your chances of ever serving simple biological purposes are quite remote. A man has no use for a sulky wife. Nor, for that matter, has God for a sulky creature."

Lucy had stopped in her tracks. "Mr Greengrave," she cried, "I didn't think you could be so horrid!"

"And now, my dear, you are being quite childish. And what is wrong with Sherris Hall, anyway?"

"Wrong! Swindle is always asleep and mama—for I call her so—is always awake. When it gets to half-past eleven and we are still at piquet I could scream aloud. Or rather I could do something much more effective. I could take a brand to the whole place."

"Take a what?"

"A fire-brand, Mr Greengrave. And raze the whole place to the ground this time. Not just an inconsiderable nursery wing."

For some seconds the vicar was silent. "Lucy," he said presently, "think of what you say. In that fire two infant children perished—and you were in a sense brought in to fill the empty place in Lady Dromio's affections. And in Oliver's, I suppose."

"No doubt I was." Lucy Dromio suddenly flushed darkly. "But I shall never forgive that fire. It brought me here."

"And where should you have been brought in life without it?"

"I don't know; I have no idea. I know nothing of my parentage. I know only that my adoption brought me to—to an impasse. I hate . . . I hate Sherris and all it stands for."

Mr Greengrave looked at her. "No," he said slowly; "no, it isn't true."

And Lucy shuddered. "Love turns to hate if it isn't let get anywhere. I was prepared to do a lot of loving. But the place has no use for me, really. I'm an outsider, after all. And I ought to have got outside—and right away—as soon as I was old enough to recognise that it was no go. Of course what you say is quite true. It's filthy and weak to fall into a chronic discontented way. But there it is."

Mr Greengrave considered. "But isn't this," he asked, "just a phase? Your brother is away—"

"Oliver is not my brother and I hate to hear him called so."

"I see." Mr Greengrave thought this information worth meditating. "Sir Oliver is away and you and Lady Dromio are much alone. That may well generate little frictions. And, indeed, I seem to sense some quality of suspense—"

"There's that, all right." Lucy spoke grimly.

"Everything is in a bad way, you know. The firm is in difficulties and the investments are shaky—that sort of thing. I think I know what Oliver is up to in America, and a certain amount of anxiety is natural."

"Am I right in thinking that for some time there has been an absence of news?"

"You certainly are. We can't understand it. Oliver is usually not a bad correspondent in a non-committal way."

"Then here is an explanation of much of the sense of strain which has been upsetting you, my dear." Mr Greengrave spoke confidently. "It is natural that Lady Dromio should feel anxiety. She is a most affectionate mother."

Lucy laughed and—all the more because it was unforced and natural—the laughter grated on her pastor's ear. "Really, Mr Greengrave, it is mama you should have picked on for a walk full of cosy confidences. You might have begun to learn the elements. Why ever should you suppose her affectionate?"

Again the vicar was shocked—as also rather nonplussed. A substantial majority of mothers are on the whole affectionately disposed to their offspring. Lady Dromio's manner was affectionate. His judgment had been founded on nothing beyond this.

"She can't forgive him, you know." Lucy tipped her letters into the pillar-box as she said this, and turned to look the vicar straight in the eyes.

"But whatever for?" Oliver, Mr Greengrave recalled, had not as a young man been of unblemished moral character, but he had always supposed Lady Dromio to bear if anything too broad a mind in matters of that sort.

Lucy raised her eyebrows. "Well, what is it that a

21

mother can't forgive her son? That son's father, I suppose."

Very seriously, Mr Greengrave shook his head. "My dear, gobbets of the new psychology do none of us any good. It is an infant science, full of half-truths dangerous to our faith and happiness. After that fatal fire nothing was left to Lady Dromio but this one baby son. She must have been devoted to him."

"Not a bit of it. She showed how she felt about her Dromio son by first waiting to have a good look at him and then adopting a non-Dromio daughter. And what I say isn't just a gobbet from an infant science. You'll find it in your own text-book as well, Mr Greengrave."

"My text-book?"

"Yes. The sins of the fathers shall be visited upon their children to the—"

"Lucy, this is bad—very bad, indeed. We know nothing about Sir Romeo's sins."

"Don't we know that he died quite mad because of something dreadful he had done?"

"We know that rural communities are always full of evil gossip." Mr Greengrave raised his stick and pointed down the little village street before them. "You see those cottages—so picturesque, so peaceful, so suggestive of the comfortableness of calendars and Christmas cards? There is scarcely one about which some foul story is not current among its neighbours. And about the gentry they have all sorts of extraordinary beliefs. But our own minds surely we should keep clear of such stuff."

The vicar's brow had darkened as he spoke and his words had come with unusual energy. Lucy seemed impressed and anxious to make herself understood.

"You think me cynical and ungrateful. It all isn't easy to explain. But this waiting for Oliver during the past few weeks is only an intensification of something that has been going on for years. There is a queer perpetual expectation about mama, and it spreads to Oliver and myself without our at all understanding it. We're like Mr Micawber—always expecting something to turn up. Not Dickens's cheerful Mr Micawber, of course. If you can imagine a Micawber invented by Chekhov and given touches by Dostoevsky—"

Mr Greengrave frowned; he disapproved of serious conversation being given these literary embellishments. "Beneath Lady Dromio's placidity," he said, "I have more than once felt something of the sort. I confess that I have hoped that it might be a scarcely recognised craving for deeper spiritual experience."

"Well, it isn't just that she became very early a widow and obscurely feels that she has always been cheated of something." Lucy delivered this by way of concession. "Rather it has been a constant muted expectation of some definite event, as of somebody coming in at the door or—or of a skeleton coming out of a cupboard. I have always had the feeling that I was brought in just to pass the time until something happened—and that I fell down on the job. Mama stroked my little curls in a very becoming way and we were the admiration of visitors. But her eyes were on that cupboard all the time. They are on it still. And I almost believe that she has lately done something to—well, to make the door give a preliminary creak."

"Lucy, my dear, this is mere mystery-mongering." But the vicar's voice lacked confidence. "We must find better things to think about."

"I don't agree. If one could think—but can one?—this would be a very useful thing to think about. It ought to be cleared up. I should be less of a mess—more of a credit to you as a parishioner, Mr Greengrave—if it were got out into the open. And I think it would help Oliver. Won't you try?"

"Try, Lucy?" The vicar was startled.

"You like finding out about people. I can see that."

"I don't at all like doing anything of the sort. It is apt to seem officious and impertinent, even in a priest."

"Yes, I know that too. You find personal relationships rather a trial. But you happen to have the sort of brain that does eventually piece people together and see what a thing is all about."

Mr Greengrave laughed. "You seem already to know much more about me than I can ever hope to learn about you—let alone about this rather hypothetical skeleton in Lady Dromio's cupboard. But of course if I could help it would be my duty to do so. And I should be very pleased to help you, my dear. I am afraid I spoke to you rather crudely at the beginning of our walk."

"Not a bit of it." Lucy sighed. "Well, I hardly suppose you can come back to the Hall now and begin turning out the cupboards straight away. Still"—her voice took on a resigned tone—"there's plenty of time. We take our tempo from Swindle, I think. There's always oceans of time with the Dromios."

But in this, as it happened, Lucy was mistaken.

2

To talk in one's sleep is common enough, and only occasionally dangerous. To walk in one's sleep is a frequent vagary, much exploited by sensational writers long before Wilkie Collins wrote *The Moonstone*. To drink in one's sleep is an accomplishment altogether more unusual, and one the possibilities of which fiction has left unexplored. Swindle, the ancient butler at Sherris, was said to do all three of these things.

Swindle was sleeping now. A cheerful fire burnt in his sanctum; every now and then it was noiselessly replenished by one of the two able-bodied young men whom Swindle kept in thrall. Before this the feet of Swindle, unprofessionally encased in felt slippers, comfortably toasted. His snowy head reposed upon a handsome cushion which Lady Dromio had for some time missed from her favourite corner of the drawingroom. Beside him was a decanter and a glass of port. From this, and without calling upon the unnecessary intervention of the conscious mind, Swindle recruited himself as he slept.

Port wine has long since ceased to be regarded as a normal before-dinner drink. But Swindle—apart from the half-pint of sherry which he was used to consume after his morning stroll in the park—drank nothing else, and this for a curious reason. Fifty years ago it had been discovered that of all those who served the then vast and ramifying Dromio interests it was Sir Romeo's butler who had the most exact and finely discriminating palate for wines. As the years passed, and Swindle's experience and virtuosity grew, he had become increasingly without challenge the firm's final court of appeal, being often whirled away to pronounce, before an anxious board of directors, a verdict upon the Beaune of Les Fèves, Les Grèves, or Le Clos de la Mousse. And Swindle, holding to the persuasion that if one is to taste wines one must certainly not acquire the habit of *drinking* them, confined himself to the exports of Jerez and Oporto. It is possible that had Swindle regularly allowed himself recourse to the mollifying and mundifying influences of one of the *grands crus classés* his character would have resisted that corruption which —the historian tells us—all power brings. As it was, Swindle's was not an amiable disposition. By pride or covetousness he was not notably distinguished. But of the five remaining Deadly Sins he was a very sufficient licentiate of four, while to the fifth it was believed that he had said good-bye only round about his eightieth birthday. And chiefly Sloth and Ire struggled for the masterhand within him. If Lucy Dromio for her own convenience wished his slumbers shorter the menials subordinate to him heartily wished them coterminous with the clock.

Swindle slept. And Sherris Hall, like some palace appropriately disposed round its Sleeping Beauty, slept too. Doves cooed behind the stables; faintly from woods beyond came the caw of rooks; in the rose garden the last belated bees were making their rounds. Cobweb and dead leaves possessed the raquet-court; the billiard-table showed white and shrouded like some gigantic mortuary slab; in the kitchens culinary preparations proceeded on the unambitious level and restricted scale proper to a masterless house. But it was over Sir Oliver's study, a handsome room giving on the west terrace, that the heaviest sense of suspended animation hung. Dust and soot were gathering on the elaborately laid fire in the enormous fireplace. On one side of the desk was ranged a row of unopened financial journals and on the other, ominously high, a pile of bills. In the tantalus nearby the decanters were filled to the brim and beneath them stood a file of glasses in undisturbed repose. Every day housemaids went dutifully through the room with dusters. But for weeks, and apart from this, almost nothing had been touched except the cigar-cabinet, a repository which Swindle found occasion to visit each morning shortly after breakfast.

Everyone was idle.

In the slanting rays of the declining sun Grubb the gardener sat on a borrow and smoked his pipe. His day's work had consisted in walking slowly through the greenhouses and pinching off appropriate parts of the tomato plants. Although only in late middle age, Grubb had memories of Sherris stretching back to very different times, and he mingled the irritating role of *laudator temporis acti* with some immemorial grudge against the whole establishment for which he labored or was employed to labor. Now he was watching, censoriously but without any prompting to appropriate action, his assistant William neglect the necessary repair of the lawn-mower to gossip with a groom who was failing to exercise Miss Lucy's mare.

Nor were matters anywhere more actively ordered within doors, and Miss Lucy herself was now sitting idly at her bureau, a bookseller's bill and two letters from a dressmaker lying forlornly before her. Lady Dromio alone was unaffected by the spell; she prowled from room to room, vague but yet alert, and whenever her eye fell upon a calendar she paused before it and her lips moved in silent calculation. And silence held the house. Only in the dining-room where the parlormaid, being sulky, was contriving to extract noise out of laying silver for three, could a sound be heard. Sherris, like the house of Morpheus in the poem, might have been conceived as wrapt in eternal silence far from enemies. But this, as it happened, would have been an error. Fate was marching upon Sherris now.

High above the offices the hands of the stable clock moved to the minute before seven. A deep whir, as of the clock gathering its forces to strike the hour, floated down and through the nearer gardens and the house itself. Almost imperceptibly the household stirred uneasily. Swindle set down his glass and opened an eye. Grubb took his pipe from his mouth as if about to admonish William in the matter of the mower. The parlormaid set two forks silently on the table and turned briskly for the spoons. Lucy made as if to take up her pen. Lady Dromio laid a decisive finger on the calendar before her. . . .

But only silence followed. Some months ago the stable clock had ceased to strike and any preliminary mustering of its powers was in vain. Swindle closed his eye, Grubb returned to sucking his pipe, the parlormaid set down the salt-cellars with a slap. Lucy's hand fell to her side, Lady Dromio turned and drifted restlessly to the next room.

At five minutes past seven the blast of a motor horn sounded from the high road half a mile off. Not many seconds later it was heard more loudly at the lodge gates. Then again, and most unnecessarily, it blared out on the drive.

Instantaneously Sherris came to life. Grubb seized his barrow and trundled it away. William bent to his mower, the groom vanished, the parlormaid scurried from the dining room. Swindle drained his glass, woke up and reached for his shoes. Lucy jumped to her feet. Lady Dromio sat down.

Lady Dromio sat down, took up a piece of embroidery, and looked extremely composed. "Swindle," she said as the butler shuffled through the hall, "what was that horrible noise?"

Swindle gave his mistress a sidelong malevolent glance. "Urrr!" he said disagreeably, and proceeded on his way.

Lady Dromio sighed, with the air of one whom the insolence of an old retainer has long since subdued. But the eye which she directed upon the doorway was keen and cold. She had not long to wait. There was a screech of brakes beneath the portico beyond, a bang and a clatter in the vestibule, and the door was flung open to admit a hurrying man somewhat past late middle age. "Well!" His glance seized upon Lady Dromio at once. "Is he here?"

Very deliberately Lady Dromio completed a stitch. She rose. "Sebastian," she said, "how nice to see you. But we were afraid you would not arrive till after dinner. I do hope that the water is reasonably hot. Swindle—"

Swindle made a displeasing snuffling noise in his nose. He was looking at Mr Sebastian Dromio with a dim but questioning eye. "We do our best, your ladyship," he said. "But the boiler isn't what it was, not by a long way." It would have been charitable to say that Swindle's voice croaked, since this is a quality that may be induced merely by age. It contrived at once to croak and snarl. "It might run to a shower —not but what that looks less than Mr Sebastian needs."

It was true that Sebastian Dromio gave the impression of being extremely hot and dusty. Now he sent his hat skimming towards the stomach of an advancing footman and himself strode over to his sister-in-law. "Well," he reiterated unceremoniously, and on a rising note. "Has he turned up? This afternoon I found out—"

Lady Dromio's eye travelled from Swindle twitching his wrinkled nose to the second footman retrieving the hat, and then on to the first footman who was coming through the vestibule with Sebastian's bags. "I think," she said, "that I will come upstairs with you myself, just to see that things are as they should be. Robert, those suit-cases are very dusty; take them away and clean them before bringing them to Mr Dromio's room." Lady Dromio turned and mounted the stairs. "Really, Sebastian," she murmured, "you might be a little less dramatic, whatever the occasion may be. I have been reading a very interesting novel, all about a big hotel, and there is a man who keeps rushing—"

"Damn your novel! Has Oliver not turned up?"

"He has not turned up." Lady Dromio's placidity was unruffled. "There is quite enough remark about it all already, without your shouting the house down. And a great deal of practical awkwardness, too. The local bank manager came to see me this morning. It seems that there has been some hitch in the money that comes through from London—"

"I can well believe it."

"And, as you know, the mere monthly outgoings here are very large. It is absurd in Oliver to keep so many servants, particularly those tiresome men. But here is your room, and everything seems in order. I expect that Lucy has given an eye to it."

"Very kind of her." Sebastian was perfunctory. "But the point is that there's more than awkwardness round the corner. There's some deuced odd revelation."

"Some revelation!" Lady Dromio had gone very still. "What sort of revelation do you mean?"

"Money, of course." Sebastian Dromio threw off his dustcoat and sat down by a window which commanded the park. He was old, his sister-in-law thought as she looked at him in the level evening light. In fact, he was just as old as her dead husband would be now. . . . She shivered—and at the same time relaxed. "Money?" she questioned vaguely.

"Have you never felt that there is something odd about Oliver and money? Has he ever told you anything? After all, his mother—"

"Oliver seldom mentions such things. Of course I know he *needs* money. But about that, you must admit, he has been doing his best."

"A damned poor best, if you ask me." Sebastian lifted a tired chin, and the action seemed to show him not a tired man merely but a sick man as well. "I don't care for your son, you know."

"I realise that. Oliver is not a very attractive person, I suppose. Although I believe that Lucy—"

"The more fool she." Sebastian Dromio's harsh tone seemed momentarily to soften as he mentioned the girl. "I've sometimes thought that your abominable fire couldn't have done worse. If it had been one of the others that Romeo got out the brat might have proved a less poor fish than Oliver."

Lady Dromio flushed—but with what emotion it would have been hard to discern. "That is rather a brutal thing to say—and gets us nowhere."

"No more it does." Sebastian's face—one of those faces that harden as they grow old—contrived an appearance of contrition. He shifted restlessly in his chair. "The business," he said, "—I have my finger pretty well on the pulse of that. And I keep liking it less and less. But there's something else." His fingers drummed on the arm of his chair. "Look here, Kate, about that Mrs Gollifer—"

"Mrs Gollifer!" Lady Dromio drew a careful stitch through her embroidery and then looked up blankly at her brother-in-law.

"Yes, Mrs Gollifer. Is she Oliver's mistress?"

Lady Dromio's expression of astonishment grew—but there was an obscure horror behind it. "Sebastian, Oliver is forty, and Mary Gollifer is old enough to be his—"

"Yes, yes, I know all that. Only some people have queer tastes. Otherwise I don't see—" Sebastian hesitated. "Tell me," he said quietly, "do you know Oliver to be hiding?"

"I have no idea what you mean."

"He hasn't been down here—quietly?"

"Of course not! He's in America still."

"He's no such thing, Kate. I saw Oliver in London at lunchtime to-day."

Lady Dromio said nothing. She rose, walked to another window, and searched the park rather as if expecting her absent son to be lurking behind an elm or in a ha-ha. "You spoke to him?" she asked.

"No, I did not. It was a deuced queer thing. I'd gone into a restaurant to lunch—sometimes, you know, I feel I can't stick the faces in that damned club—and I had got pretty well through a filthy meal when I became aware of two men getting up from a table on t'other side of a pillar. As they rose their voices reached me for the first time—or I attended to them for the first time—and I'll be damned if one of them wasn't Oliver's. I swung round, pretty thoroughly surprised. I had no more notion than you"—and Sebastian glance swiftly at Lady Dromio, silent by her window—"that he was back in England. There he was, pretty well within a couple of yards of me. But I saw him only for an instant, for no sooner had our eyes met than he whipped out a handkerchief, buried his nose in it like a fellow being let into a police-court and hoping to dodge the photographers, and bolted through the door. Fishy way for a nephew to behave towards his uncle, it seemed to me."

"It was certainly strange." Lady Dromio returned

from the window and sat down quietly in her chair. "But didn't you follow?"

"I sat tight. It was too queer to be comfortable, and it struck me at once that Oliver might have got into some pretty stiff pickle. Mightn't want to be greeted, you know, before this other fellow. You see, I've had my doubts for some time. This disappearing into America and not being heard of—" Sebastian broke off. "Look here, Kate, what was the last you heard?"

"Money." Lady Dromio smiled faintly. "He had some heavy call for money over there about six weeks ago, and for some reason he couldn't get it from our New York office."

"I'm sure he couldn't." Sebastian's tone was grim.

"And of course there is fuss about getting sterling to America and old Mr Pomeroy had to ring me up to fish out some papers. That was how I heard of it." Lady Dromio paused, picked up her embroidery and executed a couple of stitches. "But what," she asked abruptly, "about the other man?"

"In the restaurant? I just didn't notice him. Too dashed dumbfounded by Oliver's behaving that way."

"You are sure it was Oliver?"

"Good God! Of course I am. There he was. And I heard him talk as well. I tell you, Kate, I don't like it."

"Clearly not. By the way, Sebastian, how are *your* money affairs?"

"How are any Dromio money affairs these days? I can tell you, I don't want any sort of rumpus at the moment. Let the world hear that one of us has bolted or lost his nerve—"

"I see. And that is why you arrive at Sherris as if

you were bringing the bad news from Aix to Ghent."
And Lady Dromio, unconscious of having achieved
any witticism, took another stab at her embroidery.
"Here is Robert with your cases." She rose. "We shall
dine, as usual, at eight."

"Very well. I could do with something to eat after
that beastly luncheon. Nobody coming in, I suppose?"

"Well, yes. We didn't expect you, you know, until
long after dinner. And so I asked Mary Gollifer to
come across. And now, as you seem interested in
her—"

"I'd like to know a little about her past," Sebastian
Dromio said.

And Lady Dromio shivered.

Grubb locked the tool-shed and, as was his invariable
custom, thrust the key beneath a piece of sacking on
the windowsill. It was twenty to eight. Having spent
a particularly long day in substantial vacancy of mind
and idleness of limb, Grubb felt tired and glum. He
climbed to the terrace and walked heavily round the
house, dimly hoping that his leaden and exhausted
gait would attract the compassion—or if not the
compassion then the resentment—of his employers.
But the house turned upon him only a succession of
blank windows. They would be upstairs, he reflected, getting into their tomfool clothes. Between
that and eating and ordering folk about they passed
their days. Grubb's thought turned to the cold bacon
waiting him in his solitary cottage. Actually, and at an
instinctive level, the image of this rose before him
accompanied by sensations of simple pleasure. But
quickly, and because he had long schooled himself in

35

the prime duty of being disgruntled, Grubb achieved the darkest view of his supper. He commiserated with himself as one iniquitously defrauded of his just inheritance of caviare and champagne. It was not that Grubb held levelling views. He would altogether have disallowed William's claim to caviare, and even Swindle's to port. But it seemed to Grubb that he was, or ought to be, a man exceptionally privileged. Such was the monstrous unfairness with which the world had treated his beautiful nature that the Deity, as a special recompense, had excused him—and him alone—from the observance of certain of the more irksome moral laws. Grubb was no doubt unaware that he thus possessed what was technically a criminal psychology. Nevertheless his next action was dictated by this feeling. He paused outside the study and his eye swept the terrace. A particularly morose expression came over his face. He looked round again—this time plainly to make sure that he was unobserved—and moved with a rapid shuffle towards the French window.

Ten minutes later Grubb was trudging across the park—not directly towards his cottage and waiting bacon but by a slightly circuitous route. This route represented his settled choice at the end of his day's labors, and often enough it had cause speculation among the outdoor servants. A sort of ritual attended it.

Grubbs trudged across the park, muttering strangely as he went. Such browsing sheep or cattle as he met with he cursed heartily. Eventually he reached the boundary of the property and paused. Before him here, and almost on the highroad, stood a cottage evidently long untenanted. Its windows were boarded up and in places the roof had fallen in. Even amid the pervasive disrepair of Sherris it was arrestingly dreary and forlorn. Grubb halted and for some moments stared. Several times, and with a curious effect of unsuccessful experiment, his features worked, contorting themselves into a semblance of sudden inspiration. Then they clouded again; moroseness took up its settled stance; with a gesture baffled and discouraged Grubb scratched his jaw.

It was eight o'clock.

It was eight o'clock and Mrs Gollifer would be late; nevertheless she found it difficult to throw away her cigarette, press the self-starter and complete her drive to this awkward dinner. Oliver Dromio presumably was still abroad, so there would be no call for the final and fantastic insincerity involved in a meeting with him. But was there not insincerity enough?

Kate Dromio was an old friend. She was—yes, surely she was—deeply beholden to Kate. Kate could not have foreseen this eventual disaster, and she would be heart-broken if she knew. Or would she? Making an effort of will and throwing away the cigarette, Mary Gollifer frowned. You just couldn't tell with Kate. Her feelings about Oliver, her feelings about Lucy—there was something oblique or uncertain in them. And she was correspondingly uncertain about the feelings of others. Otherwise she would not give little dinners of just this sort.

The truth was that she, Mary Gollifer, should have stopped knowing the Dromios long ago. She should have stopped her son Geoffrey knowing them. . . . They were not a satisfactory spectacle. And all the trouble—or all the trouble as Mrs Gollifer saw it—proceeded from Lucy's position in the household. With Kate Dromio, and as an adopted daughter, Lucy had failed to come off. And the girl knew it. Not that she was a girl; she was a woman who ought to have been married and away from the place long ago.

But what if Lucy wanted to marry Oliver? And what if her own son Geoffrey wanted to marry Lucy? Mrs Gollifer felt anger leap in her like a flame; felt consternation and panic gather round her like a cloud. She let in the clutch and drove fast for Sherris, reckless in these winding lanes.

She brought her mind back to dwell on the Dromios as the mind of a disinterested acquaintance might do. And she saw that with Lucy, clearly, Kate Dromio had bitten off more than she could chew. In personal relationships one can commit no greater crime—and mere generosity and lack of self-knowledge can lead to it. Long ago, and after tragedy and disappointment, Kate had wanted the child. But she had not wanted her enough. Or not enough to weigh against something else. But against what? Mrs Gollifer had no idea. Kate's tragedy had been deeper than was known and the little girl—a waif, thought Mrs Gollifer, no more than a waif—had failed to ease it into oblivion. Between mother and adopted daughter the right things had not grown, and when that happens the wrong things grow instead. Nothing very wrong, surely, but enough to make frustration and disillusion the dominant notes at Sherris. Frustration and disillusion. . . . Who would willingly dine —or live—with these?

Kate was not to blame; in fairness it was necessary

to hold to that. Mary Gollifer's foot pressed the accelerator as she made the assertion. If disillusioned and defeated, that was to say, Kate Dromio had ample cause. She could hardly be unaware that Oliver was —well, that Oliver was no good.

It was nearly ten past eight. Mrs Gollifer's car swept round the last curve of the Dromios' drive and the house was revealed to her. The property of Sir Oliver Dromio, fifth baronet. But if Lucy had actually become. . . . Again the flame of anger licked up in Mary Gollifer. Then her heart sank for a moment to her evening shoes. A figure in a dinner-jacket was pacing the terrace with overt and uncivil impatience. She looked again and sighed with relief. It was not Oliver but his uncle, Sebastian Dromio. He was a disagreeable old man to whom she was entirely indifferent.

In large houses and among well-bred people guests do not commonly overhear embarrassing conversations about themselves. That Mrs Gollifer did so was substantially Swindle's fault.

Just before leaving home Mrs Gollifer had told her butler, a retainer almost as far declined into the vale of years as Swindle himself, to telephone Sherris Hall with the information that she might be late. Swindle, being hard of hearing, had made no more of this than a mere mumble. Whereupon, with the obstinacy or malice of the aged, he had chosen to announce to his mistress that Mrs Gollifer was unable to dine. When Mrs Gollifer actually arrived she was shown, according to the familiar habit of the house, into Lady Dromio's boudoir. At that moment Lady Dromio and her adopted daughter were conversing over some final adjustment of dress in the elder lady's bedroom next door. Mrs Gollifer would have interrupted them at once. But the first two words stopped her.

"Oliver's Gollifer!" Lucy Dromio's voice held what was not a sympathetic laughter. "How many of the silly stories about Oliver are nasty too, mama. But not many are so exquisitely cacophonous."

"Lucy, dear, it is to be wished that you would not color so when Oliver's name is mentioned in such connections. It will be remarked."

"Then why mention it?"

"Because before Swindle told me that Mary Gollifer was not coming to dinner I thought I had better warn you of this piece of scandal in Sebastian's mind. Not that I really understand it. He seems to think that Mary has been getting money from Oliver."

"Because she is his mistress? Was ever anything so absurd! For surely it would be the other way round. Oliver would require quite a lot of money from the lady."

"Lucy, that is not nice." There was unusual agitation in Lady Dromio's voice. "And I wonder that you can make such jokes about Oliver. Especially when you—"

"Yes, mama. But uncle Sebastian must be mad. For surely Mrs Gollifer has lots of money. Her son Geoffrey is enormously wealthy."

"Well, dear, I do not know that Mary has as much money as she had. So many people haven't. And, as I say, I don't at all understand what Sebastian means. He seems merely to have come upon some hint of money transactions between these two, and he may have got it quite muddled. But I mentioned it because he might have been very tactless and brutal and I should have needed you to help me head him off. But as Mary isn't coming—"

"She has come." And Mrs Gollifer, gathering her skirts and her courage about her, swept through to the adjoining room.

3

It was a quarter to nine when Geoffrey Gollifer drew up outside his mother's house and ran indoors, almost colliding with Martin, the butler who had held so luckless a telephone conversation with Swindle an hour before.

"Good evening, Martin. Is my mother at home?"

"Why, good evening, Mr Geoffrey. This is a great surprise. And Mrs Gollifer is out, sir, I'm sorry to say. Dining at Sherris and drove herself over in the car. I understood her to say you would be sailing tomorrow morning, sir."

"And so I am, Martin. That's what I've come about. It seems that when I brought my mother back from Switzerland in January I left my passport with hers. I think I'll drive over and ask her about it. . . . I suppose Miss Lucy is at Sherris?"

"I suppose so, Mr Geoffrey." Martin's tone was benevolent.

Geoffrey Gollifer glanced at his watch. "Would you

say they'd have finished dinner?"

"Why, yes, sir. By the time you arrive there I venture to think they'll be taking their coffee."

"Good." Geoffrey Gollifer turned to the door. Then he hesitated. "Sir Oliver not back there yet, I suppose?"

"I couldn't positively say, Mr Geoffrey. But, come to think of it, it seems very likely, sir. He has been in expectation for some time. There has been quite a mystery, if I may say so, sir."

"Mystery, Martin? Tommyrot. Lot of country gossip, I suppose."

"As you say, sir. But I do think he may be back, and this little dinner a-celebrating of the fact. Not that the mistress mentioned anything of that kind, Mr Geoffrey."

"I see." Geoffrey Gollifer did not sound particularly pleased. "Well, I think I'll just telephone across and ask where the passports are kept. It will save time. Just see if you can get Sherris on the line."

"Very good, Mr Geoffrey."

But Sherris for some reason was unobtainable. And Geoffrey frowned irresolutely. "Dash it all," he said, "where are such things kept? Would my mother lock them up?"

Martin, perhaps because his mumblings to the girl on the local exchange had been ineffective and half-hearted, was eager to help. "Very probably your passport would be in Mrs Gollifer's bureau, sir. I believe that one or two of the drawers are kept locked, but as likely as not the document would not be in one of those."

"Very well, I'll have a look. I don't suppose my

mother will mind. Just come along, Martin, and lend me a hand."

The bureau was ancient and capacious, and for some time Geoffrey rummaged in vain, Martin making ineffective fumbling motions beside him. "Dash it all, Martin," he said irritably, "don't you think you could get through on the telephone, after all? We might be a couple of burglars."

"Well, sir—"

"And now this drawer is stuck. Damn!" The drawer at which Geoffrey was tugging had flown open with a splintering crash. "It must have been locked after all."

"Yes, sir. The piece is an old one and the woodwork must have been unsound." Martin was respectfully malicious. "Mrs Gollifer has always been particularly attached to this bureau."

"And here I am behaving like a bull in a chinashop." Irritably and rather shamefacedly, Geoffrey Gollifer was flicking over papers in the drawer. Suddenly his hand stayed itself and turned a couple of papers slowly. "Martin," he said, and his voice had sharpened unaccountably, "go and fetch me a brandy-and-soda."

"Very good, Mr Geoffrey."

"But first, just find Thomas and ask him to make sure that there is plenty of petrol in my car."

It was nearly ten minutes before Martin returned. The bureau was closed. Geoffrey Gollifer was standing by the window, looking out into the gathering dusk. His passport was in his hand. "I found it," he said.

"I'm glad to hear it, sir." Martin, as he set down his tray, glanced at his employer's son in some surpirse.

Mr Geoffrey it seemed to him, had spoken with altogether disproportionate emphasis.

"Yes, I found it. I had a notion it was there—quite dimly. And—by Jove!—it was. . . . You say Sir Oliver is probably at Sherris?"

"I believe he may be, sir."

"Well, I suppose I had better be off." And Geoffrey Gollifer drained his glass. "By the way, Martin, where have they put those army things of mine?"

"In your old dressing-room, sir. I put them carefully away myself."

"Good. I'll just run up and get something."

Geoffrey strode to the door. Martin followed. "Can I be of any help to you, sir?"

"No, thank you, Martin. I'm pretty sure I don't need any help."

And Geoffrey Gollifer went off upstairs. In the old way, Martin thought—with a sort of jump at the bottom and then two steps at a time. And Martin shook his head doubtfully. He was getting on, he knew, and the mistress was already hinting at a pension. But was it so bad that he had come to fancy things? For he thought he had seen a young and handsome face suddenly transformed—pale, strained, and the forehead showing beads of sweat.

Smoothly the car slid away from the little inn. The hands of the clock on the dash-board were at nine-fifteen. It was growing dusk.

The two men drove silently for some time. "Not a bad idea," said the first, "turning off the main road to dine. The bigger places are most of them a bit spoilt nowadays. It was a quiet spot, that."

"Yes," said the second, "quite out of the way."

The first glanced at a sign-post. "Getting near," he said, and paused. "You know, I just don't see how I can face it."

"Oh, come, my dear chap. That's quite morbid, surely."

"I suppose it is. But I've always been a bit like that. And you just don't know what it—"

"Say!" The second man, who was driving, braked sharply and drew into the side of the road. "Did you see that? Looked as if it might have been a hit-and-run accident. Fellow knocked into the ditch."

"Good Lord! I didn't notice." The first man spoke not altogether attentively, as if his thoughts were far away. "Better get out and look."

"Don't you bother. I'll just run back."

And the second man climbed out of the car. He was absent a couple of minutes. "Nothing at all," he said casually when he returned. "Just a tramp dead drunk and fast asleep. He'll come to no harm. We'll drive on."

And the first man nodded. "Right-ho," he said. "Better face it. And the fellow will come to no harm, as you say."

Oliver's Gollifer. It rankled, Mrs Gollifer found as she bent down to admire Lady Dromio's embroidery. That she should be supposed at her age to be any man's mistress was—or ought to be—merely comical. Doubtless there were such horrible old women, and what did it matter if she were taken for one of them by a horrible old man? And Sebastian Dromio was certainly that. It had become clear during dinner that he was worried, but he had seemed to take this as licence for being as disagreeable as he pleased—

except to Lucy, for whom he seemed to have some slight affection. A horrible old man spreading a horrible slander. . . . But it was not the slander itself that really stung. It was—Mrs Gollifer discovered with some surprise—the disgusting collocation of gobbling sounds with which Lucy Dromio had ridiculed it. Oliver's Gollifer. . .

She had greatly disrelished wedding herself to a Gollifer. The outlandish name had been one of two considerations which had weighed almost decisively against her going to the altar with the very wealthy man who bore it. . . . But she had gone, all the same. And Samuel Gollifer had proved a very decent fellow. They had teamed up well. She had been very sorry when he died.

It was not all that man desires (thought Mrs Gollifer, looking thoughtfully at Lucy laying out a cardtable, and at the same time letting her mind stray back across the years). But it was all that man requires—or approximately so. And, for good measure, there had been Geoffrey, her only son. Mrs Gollifer was sometimes puzzled to know where her love for Geoffrey came from. But it was there. . . . Mrs Gollifer's finger made a little arabesque in air, tactfully picking out some special elegance in Lady Dromio's needlecraft. If only, after all, Geoffrey and Lucy—

Mrs Gollifer sighed. Unfortunately there was no possibility of that.

The little silver clock on the mantelpiece struck half-past nine. Lady Dromio looked at it and then at the empty hearth beneath. "I had rather hoped," she said, "that we might have a fire. But Swindle advised against it. And no doubt it is rather warm."

Kate Dromio, Mrs Gollifer thought, increasingly liked conversation of a comfortable inanity. She liked the convention that life was comfortable and unexacting—not merely on its surfaces but basically as well. That woman in Jane Austen—or was it the Brontës? Mrs Gollifer wondered—who just sat on a sofa with a pug: Kate liked to suggest that for her life was like that. But it was not, nor probably would Kate have found it tolerable if it were so. For in her old friend there was something lurking and unassuaged, something that Mrs Gollifer by no means understood.

"Then for once Swindle was right in his notion of what would be comfortable." Lucy had opened a pack of patience cards and now came to sit down beside Mrs Gollifer. "It's one of those close nights that seem to go on getting warmer until midnight. And I'm sure there is only one fire in the house, Swindle's own. He sits before it, you know, all the year round, drinking port. If we ever see the end of Swindle, which I doubt, it will surely be as the result of spontaneous combustion. He is much too wary just to tumble into the fire—"

"Good gracious!" Lady Dromio was alarmed. "Swindle is getting rather old. And they say he walks about in his sleep. It would be dreadful if—"

"No." Lucy shook her head. "It will be spontaneous combustion, like the man who drank too much gin."

"I don't think I heard of him. No doubt it comes of not reading the newspapers carefully. Such odd things, Mary dear, Lucy knows about, clever girl. Not that I don't do a great deal of reading myself, particularly when Oliver is away and we hardly en-

48

tertain at all. Or only as we are doing to-night, which is the nicest way, I think. Mary, I wonder if you have read a novel, a most unusual novel, about a big—" Lady Dromio paused, frowned and looked about her. Apparently the book itself was necessary if she was to be quite sure of what it was that was big in it. "Lucy, can I possibly have mislaid that absorbing story? The one old Mrs Rundle recommended to Mr Green-grave's niece on that dreadful ship. They had storms all the way, you know. And although Mr Greengrave himself—not that he was on board—is an excellent sailor—indeed, he was in the navy as a chaplain, I believe, when he was a young man. . . . or was that old Canon Newton at Sherris Magna?" Lady Dromio paused, herself rather at sea. "Well, Mr Greengrave has a niece—"

"Talking of ships," said Mrs Gollifer, "is there any news of Oliver returning? When I drove up and saw Sebastian on the terrace I thought for a moment that it was he. I was quite disappointed."

"Were you?" Lady Dromio was surprised and vague. "But of course. Oliver has really been away for quite a long time."

Mrs Gollifer was silent. This was surely a company far too intimate for such ghastly insincerities. Or it ought to be that. Oh, what a tangled web we weave, when first we practice to deceive. Indeed, the web can eventually become a noose. Or an ulcer. Or a secret wound through which one may be bled to death. . . . There were only the three of them in the room and Sebastian was unlikely for some time to abandon such port as Swindle resigned to him. Mrs Gollifer stubbed out her cigarette, and knew as she did so that a resolve had formed in her mind like a suddenly precipitated crystal. "Lucy——" she began.

Lady Dromio dropped her embroidery.

Down below, Swindle stoked his own fire. He had locked the door—a very definite indication that the household was to expect no further directions or services from him that night. He poured himself out a glass of port and put on his carpet slippers. But his expression held no suggestion of a desire for slumber. Perhaps he was by nature nocturnal; certainly his complexion suggested a creature habituated to emerge from a hole after dark.

And yet Swindle in his solitude was looking rather more human than usual. Signs of doubts, of uneasiness, of an obscure internal debate were apparent in him. He sat down at his table and brought out a sheaf of papers from a drawer. These he fell to studying with concentration, occasionally making a pencil jotting in a notebook at his side. He shook his head peevishly, dolefully; at the same time the gesture suggested resolution. He made more jottings, sifted the papers with care into three piles, produced a column of figures relating to each. They represented (an observer might have guessed) bills of various degrees of urgency. Swindle turned to the drawer again and brought out three rubber bands. Whatever were the affairs in hand it was evident that he had no power to achieve more than a preliminary ordering of them now.

Again Swindle looked uneasy. He pushed away the papers, hesitated and looked round his room as if to make quite sure that he was unobserved. He drew from the pocket of his ancient tail-coat an orange-colored envelope and with fumbling fingers drew out the telegram inside. He read this through, frowned in indignation or protest, thrust it away again, eased himself into his arm-chair and drew the glass of port to his side. The fire was blazing, the little room stifling, everything invited to sleep. But Swindle sat wide-eyed, staring at the toes of his slippers. The house was silent. The only sound was the ticking of a watch. And this watch Swindle presently produced and eyed with hostility—a handsome half-hunter on a gold chain, such as elderly and valued retainers sometimes receive from their employers. He shook his head once more, muttered some protest and rose painfully from his chair. He reached for his shoes, thought better of this, and in his old slippers shuffled noiselessly to the door. Softly he turned the lock, cautiously he put his head out and looked to right and left. Reassured, he stepped into the corridor and made his way silently, like a burglar, to the service stairs.

The time by the half-hunter had been ten minutes to ten.

Mr Greengrave had dined with old Canon Newton at Sherris Magna and now he was on his way home. If he had excused himself a little earlier than his host would have wished—perhaps a shade earlier than was civil, indeed—it was the innate caution of his nature that was responsible. The Canon was a lover of good talk, and in an age in which it is unusual to be able to converse at all this accomplishment had made his society much prized throughout the diocese. But the Canon was also a lover of good wine, and he was equally esteemed because of this. The

Bishop and he, it was averred by the irreverent, bartered spiritual for spirituous advice; there were few considerable cellars in the county in the replenishing of which Canon Newton did not have a say; he even enjoyed the unstinted confidence and regard of Mr Swindle of Sherris Hall.

It would be crude to boil this down to the statement that Canon Newton drank. Nevertheless this was how Mr Greengrave secretly regarded the matter. Mr Greengrave had no head for liquor. It quickly made him argumentative rather than merely talkative, and this was an embarrassment when one's host expected—as Canon Newton did—an unfaltering standard of polished Landorian prose. And if wine made Mr Greengrave argumentative (so that he was uneasily aware, as he talked, of the image of some rather quarrelsome and quite unrefined person emerging volubly from a pub) it by no means left him there. The painful fact was that even Canon Newton's good wine rapidly produced the sort of consequences exploited in comic papers—in those less seemly comic papers that do not ban drunkenness as a staple of humor. Upon Mr Greengrave after a party the tangible and visible surfaces of life were liable alarmingly to advance and recede, tilt and rock. And although rats, mice and dogs invariably, so far as he could remember, retained the hues with which Providence had endowed them, their number was liable to become variable and uncertain, much as if they had ceased to be the creatures of God's hand and become symbols of the higher physics. All this Mr Greengrave disliked, and particularly when he had to drive himself through the little watering-place of

Sherris Magna on the way home to his country rectory.

So he had left early and Canon Newton, after amiable farewells, had returned to the golden cadences with which he was entertaining his other guests.

The night was pleasant, although a shade close and surprisingly warm. Mr Greengrave let down the hood of his lumbering old car and decided that fifteen miles an hour represented what it would be judicious to attempt. He also decided that although much attention must be given to the road it would be advantageous to choose some substantial but not too difficult theme for meditation. This, he felt, would assist him to maintain the higher brain centres in operation and minimise the risk of an untimely nap. He might, for instance, plan out the heads of a sermon for the Sunday after next. There had been some heavy drinking at the cricket club; he might well choose a text which would enable him to take glancing notice of that. But then again an orchard had been robbed and, even more serious, a good deal of poultry had been disappearing in Sherris Parva. Only two days ago Mrs Marple had missed two Khaki Campbells. And although it was likely enough that toughs from Sherris Magna were responsible Mr Greengrave had by no means liked the look of young Ted Morrow when the matter had been mentioned in his presence that very morning. . . .

Communing thus with himself, Mr Greengrave drove sedately on his way. The landscape, he noted with satisfaction, was behaving tolerably well. He looked up at the moon—a trifle apprehensively, recalling Shakespeare's words:

> My Lord, they say five moons were seen to-
>   night. . . .

But the heavens too were behaving well; the mild
luminary shone single in its element; nor did certain
stars shoot madly from their spheres, a disconcerting
phenomenon which Mr Greengrave had on certain
previous occasions observed.

Mr Greengrave was so pleased by this that he for-
got about his sermon—whether on pilfering or
drunkenness—and began to sing. Mr Greengrave
sang loudly. The words were those of *Onward,
Christian Soldiers,* so that nothing but edification
could have resulted had he at this time been encountered by any of his flock. Nevertheless under the in-
spiriting influence of this war-song Mr Greengrave's
foot pressed imperceptibly down on the accelerator,
and fifteen miles an hour was very soon exchanged
for thirty. He pulled himself up with a jerk. Jollity,
even a robustly clerical sort, plainly would not do. A
more chastening—nay, depressing—theme had better be sought. It was thus that Mr Greengrave, with
results unpredictable at this juncture although already imminent, turned his thoughts to the people at
Sherris Hall.

From the point of view of pastoral care the view in
that quarter was commonly bleak enough. But even
here Mr Greengrave, thanks to Canon Newton's vin-
tages, found cause for mild satisfaction now. Lucy
Dromio, Lady Dromio's adopted daughter, was a
young person open to much pastoral censure, and he
had himself spoken to her with some severity that
afternoon. And Lucy's reply had been to say something flattering—flattering because obscurely true.

Mr Greengrave liked finding out about people. Well, there was perhaps nothing particularly gratifying to self-esteem in a diagnosis such as that. But Mr Greengrave—Lucy had added—had the sort of brain that pieces people together and sees what a thing is all about.

Now, in a way this was outrageously untrue. Mr Greengrave was not really at all clever (he had only to think of himself in colloquy with Canon Newton to realise this) and therefore it was impossible that he should have the marked powers of analysis and synthesis that such an opinion suggested. But in a way Lucy was right—because often Mr Greengrave did successfully piece people together and see what a thing was about; only he did this in a substantially intuitive way. From time to time he would see, and in doing so would leave more abstractly perceptive people standing.

He had seen that in the Sherris hinterland some enigma or mystery reposed. And Lucy saw this too —or perhaps Lucy had less an intuition than some positive if fragmentary knowledge. It was a bond between them. And she had actually asked him to investigate—to tackle some ill-defined problem of family relationship troubling the awareness of each. That in a situation so nebulous the two of them might have quite different notions of where the mystery lay was an intellectual conception which did not occur to Mr Greengrave. Now, driving carefully through the deepening summer dusk, he was about to let his mind play upon the Dromios with whatever result might come. But this never happened. For, quite suddenly, he saw.

Really saw. For it was a revelation as purely visual

55

as it was spontaneous, and it was won sheerly from the void, without preparation or labor, like some line that precipitates a great poem. And this vivid and revealing appearance, astounding in itself, of course rendered much more disconcerting what was to happen to Mr Greengrave a few minutes later.

He continued to see the winding road to Sherris Parva, familiar in the lengthening shadows. But floating upon this he saw two faces—faces which were also familiar enough, but which had the superior reality of images compelled upon one by powerful forces deep in the mind. The two faces floated before him more or less at opposite ends of the windscreen. And then they coalesced, drifting together rather like complementary pictures viewed through a stereoscope. And at the moment of their coming together Mr Greengrave exclaimed aloud. "Well, I'm damned!" he said.

Instantly the vision vanished. Mr Greengrave was astounded and shocked at what he had seen, but he was perhaps even more distressed at what he had said. What would Canon Newton think of an ejaculation so little pious—so profane, indeed? And it was the more offensive in that what was untrue of himself had been revealed to him as a painful approximation to plain fact in the case of certain other persons. People among whom such things happened must surely feel like lost souls. . . . Mr Greengrave drew into the side of the road and stopped his car. The thing needed thinking out. Moreover the shock of his discovery—for he never doubted that it was that—had upset whatever precarious control he had achieved over the physical world about him. The ditch was in motion; it was behaving less like a ditch than a reptile. The poplars undulated like great dark flames. The road flowed as if it were water.

Mr Greengrave closed his eyes and laid his head on his arms, the better to cope with the situation which had started upon him. His discovery, he knew, imposed some duty, but for the moment he could by no means discern what that duty was. He was not a policeman, nor was he yet assured that there was matter in which the law would interest itself. For instance, questions of inheritance might be involved. Supposing there had been a marriage—

At this moment Mr Greengrave's interior counsels were interrupted by the sound of an approaching motor car. He looked up, turned round and saw that it was about to overtake him. Twilight had barely fallen; the moon was still mere tissue paper in the sky; at close range visibility was scarcely affected. Nevertheless the shades of evening lent something insubstantial to the scene, and would have done so even were that scene not faintly gyrating under the influence of Canon Newton's wines. The car approached. And once more Mr Greengrave saw two faces. Once more they were familiar. But this time they did not drift together; rather it was as if by some monstrous alchemy they had been torn apart. Moreover this was no vision, no mere retinal image. To what he now saw something in the external world did after some fashion correspond.

The car passed on. To Mr Greengrave what had happened was at once clear and humiliating. There was still only one moon in the sky and he himself (for he investigated this) had four fingers and a thumb on each hand. Nevertheless, and like any bibulous person in a vulgar print—

And then Mr Greengrave wondered. Did not this plain betrayal by the senses cast very substantial doubt upon the reliability of that earlier and purely inward vision?

At least it would be necessary to go carefully. In every sense to go carefully, thought Mr Greengrave. And he drove on in third gear.

4

There was silence among the three ladies in the drawingroom. It had lasted for some time. Lucy played patience, her head bent as if she were listening to a whispered message from the cards. Mrs Gollifer was lost in reverie. Lady Dromio stirred uneasily, rose and walked to the window. "It must be put an end to somehow," she said.

Mrs Gollifer laughed. Beneath the standard lamp where she sat she looked old and ill. "The evening?" she asked. "It is true that I must certainly be getting home."

"Perhaps Lucy would like the drive and a tramp home by moonlight. It is quite her sort of thing." Lady Dromio had tossed her embroidery into a corner, much as if whatever purpose it had served was over. "Lucy, would you care—?"

"It is so complicated." Lucy spoke quietly, but both ladies turned to her at once. They looked hopeful, relieved.

"So many points to consider. One doesn't know where to begin."

Lady Dromio nodded. "If only Oliver—"

"For instance, here are two five of Spades, and I know what is under each."

Mrs Gollifer sank back in her chair. Lady Dromio uttered a sound which might have been merely exasperation, or might have been desperation of a very different quality. Lucy glanced briefly at each of them in turn. Her face was pale and expressionless. "I wonder why Sebastian didn't come in," she said. "Possibly he might be able to help."

Lady Dromio turned round. "Certainly not!"

"Since he is a capital bridge player and must have an eye for cards in general."

"Really, Lucy, this is most—"

"Unfilial, mama? Queen on King and here is the Knave."

Lady Dromio was silent. She may have been reflecting on the sundry small ways in which she had found an obscure nervous release in plaguing her adopted daughter in former years. But now she turned back to the window and with an agitated gesture threw it open. "It is insufferably close tonight. There must be a storm coming."

"Assuredly there is that." And Lucy nodded. "It is the wind and the rain for all of us, I am afraid. As for Oliver"—she paused—"I think it is likely that I shall kill him."

"Lucy, dear, that is idle and horrible talk."

"It sounds silly, doesn't it? Nevertheless that is what I think I shall do. To—to be stained so."

There was something in her voice that stirred Mrs Gollifer. "Drive home with me," she said. "I can rouse Evans and send you back in the car. Or—or you might stop the night."

Lucy was silent. But she had abandoned her cards and was slowly, petal by petal, tearing and shredding a rose which she had worn in her bosom. The clock ticked. Lucy glanced down at her hands. "A rose is a rose," she said. "A rose is a rose is a rose." She looked with the faintest of smiles at Lady Dromio, who appeared alarmed at this mysterious incantation. "Only a poem," she said. And there was silence again.

"It isn't quite dark yet." Lady Dromio spoke matter-of-factly, as if determined that something without an inner meaning should be said. "And I think I have seen Sebastian in the garden. Probably he is prowling with a cigar. I shall go and take a turn with him. There is nothing like a cigar in a garden at night." With nervous haste, or with an odd resolution, she stepped out to the terrace and disappeared.

Lucy looked first at Mrs Gollifer and then at the clock, which stood at ten-forty-five. "It is funny," she said, "but there really seems nothing to say."

"Then let us not try to say anything." And for several minutes Mrs Gollifer was silent. "But there is surely something to be done."

"Is it not a little late in the day? Or do you feel that the situation is happily covered by the adage Better Late than Never?"

"I said that something must be done, Lucy. I realise that, for you, the chief shock is about Oliver."

"I love him."

"I know you loved him. I think we have all already understood that."

"It is not what I said. I love him. Now."

Mrs Gollifer's expression flickered; there might have been read in it a mixture of perplexity, mortification and relief. "Then," she said, "you can hardly feel—"

"Oh, dear me, yes. Do you remember the poem which says that each man kills the thing he loves? In certain circumstances it is likely to be true."

But now Mrs Gollifer was looking at the younger woman with dilated eyes. "Lucy," she cried, "was Oliver . . . all the time . . . encouraging you?"

Lucy's lips moved; she seemed to be seeking a precise form of words. "The phrase, I fear," she said, "is inadequate to the specific nature of what has occurred."

Mrs Gollifer seemed to take unnaturally long to elucidate this grotesque little speech. When she did so, however, she began to weep.

"How does it go?" And Lucy let the shreds of the last rosepetal fall. "Some kill their love when they are young, and some when they are old; Some strangle with the hands of Lust, some with the hands of Gold. Well, that's very appropriate. My love has been strangled with the hands of Gold, exactly."

"We have had more than enough." Mrs Gollifer controlled her weeping and rose. "Tomorrow, perhaps, we shall be of a better mind. And now I am going. Don't stir. I shall go up for my cloak and then find my car. Kate will understand." And Mrs Gollifer left the room.

For a long time Lucy Dromio sat quite still, her hands limp on a table where lay the ruined rose. Then she got up and went to the window. The summer night had fallen. For minutes longer she stared into it, motionless and absorbed. She shivered. Very silently, she slipped into the garden and vanished.

"Look here, what's all this?"

Sebastian Dromio strode into the drawingroom where his sister-in-law and Lucy were sitting. His entrance had rather the effect of the knocking on the gate in *Macbeth*. A spell painfully broke itself. Lucy picked up her patience cards and shuffled them. Lady Dromio looked about her for her embroidery.

"But, Sebastian, what are you speaking of? And is half-past eleven a companionable hour at which to join us?"

"Companionable hour be damned. You don't look companionable, either of you, if it comes to that. And there's something uncanny about this house to-night. I don't like it." As he spoke to his sister-in-law thus, Sebastian cast at Lucy a considering and almost fearful glance.

"Old houses do sometimes get like that. Or any large building, for that matter. Lucy will tell you that I have been reading a most unusual novel about a big—"

"Stuff and nonsense!" Sebastian gave short shrift to this dive of Lady Dromio's towards her old refuges. "Either of you been outside?" he asked sharply.

"We have both of us been outside at one time or another. The night is mild."

"No doubt." Sebastian took an irresolute pace about the room. "Look here, there's something queer going on. And I knew there would be as soon as Oliver behaved in that deuced queer way this morning."

"As soon as what?" Lucy had sprung to her feet. "Uncle Sebastian, whatever are you saying?"

"Good heavens!" Sebastian swung round upon his sister-in-law. "Haven't you told the girl?" He crossed to the window and appeared to be listening uneasily. "Secrets all the time! And where's Mary Gollifer?"

"Sebastian," Lady Dromio explained, "says that he thought he saw Oliver in London this morning. I didn't mention it. We—we seemed to have enough on hand."

"I see." Lucy too appeared now to be listening. "And did you tell—" She hesitated.

"Mary? No, I did not."

"Well, where's the woman got to?" And Sebastian peered round the drawingroom much as if Mrs Gollifer might be crouching behind a sofa.

"She left nearly three-quarters of an hour ago." Lucy was gathering her cards together and putting them away in their box. "It was when mama was in the garden, so she went without saying good-bye."

"Three-quarters of an hour ago?" Sebastian snorted nervously. "Lucy, you must be dreaming. I saw the woman within the last ten minutes."

Lucy's eyes rounded. "But I heard her car!"

"Well, she was down in the garden. I couldn't think what I had stumbled on. Some blubbering old hag."

"How dare you!" And Lucy turned upon her uncle, inexplicably flushed and quivering. "Mrs Gollifer is mama's friend. Only a horrible old Edwardian bounder would speak of her in that pot-house way. And that's what you are."

"Lucy, dear!" Lady Dromio was very pale. "Perhaps Mary was taken ill and came back. And then

64

perhaps she was—was reluctant to return to the house."

"She looked ill enough." Sebastian, who had unexpectedly winced beneath Lucy's reproaches, now nonchalantly shrugged his shoulders. "But that's not all. I met Swindle some time back and he looked ill too. He looked like something out of a coffin. And when he saw me he bolted. Did you ever see Swindle bolt? It's out of nature."

Lady Dromio opened the window. "I shall go and look for Mary, though I hardly believe that what you say can be true. And I advise both of you to go to bed, and to practice more moderate language in the morning." And Lady Dromio lifted her chin and glanced from one to the other. The woman thus momentarily revealed had not entirely the appearance of one made to live a fantasy life in dream-hotels. "Good night."

But Sebastian had stepped to the window too. "Well," he said, "for heaven's sake let's keep civil tongues. And I'm coming with you. There's something queer outside this house as well as in. Not long before I saw Mrs Gollifer I saw—" He hesitated and glanced swiftly at Lucy. "I saw a fellow skulking in the laurels. And he appeared to me to be carrying something damned like a bludgeon."

Lucy too was at the window. "Is that why you went and got a revolver?"

"What the devil do you mean?"

"I can see the shape of it in the pocket of your dinner-jacket."

"Well, yes it is." Somewhat shamefacedly, Sebastian produced the weapon. "Didn't want to alarm you unnecessarily, you know."

Lady Dromio was on the terrace. "If Mary is being dogged by a man with a bludgeon," she said, "there is some cause to be alarmed. Sebastian, you may come with me. But put that thing back in your pocket."

Sebastian did as he was bid. "Look here, Kate, you two had better stay behind. It's not chilly, but there's no sense—"

Lady Dromio, however, had gone. They followed her. The air was stifling and still; frogs could be heard croaking very far away; and from farther yet, with an effect of inconceivable distance, a train whistled in the night. To the west heavy clouds were banked, but overhead the stars were clear. They moved down into the garden and behind them the house stood silhouetted in moonlight. The lawn where Lady Dromio had entertained Mr Greengrave that afternoon gleamed like a pale velvet; across it sprawled the distorted shadows of two stone hippogriffs pedestalled high in air—a pomp with which some long-dead Dromio had thought to embellish a large formal garden which had never been brought to completion. The creatures stood with wings outspread and a raised and threatening paw; the shadows seemed crouched and waiting to strike a premeditated blow.

"It was here I saw her." Sebastian Dromio, peering apprehensively about him, tapped a stone seat which commanded a view of the terrace now at some little remove above. "What about giving a shout?"

"Not yet." His sister-in-law, although anxious for her friend, was reluctant to make the night hideous with clamor. "If we look in the courtyard and the avenue for her car—"

"Mama, isn't there something funny about the house?"

They turned round, startled by the perplexity in Lucy's voice. Then Sebastian spoke impatiently. "Funny? I don't notice anything funny about it. Dash it all, one can't see much more than the outline of it."

"That's so. But—"

Lucy's sentence was left unfinished—interrupted by the sound of a car-door violently slammed somewhere round the side of the house. This was followed by the roar of a powerful engine starting into life, and then by a series of rapid crescendos as gear after gear was engaged in a swift acceleration.

"Well, I'm blessed!" cried Sebastian. "Somebody going hell for leather down the drive—and without any lights on, either. Look, there he goes." For a second it had been just possible to distinguish a dark, hurtling object beyond the line of elms that ran from Sherris to the high-road. "Whoever is in that is asking for a broken neck. Surely your Mrs Gollifer wouldn't be so crazy."

Slowly the uproar died away—and as it ebbed it seemed to drain from the three people standing on the lawn any reserve of nervous calm they had left. Lucy shivered. "Nobody," she whispered, "would drive away like that except from—from something horrible."

Sebastian Dromio took a handkerchief from his pocket and with trembling hand wiped his mouth. He was an old man and physical fear had suddenly gripped him. "Better get up the servants," he mumbled. "Better—"

"But what is this about?" Lady Dromio's voice was a pitch higher than usual. "Why are we behaving in

67

this way? We've seen a car—"

"And there's something funny about the house."
Lucy had turned and was again staring at the silhou-
ette of Sherris Hall. "The chimneys!" she cried.

"Lucy, whatever do you mean?"

"We can't see the kitchens from here, or the furnace. But there are two chimneys smoking, and
there should be only one."

It was true that two trails of smoke, one small and
the other larger, were rising straight into the sky,
clear against the moonlight.

Sebastian snorted. "Chimneys!" he said. "Who the
deuce cares whether there's smoke from every chimney in the house."

"I do. No smoke without fire."

"Fire?" Lady Dromio's voice rose still further.

"There ought to be only one—Swindle's. Nobody
else would dream of lighting a fire on a night like
this. And it must be a big fire to make all that
smoke."

"Nonsense!" Lady Dromio was driven to a panic
denial of the evidence of her senses. "Nobody could
light a fire at this hour. I don't believe there is a
single fire laid in the house."

"But there is—in the study. Oliver has come
home."

There was a moment's silence. Startlingly it was
broken by a new voice—no human voice, but a
nightingale's, piercing and full from a moonlit cedar
beyond the lawn. They stood transfixed and the song
rolled over them in burst upon burst of triumph and
agony.

"Oliver has come home." Lucy repeated the words
almost in a whisper. Then her voice rose wildly. "*And*

sang within the bloody wood—"

"Lucy, be quiet!" Lady Dromio turned upon her adopted daughter, her face blanched and ghastly in the moonlight.

"While Agamemnon cried aloud—"

From the house came voices, calling, and the sound of someone running along the terrace. Again the passionate song came from the cedar. They were hurrying, all three, between tall hedges, past the menacing hippogriffs, up a flight of stone steps. And to meet them came Swindle, grotesque in carpet slippers. His face was convulsed and twitching; his mouth hung open; he made as if to work it and only a horrible slobbering sound came. Sebastian grasped him and shook him roughly. "What the—"

And Swindle found his voice. "Your ladyship," he cried, "your ladyship—it's Sir Oliver! He's dead, your ladyship—burnt to death in his study."

They looked at each other fearfully and in a sick silence. Unheeding, the nightingale sang out its ecstasy beyond the lawn.

5

"Would you care to come and look at something?" said the voice.

Appleby glanced at the clock. "My dear man, it's nearly midnight."

"Quite so. But that's when these things are apt to happen. Of course"—and the voice took on the faint irony of the bachelor—"if your wife—"

"Judith's away visiting her people at Long Dream. When what things are apt to happen?"

"Murder." The voice spoke in plain triumph. "Murder most foul, as at the best it is—"

"Good heavens, Hyland, don't tell me you've taken to Shakespeare."

"Well, haven't you taken to bees? The force must keep its cultural end up, you know. But this most foul, strange and unnatural."

"Why unnatural?"

"Look here," said the voice most unfairly, "you're simply wasting time. Will you come? It's a baronet."

70

"No, no, Hyland—it won't do. I've had my fill of murdered baronets—and especially at midnight, as you say. The annals of the Yard are glutted with them. It was hard at times to believe that any could be left alive in England. For you must add, you know, all those we were obliged to hang. . . . Who is it?"

"Sir Oliver Dromio—quite one of our local bigwigs. And a beautiful murder. Hit on the head— they think perhaps with the butt-end of a revolver—and then burnt to a cinder in his own fireplace."

"Rubbish. Burning to a cinder takes more than that. When I was looking into the burning of old Gaffer Odgers back in—"

"To be sure—one of your most famous cases." The voice over the telephone was momentarily deferential. "But, you know, since you came to settle in these parts I've always hoped we might have something to show you one day. And here it is! Of course I can't promise, but I do think it may be interesting. I've heard some queer things about these Dromios. Why, in this office there's record of an investigation we thought it necessary to make into them about forty years ago."

Appleby laughed. "And endorsed 'How will it be with them forty years on?' Well, the answer's a cinder. I'll come."

"Good. I suppose Mrs Appleby took your car?"

"No, she didn't. Billy Bidewell came over for her with Spot."

"Then that's capital. I'll meet you at Sherris Hall. You must have noticed it? Big place rather falling to bits. I'd better get along there myself now. I've only had a telephone report so far."

"All right, Hyland—and thank you very much. But I rather think you'll find more than a few calcined bones."

"Possibly so. But that's all they found forty years ago. It's always stuck in my mind, that. I rather see this"—the voice was again full of gusto and excitement—"as a grim crime of retribution."

"As what?"

But Inspector Hyland of the Sherris Magna police had rung off.

Appleby smiled as he hung up the receiver. A thorough-going fellow, this Hyland, and evidently resolved to begin at the beginning. Few crimes have their roots a couple of generations back. But a murderer would get a good start if, for a romantic police officer, he contrived to give his crime so cobwebby a *décor*. . . .

And Appleby quieted the dogs and got out the car. As one grows older one's pleasures become less sophisticated, and he was fond of the smooth power locked up in the big yellow Bentley. It had bound itself up with his career; more than ten years ago it had taken him to his first big case—that queer, rather creaking case at St Anthony's College; the Commissioner had acted with the amiability of the truly great when he arranged that it should be sold to him shortly after his retirement. Routine had improved his technique since then, but it had also dulled his faculties; where was the sparkle now of those first clear runnings of detective investigation? He had done well to retire upon his marriage. And now here he was poking out his head again.

The Bentley purred through the night. It would

take more than ten years to rob that engine of its sparkle. The moon was riding high. The road was a white ribbon. The night air was close but obscurely stimulating. "*I am old, I am old*," sang Appleby, "*I shall wear the bottoms of my trousers rolled . . .*" Yes, one grows old; one's tags and quotations begin to date; it is very sad. "*Agnosco*," Appleby chanted "*—agnosco veteris vestigia flammae.*" The delicious and mellow melancholy of early middle age possessed him. An owl hooted and he hooted back. He could not have comported himself so when driving down to St Anthony's to survey the remains of Dr Umpleby.

The road curved and as Appleby swung the wheel he noticed a car ahead, drawn into the hedge. He slackened speed and then his eye caught something which made him pull up hard, abruptly attentive as any constable on a beat. He got out and walked back. The car was an ancient sedan with its hood let down. And a man was slumped across the wheel.

Appleby laid a hand on his shoulder. "Hullo!" he said, "can I be of any help to you?"

The man stirred and sat up, making Appleby immediately feel officious. Still, he could hardly have passed by what might have been a corpse or a case of serious illness.

"Help?" said the man, blinking sleepily at Appleby in the moonlight. "Dear me, no. But I am obliged to you for your kindness."

Appleby realised with some embarrassment that he was talking to a clergyman. "It is a mild night," he said, "and pleasant enough for a nap in the open air."

"Quite so—precisely so." The clergyman appeared to consider whether this was an adequately civil end to the encounter. "But it is not a thing I commonly

73

do. Indeed in my parish—I must explain that I am the incumbent of a neighbouring parish—the habit of sitting in parked cars at night gives me not a little anxiety. People come out from the towns and misconduct themselves, and the example is a bad one for our own young folk."

"No doubt," said Appleby. The gentleman, thus discharging himself of professional anxieties, he saw, was still half asleep. Appleby wondered if he had been drinking.

"The truth is that I have been dining with a friend —with a colleague, that is to say—"

"That sort of thing can be very soporific, I am sure." Appleby nodded sympathetically and prepared to beat a tactful retreat.

"Well, yes; Canon Newton's conversation is so polished that it is a little like an elderly lullaby—though I should hate him to hear I had said so. The real truth is that I have a very poor head for wine. So much so, indeed, that I have sometimes contemplated a total abstention. But then one is reckoned a dull dog—and even a clergyman does not care for that. The bishop would laugh at it."

This in a bishop, Appleby thought, was somewhat unepiscopal conduct. "It is a difficult situation, no doubt," he said vaguely.

"So I set off for home early. I was singing."

"It's like that at night. I have just been doing a bit of reciting myself."

"Now, that is very interesting." The clergyman was still sleepy. And sleepiness made him not morose but friendly—which Appleby judged a pleasant trait. "My name, I should say, is Greengrave."

"Mine is Appleby."

74

"Good gracious! Are you the young man who has married Judith Raven? I am delighted to meet you." And Mr Greengrave shook hands—rather with the air, Appleby thought, of a cricketer bringing off a difficult catch. "Well, as I say, I was singing; and then I fell to meditating a matter of some perplexity; and then"—Mr Greengrave hesitated—"I had rather a curious experience. It sobered me, so to speak, and I went along cautiously. And then I grew so sleepy that I judged it safer—"

"Very wise," said Appleby; "very wise, indeed."

"But I must not weary you with my affairs. I hope we may meet again." And Mr Greengrave made as if to proceed on his way.

Appleby stepped back. "By the way," he asked, "can you tell me if I am right for Sherris Hall?"

"Sherris Hall?" There was something startled in the clergyman's voice.

"Yes, I am making my way there in rather a hurry. I suppose it is an odd enquiry at this late hour."

"Has—has anything happened there, may I ask?"

"Something rather serious, I am afraid." Appleby was less cautious than he would have been before he became a private citizen. "Inspector Hyland of Sherris Magna rang me up—"

"The police!" Mr Greengrave's face took on a paler shade in the moonlight.

Appleby looked curiously at the agitated man before him. His indiscretion was deliberate now. "Yes, the police. I was a policeman myself, you know, once. Something bad has occurred, it seems. And Hyland thinks it has started up from some hiding-place no end of years back."

"Good heavens! Only this evening—" Mr Greengrave checked himself and looked cautious. "The truth is," he said, "that I have suffered from something in the nature of an hallucination, and I am still somewhat confused. I had better be off to bed. As for Sherris Hall, take the first to the left and you can't go wrong. Good-night."

And Mr Greengrave departed amid a grinding of gears. Appleby watched him go, and noted that the course he steered was very tolerably straight. It did not look as if the hallucination and confusion of which he spoke had any very substantial origin in alcohol.

"Odd!" Appleby murmured and walked back to the Bentley.

But this was not his only untoward encounter on the way to enquire into the death of Sir Oliver Dromio. And inebriety of one degree or another seemed to be the rule round about Sherris that night.

He found the drive and turned into it. Within fifty yards it forked. Taken by surprise, Appleby swung right and was presently convinced that his guess had been a bad one. This was a mere track. It wound through a shrubbery and petered out. And as he brought the car to a halt and prepared to back he saw that his headlights were focussed upon a sleeping man. He lay sprawled on a bench before a ramshackle shed. And on the ground, partly obscured by his dangling legs, lay an object that gleamed and sparkled like a gigantic firefly.

A tramp, Appleby thought, and slipped into reverse. But what, after all, was that object that lay at his feet, throwing back every colour in the spectrum? Had Sir Oliver Dromio been killed by a burglar, and were these the Dromio family jewels? It is astonishing how many burglars, when about to make off with a highly successful haul, get themselves hopelessly drunk on a purloined bottle of whisky. Liquor disposed freely about the house, indeed, is as effective a precaution as all but the most expensive sort of safe. And Appleby stopped the car. As he did so the man woke up and stared dead into the headlights in a sort of stupid terror.

The stupidity, it could be discerned, was natural to that coarse face. And the terror, surely had not come upon it on the instant. Terror, Appleby intuitively felt, had been upon the man when he fell into his drunken slumber, and the same terror was with him now as he awoke to that blinding glare.

It was clear, at any rate, that constabulary work was to be done. And Appleby leapt from the Bentley. But as he did so the man—who looked more like a farm-labourer than a tramp—found possession of his wits and limbs. He staggered to his feet, grabbed the strangely prismatic object from the ground, and with surprising speed rounded the shed and vanished into the shrubbery. Appleby followed, stopped, listened. Not a sound was to be heard. Among these thick shadows the fellow was creeping away or lying concealed with the cunning of a redskin. To play hide-and-seek with him would be useless. Lady Dromio's tiaras and necklaces—if indeed it had been these— were gone for the moment. But with the police of the countryside roused by murder the fellow had little chance of escape. Appleby returned to his car, backed to the drive, and drove ahead. He rounded a final curve and the house lay before him, its leads gleaming in the moon and yellow light pouring from a dozen windows.

And above it two straight pillars of smoke rose into the sky. Perhaps Sir Oliver Dromio was indeed reduced to cinders. But Appleby, recalling the charred hovel and carrion stench that had marked the end of Gaffer Odgers, again doubted if anything so dramatic had occurred.

And, of course, he was right. A stench of sorts there was, but it was incongruously suggestive of no more than half a dozen sausages incautiously left on a gas-ring. Through an open French window came the warm breath of this strangely Mediterranean night. Inspector Hyland sat at a table, stiff in silver buttons and black braid; he had clearly judged the violent death of a baronet to call for an appearance *en grande tenue*. White gloves and a silver-headed cane lay beside him. A constable was walking up and down on the terrace outside, apparently to guard his chief from sudden nocturnal assault. Another stood by the door, his attitude suggesting an intention to collect tickets from those desiring admittance to the spectacle within.

The body lay before the fireplace on a grotesquely deflated polar bear. The bear's mouth gaped open as if the last gasp of air had been forced out of it by the fall. The mouth of what had been Sir Oliver Dromio gaped open too. And the back of the head was all bashed in.

Would you care to come and look at something. . . . Appleby glanced from the body in its sprawled indignity to Inspector Hyland, neat and dapper at his table, naively rejoicing in being still alive. "I should be inclined," he said mildly, "to send for a sheet."

Hyland shook his head disapprovingly. "We must wait for the photographers and people from the borough, my dear chap. Nothing must be touched till then."

"I see. I just don't like the flies crawling over the tongue. Or that fat one perched on the left iris."

"Nasty, of course." Hyland rubbed his nose, uncertain how to receive these unexpectedly unprofessional remarks. "Very distressing for the family. They are prostrated, naturally."

"Naturally. . . . I suppose he *is* dead?"

"He's dead, all right."

"And he *has* been touched?"

"Well, yes, of course. He had to be dragged out of the fire, you know. Couldn't let him roast until we got up a battery of cameras."

"No, one couldn't do that." Appleby during these flat responses was looking carefully round the room. It was insufferably hot. "Who did drag him out?"

"The butler, Swindle. A disagreeable old man, who's been with the Dromios for ages."

"Is the butler prostrated?"

"Dear me, yes." Hyland was confident. "Terrible experience for the poor old chap. Fairly slavering."

"Nothing known to have been stolen, I suppose? Jewels, bonds, anything like that?"

"Nothing like that—nothing like that, at all." Hyland shook his head. "That's to say, of course, so far as I know at present. But I think we'll find this is quite a different sort of affair." He lowered his voice. "What you might call a domestic tragedy. They were expecting Sir Oliver back, you know, and were all very edgy one way or another, it seems. And then he came back. And immediately this happened. So it doesn't look like being the work of a cornered thief, or anything commonplace of that sort."

"I see." Appleby looked at the gaping jowls of man and brute on the floor. "The result of a family reunion, you might say?"

"Well, that's one way of putting it." Hyland found irony disturbing.

"No wonder they are all deflated." Appleby was glancing again at the bear. "Or did you say prostrated? It's more or less the same thing." Abruptly he changed his tone. "But how on earth did the arms get like that? There's something queer there."

Hyland nodded. "That's what they meant by saying he had been burnt to a cinder. Stupid exaggeration, of course. But the forearms and hands are just like that, as you see. I'd say it rather helps us to envisage the actual assault."

Appleby knelt by the body. The hands and forearms had indeed been consumed almost to the bone. The jacket, of dark blue cloth, was scorched over its upper part, and on the shoulders in places charred away. Appleby shook his head. "Helps us? I don't know that I see it."

"You notice how high this big fireplace is, with a mantelpiece nearly seven feet up? He must have been standing facing it, I think, when he was taken by surprise from behind. He would throw up his arms as he fell, trying to catch at the mantelpiece and save himself. But his grasp would fall short of it and he would go straight into the fireplace just as he was found." And Hyland looked at Appleby with a poker face. "That's all right?"

"It's nonsense from beginning to end. If a man got a blow like that his arms couldn't conceivably go out and above his head to save himself from a fall. He would simply crumple where he stood. And your reading of the affair implies that he was standing in front of a roaring fire before the attack was made. But who would think of lighting a fire on a night like this?"

"A man sometimes feels chilly when he's been travelling, even when the temperature is warm enough. Or he may have been proposing to burn papers."

"Or to roast chestnuts, or make hot-buttered toast?" And Appleby shook his head. "I'm terribly rusty, of course. But not so rusty as all that."

And Hyland chuckled, much pleased. "Exactly so! The fire was lit after the murder, not before it. And it wasn't lit for any of the common purposes for which one lights a fire. It was lit as a symbol."

"A symbol?" Appleby frowned. "Arson when committed by insane people is generally considered as some sort of symbolic act. But I can't see that anything of the sort fits here."

"No more it does. You see, we've come on something that goes back forty years. When Sir Oliver here was an infant there was a big fire at Sherris. His two brothers—he was one of triplets—were burnt to death in it. And there was something fishy about the whole business. We've got a record at the station."

"So you told me on the telephone." Appleby was now prowling round the study. "You also said that this was a grim crime of retribution. But what sense is there in that? The infant Oliver can scarcely have planned to burn up his brothers himself. So why should somebody part-burn him now?"

"I don't know." Hyland was honest. "But that old

fire is a sort of starting-point of recent Dromio family history. And now there is this senseless fire on a hot summer night. I just have a hunch the two things link up."

Appleby walked over to the fireplace and peered into a coal-scuttle. It would be interesting to know of anything emanating from the prostrated family by which this hunch of his colleague's had been activated. . . . He turned to Hyland. "By the way," he asked, "who rang you up?"

"Fellow called Sebastian Dromio. He's an uncle of the dead man, and came down to Sherris, it seems, only this evening. Pelting funk he was in too."

"I see. Did he say anything to suggest—" Appleby checked himself. If he was going to have a clear run in this matter—and it was beginning to interest him —he must not put Hyland out of humour. He turned to the door. "Here they are," he said. "Cameras, insufflators and all. And behind them your police surgeon with his little black bag. I think I'll go out and take a turn on the terrace. It's a lovely night, after all."

It was a lovely night. The constable on the terrace was enjoying it. But here was one of the two approaches to the room in which Sir Oliver Dromio had been killed. The place might with possible advantage have been examined rather closely before this heavy-footed young man was set tramping up and down on it. And Appleby brought out his electric flash and went exploring. After a fairly intensive search he went right round the house. It seemed a long time since he had treated other people's property in that way. But a notion of the layout of the place and its offices might be useful later on.

When he returned to the study the photographers and fingerprint men had finished their work and the police-surgeon was approaching the body. He was a young man who looked as if he would be most at home on a football field, but his manner was that of one who was equally familiar with occasions like the present.

"Well, well," he said, looking down at the sprawled form on the bearskin rug. "I sat next to him at dinner only a few months ago. Pleasant fellow enough, he seemed to be. And now his clothes"—and the police-surgeon produced a large pair of scissors—"have come off him in the normal way for the last time. Rather a well-cut suit to treat so cavalierly. But it causes the least disturbance before having a good dekko at him. No sign of bonds on the trouser legs. But he might have been tied up, you know, for some time before he was for it. We'll have a look at the shins."

"I doubt there being anything like that." Hyland was tapping his fingers nervously on the desk, and Appleby suspected that his confidence was waning as the night wore on. "He was heard in this room, talking in a normal way, not so very long before they found him dead."

"That so?" The police-surgeon was cutting the clothes from the body. The effect, as the white lower limbs and torso began to show, was rather that of some dark-skinned animal under the hands of a taxidermist. And the flattened polar bear grotesquely enhanced this impression. But the surgeon's mind had taken another turn. "Marsyas," he said. "Wasn't he flayed? And a fair number of saints and martyrs too, I should imagine. Not that our late friend was anything of a saint, if report speaks true. And I doubt if he had the stuff of the martyrs in him. Take a pinch at the buttocks here and you'll see he was a flabby sort of cove." The surgeon ignored the expression of disapproval with which Hyland received this. "Type of the athlete taken to living soft, I'd say. And what is nastier than that? No very obvious marks of violence on the body. But of course it would still be rash to say that it was positively the knock on the head that killed him."

Appleby stepped forward. "Not a saint?" he said casually. "Then I gather he had a bit of reputation in the county?"

"Lord, yes! Vain, self-conscious chap. Attractive to women, it seems, and none too scrupulous as to how he exploited the fact. Been between a good many sheets where he had no business, if you ask me."

Hyland frowned and jerked his head meaningfully in the direction of his subordinate at the door. But the young surgeon laughed bluffly—a nervous young man concerned to vindicate the possession of a good smoking-room manner. "Not," he continued, "that there's much in all that, is there?"

"Much?" said Appleby. "Dear me, no. Nothing at all."

"So there must have been something else that really offended people in Dromio. Well-nourished, isn't he? Tummy full of comfortable dinner, and kidneys no doubt just beginning to think of dealing with half a bottle of claret. In the midst of life we are in the county morgue."

"He offended people?" asked Appleby.

"Quite a heap. Do you know, they wouldn't have

him in the Plantagenet? My uncle's a member and he told me so."

Appleby, like an old actor picking up his tricks again, let an expression of discreet respect flit over his face. Your uncle, he was thinking, wouldn't thank you for your wagging tongue. "Is that so?" he said. "Well, that's very bad."

"Just every now and then somebody would decide that he wasn't going to know Oliver Dromio any more. Interesting to see how this damned fire and his roasting has affected the body temperature."

"Would his business affairs be in a bad way?"

"Rotten, I should say. This place is tumbling to bits. Saved appearances by keeping up a lot of servants. Cheaper than masons and painters by a long way. My uncle has quite a decent little manor house down in Kent. Help me heave him over, will you? Nothing much, but been in the family for centuries. And he says—"

"You think there was something more than just shaky finances?"

"My dear fellow"—and the young man laughed a patronising laugh—"they wouldn't blackball a man at the Plantagenet just for that. Plenty of them hard put to it, I'd say. Particularly with this damned government. Odd about those buttocks. . . . But what was I saying? Oh, yes. Every now and then people dropped him—and for good. I wonder if he could have taken money from women? Nothing rottener than that."

"Nothing," agreed Appleby. "Absolutely un-English."

"That's it!" The young surgeon gave Appleby an approving glance. "Dagoes, you know, really. Came to England in the time of Elizabeth. I have an ancestor who was Lord Chamberlain at the time. Gapes like a fish, doesn't he? Bit his tongue through, too."

"Ah," said Appleby. "I have an ancestor who followed Sir Thomas Malory. Crusades, and that sort of thing. Funny jobs we come down to, don't we? Mucking about with *parvenu* corpses."

Hyland gave an expostulatory cough. Clowning of this sort was not to his taste. But the young surgeon was delighted. "By Jove, yes!" he said. "Disgusting, isn't it? But, you know, there's a very decent girl in the house. Not out of the same stable at all. Old lady's adopted daughter. Clean-limbed lass. I wouldn't mind—"

"About the time of death." Hyland was brusque. "Perhaps you can tell us something useful about that?"

"Nothing at all, at the moment. Fire mucks it all up. Nor much about anything else. Have to be a P.M. tomorrow." The surgeon stood up. "Bloody fools, these murderers. Can't think beyond a clout on the head. And consider all the indetectable ways it could be done! You know, the physiological poisons—" And the young man, having aired a little learning, packed his bag and made for the door. "Family coming in to have a dekko?" he asked. "Better get something to cover him. He looks dam' ugly naked on that fool rug. Cremate him, I suppose. Job part done already, after all. So long."

He was gone. Appleby went to the window and took a breath of fresh air. "In five years," he said, "that youth will be the soul of tact and humanity. At the moment, he's a bit raw." He paused. "By the way, is there a family doctor?"

"Yes. Old gentleman of the name of Hubbard. He's out at a confinement and ought to be along any time. As soon as he's been here we'll get the body away." Hyland frowned. "Do you know, I doubt if Dr Hubbard will quite approve of those scissors and the skinned rabbit effect? Thomson, go and get a sheet or a tarpaulin. And tell the sergeant to ring for the ambulance." He looked at his watch and turned to Appleby. "Time's getting on. I'll give you the hang of it as quickly as I can."

"Thank you. And it is a beautiful murder, isn't it?"

Hyland greeted this echo of his first exuberance with a disapproving grunt. His bright silver buttons twinkled on him altogether incongruously now. A temperamental officer, Appleby thought—and brought out a pencil and notebook. "Well," he said, "fire away."

6

"At a quarter to twelve," said Hyland, "Mr Sebastian Dromio rang up the police station and when the sergeant on night duty realised what he was talking about he put him straight through to me. Dromio told me quite a story—which was odd, when you come to think of it. A bare summons would have been more natural."

Appleby considered. "Perhaps so. But he may have felt that when put through to you a fuller account was the proper thing."

"That may have been it." Hyland was gratified. "Well, what he told me was this. He had come down this evening with no notion of meeting his nephew Sir Oliver, whom he supposed to be in America. A neighbour, a Mrs Gollifer, came to dinner and left fairly early, driving herself home in her own car. At about half-past eleven the others—that is to say Sebastian Dromio himself, Lady Dromio and the young lady who goes by the name of Miss Lucy Dromio—

were sitting in the drawingroom when they heard a nightingale singing somewhere in the park, and as the night was warm they went out to listen. When they strolled back some ten minutes later they were met by Swindle with the news that Sir Oliver had been found dead in his study. Sebastian thereupon took the ladies back to the drawingroom, came along here and ascertained that the report was true, and then immediately phoned first Dr Hubbard—who was out—and then the police."

"All eminently correct."

"Quite so. And yet the fellow was in the deuce of a stew. Well, I gave you a call and then came straight out to Sherris. A footman showed me into this room, where Mr Sebastian was waiting for me. He said that he had returned to it immediately after telephoning, thinking it inadvisable to leave the body alone. He then asked me to hear the butler's story while he went and did what he could for the ladies. He also said he proposed to ring up Mr Greengrave, the vicar, judging that he might be of some comfort to them in this tragic moment."

Appleby raised his eyebrows. "This Sebastian sounds rather too good to be true."

"Well, I see what you mean." And Hyland considered. "But I haven't told you the one out-of-the-way thing he did say. It was early on in his telephone call, and it gave me the idea I'm inclined to work on."

"Ah," said Appleby.

"'He's been burnt,' he said. 'I knew that damned fire would come home to roost on us one day.' That was queer, don't you think?"

"Almost as queer as the metaphor it was couched in."

"Yes, I think something slipped out there, all right." And Hyland nodded with satisfaction. "There's only one way of making any sense of this thrusting Sir Oliver's body into the fire. It was by way of a nasty pointer to that conflagration forty years ago."

Appleby, with something like an apologetic glance at the corpse, lit a cigarette. "So you've suggested already."

"And I admitted I was a bit baffled. But now I think I see one possibility. Somebody was quite likely blamed for that big fire in which the two other infants were killed. I haven't looked it up yet, but it's conceivable even that there was negligence and that a servant was dismissed or sent to gaol. Well, that might rankle. And years later—"

"Forty years later."

"Well, why not? For instance, the butler—"

A knock at the door made Hyland fall silent. Appleby turned in time to see it open upon an ancient creature whom he at once guessed to be Swindle. He was followed by a robust youth carrying a tray.

"Her ladyship," said Swindle, "has given orders that refreshments should be served. Sandwiches, coffee and"—he turned and surveyed the tray—"a caraway cake the vicar didn't care for." The tone in which Swindle delivered himself of this unseemly fragment of information was displeasing: it seemed to indicate that, were he to have his way, the bloodhounds who had descended upon Sherris might more suitably be regaled on a couple of bones. "As for brandy, you'll find it on the side table. And whisky too." He stopped and peered myopically across the room. "At least there ought to be whisky. But after what happened to—"

Hyland interrupted impatiently. "Never mind about the whisky. And let the man put the stuff down and go away. We want another word with you and we may as well have it now."

With an uneasy glance at the shrouded body on the rug, Swindle gave the necessary instructions to his assistant. "I told you all I done and know," he said in a sullen croak. "A man can't do more than that."

"Quite true. But you may know more than you think. Were you in service here when there was the big fire forty years ago?"

"The fire?" Swindle was startled. "Yes, I was. Sixty-five years, man and boy, I've been at Sherris. And had six liveries under me at one time, I did. Now there's nobbut two men, a boy and a gaggle of women. And the work something chronic." His voice sank into a snarl. "You should see the boiler. Urrr!"

Senility, Appleby supposed, had robbed this toad-like being of that dignity of speech which upper servants commonly affect. But he was not sure that Swindle wholly repelled him. And as if aware that some flicker of human sympathy had come his way the butler advanced with a salver. "Take some coffee while it's 'ot," he urged unprofessionally. "It may keep you awake—which is 'ow you'll 'ave to keep to fathom this 'ere."

Appleby accepted coffee. Hyland took a piece of the rejected caraway cake without enthusiasm, hunger apparently contending with a sense of the in-decorum of this reflection in the presence of the dead. "Well, then, about that fire," he said. "Did anyone get into trouble over it?"

"Sir Romeo did. It sent him mad-like. They did say 'e died of it, in a manner of speaking."

Appleby set down his cup. "Sir Romeo was the dead man's father? Had he always been a bit mad, more or less?"

"I wouldn't care to say that." Swindle was cautious. "But none of the Dromios be common folk."

"I see. Would you say it was good service?"

Swindle considered this technicality more cautiously still. "We don't get on badly," he said at length. "The boiler's the worst by a long way."

Hyland reached unobtrusively for a sandwich. "Who else got into trouble?"

"Grubb did. Gardener's boy, he was then. The police—they was long before any time of yourn—raked about and raked about, and that very night they gaoled 'im."

"Did they now?" And Hyland glanced triumphantly at Appleby. "What would they do that for?"

"Seems 'e 'ad a grudge against the master. Sir Romeo was a great one for keeping the menservants in order. A kick on the backside, 'e'd give them. And if they wouldn't take that they could take their money."

"Dear me!" Hyland was scandalised at this glimpse of the Edwardian baronetage.

"And it seemed as not long before the fire 'e'd done something to put this young Grubb's back up. The lad swore something dreadful to the other outdoor servants as to what 'e wouldn't do to master. And when fire came 'e was skulking where 'e hadn't no business. So the police gaoled him. But her ladyship sent and got him out next day."

"Next day!" Hyland was frankly dismayed.

And Appleby chuckled. "A day in the local lock-up forty years ago. Somehow it doesn't seem a very substantial—"

"You never know. You never know what does rankle." Hyland's tone was unconvinced. "This Grubb may have been an uncommonly sensitive lad."

"Lady Dromio must have been an uncommonly conscientious woman." Appleby was frowning into his coffee-cup. "As I understand the matter, she had recently given birth to triplets and now two of them were tragically killed. But the very next day she sends down to the local police-station and sees that they let out a young lout of a gardener's boy."

"It's wonderful"—Hyland was sententious—"what the gentry could do in those days."

"Unquestionably. But she must have been pretty sure of what she was about." Appleby looked sharply at Swindle. "Do you know anything out-of-the-way about that fire the children lost their lives in?"

"Nothing at all." The butler's tone had become surly once more. "Nor what concern it is of anyone's now."

"Very well. We'll turn to other matters." Appleby paused. "But one further question there. What became of young Grubb in the end?"

"Became of young Grubb!" Swindle was astonished. "He's old Grubb the head-gardener, of course. And as good-for-nothink now as 'ow 'e was then."

Hyland brightened. "We'll look up this Grubb," he said.

"Certainly we shall." Appleby turned again to Swindle. "Would you mind," he said, "giving me what you have already, no doubt, given the Inspector here—your own account of tonight's discovery?"

And sullenly, but with a fair amount of intelligence, Swindle croaked out his story. There had been two guests to dinner: Mr Sebastian Dromio, who had come down to stay for a few days, and Mrs Gollifer. But as the one was a member of the family and the other an old family friend Swindle had not thought the occasion specially splendid, and when he had provided Mr Dromio with what he judged suitable in the way of port he had considered his day's work over and retired to his own quarters, and had there given himself to the study of household accounts. For it appeared that with the passage of years he had taken upon himself something of the function of steward to Sir Oliver, and everything went through his hands.

At half-past ten, or thereabouts, Robert had knocked on his door and informed him that Sir Oliver was home. Whereupon Swindle changed from slippers to shoes and emerged from his sanctum, apparently with the very proper intention of presenting his duty to his employer. He asked Robert, whose business it was at this hour to attend the front door, whether he had taken Sir Oliver's bags to his room. And to this Robert replied that he had himself seen nothing of Sir Oliver, who must have come in another way. The news of his return Robert owed to his colleague Joseph. Joseph at this hour had the duty of receiving from a housemaid such shoes as had been collected from the bedrooms during dinner, and these he was accustomed to polish not in the servants' quarters but in a sort of cubby-hole almost opposite the study door. There was nothing exceptional about this, Swindle reiterated upon a question from Appleby. Joseph did the same thing every night.

And while in his cubby-hole Joseph had heard Sir Oliver's voice in the study. It was an unmistakable voice, so there could be no doubt about it. And Sir Oliver was in fairly continuous conversation with another man.

Rightly judging himself to be in possession of sensational information, Joseph had dropped his brushes and hurried to Robert. Whereupon Robert had hurried to Swindle—divagating only to give the news to the cook in the kitchen, the parlormaid, housemaids and chauffeur in the servants' hall, and two kitchen maids who were helping William the gardener's boy to eat a stolen veal-and-ham pie in a scullery. And Swindle, when he had informed himself of the manner of Sir Oliver's arrival, had bidden Robert go about his business and leave any proper attendance upon their master to himself.

Appleby listened carefully to this recital. "And did you in fact," he asked, "go in and see Sir Oliver?"

"Urrr!" Swindle was contemptuous of the ineptitude of this question. "Sir Oliver made it a rule that he were never to be disturbed in there unless 'e rang the bell."

"But surely the circumstances were rather exceptional? He had been away for months—"

"'E wouldn't have heard nothing of that." Swindle shook his head decidedly. "I stayed where I was."

"I see. And you didn't think to inform Lady Dromio that Sir Oliver had returned? Doesn't that seem rather odd?" Appleby paused. "Had you any reason to suppose that Sir Oliver desired that his presence should be unknown?"

For the fraction of a second Swindle hesitated. "How could I have?" he asked surlily.

"Very well. But now about his manner of coming back. If he didn't come in by the front door how could he come in?"

"Through that there French window, I suppose."

"Would it not be locked?"

"It's Joseph's business to go round and fasten the windows at nine o'clock. But 'e may well have forgotten this one, good-for-nothink lout that 'e is."

"Well, we must ask him."

"Urrr."

"And when we do I think we shall get an answer you don't like?" Appleby turned to Hyland. "Does this man understand the risk he runs in withholding information on a matter like this?"

Hyland shook his head. "I hope he does," he said gloomily. "For it's a very grave risk indeed. Better tell us the truth, my good man."

It was conceivably this lofty manner of address, culled from the pages of fiction, that unnerved Swindle. He licked his leathery lips and let his eyes wander fearfully to the dead body on the floor. "I had a wire," he said.

"Did you, now! And have you destroyed it? Well, let's have a look at it."

Reluctantly Swindle produced a small yellow envelope and handed it to Hyland. The telegram had been despatched in the West End of London that afternoon and read LEAVE STUDY ACCESSIBLE FROM TERRACE TONIGHT CONFIDENTIAL OLLY.

"And who," asked Hyland, "is Olly?"

"Sir Oliver, of course. It be what 'e be called as a kid. Master Olly, her ladyship made us call him. Though, mark you, 'e was a baronet all the time."

"Odd." Appleby was staring thoughtfully at the telegram. "And he signed this in that way in order to occasion less remark in the local post office, I suppose. Well, what did you do about it?"

"I came in here just before ten and found that Joseph had fastened the window as he should. So I left it on the latch and came away again."

"It will be best to be frank with us, Mr Swindle." Appleby folded up the telegram. "Did any explanation of this instruction of Sir Oliver's come into your head?"

"I thought there must be a woman in it, of course." Whether guilefully or not, Swindle contrived to look surprised that any other explanation could be entertained.

"You mean that Sir Oliver, after being away all this time, wished to have a ready means of introducing a woman into his own house in a clandestine manner?"

"Urrr."

"Surely sixteen or seventeen would be the age for such an awkward stratagem? What attractions could it have for an experienced man of the world?"

Swindle's face fell into an evil leer. "There be no reckoning the queer turns will give an edge to that sort of thing. Why, 'e might have had a fancy for that there rug."

Hyland glanced down at the gaping polar bear— and at the shrouded body sprawled on it. His expression indicated severe disapprobation of this unwholesome erotic lore. "But I understood," he said, "that the footman Joseph heard Sir Oliver in conversation, not with a woman but a man?"

"I'm not saying what happened. I'm saying what I thought 'ud be happening. Like enough Sir Oliver had some private business 'e wanted quiet for. Like enough it was urgent and 'e thought to join the family later."

"Very well. You had left the window here unfastened. When the news was brought to you that Sir Oliver had returned you were, of course, not surprised. And you told Robert to go about his business. This was at half-past ten. What happened later?"

"Nothink till an hour later, or just short of that, when I was thinking of going to bed. The family was still up, it seemed, and so young Robert 'e was on duty still. Well, 'e heard a great crash from this room 'ere, and 'e hurried to it and tried the handle and found it locked. And at the same time 'e noticed the smell. Like somebody had charred a steak bad, 'e said. Well, I sent him round to the window, expecting it might be open still—which it were, so in 'e came and unlocked the door. There was Sir Oliver in the same clothes 'e sailed in, a-lying in the fireplace with his feet on the rug and his head in the coal-scuttle as you might say and his arms a-roasting as you seen them. I got him out—Robert being good for nout but whimpering—and there were no life in him, that were plain. So I went out and told her ladyship and Mr Dromio."

"You say that Robert heard a crash. How would you account for that?"

"It would be the tantalus, of course." And Swindle pointed to a remote corner of the room. "And not

98

just knocked over, either. Hurled bodily, as you might say."

Appleby had already taken stock of the appearance to which the butler referred. Lying where he pointed was the splintered debris of a rosewood tantalus designed to hold three decanters; it lay amid a litter of thick shattered crystal.

"It would certainly make enough noise." Appleby turned to Hyland. "And it was hurled across the room about an hour after voices were first heard here."

"And when there was already a smell of burning flesh from the body." Hyland frowned. "There's something uncommonly odd in that."

"Then within a couple of minutes the butler and footman were in the room. Whoever threw that tantalus must virtually have passed Robert on the terrace. But why should this unknown person, presumably alone with the dead man, pick up a heavy object and hurl it with what must have been tremendous force across the room?"

"Perhaps," suggested Hyland, "there was a third person as well."

"More like 'e were seeing things." Swindle croaked out this reading of the matter unexpectedly. "And who wouldn't be seeing things after doing the like of that?" He poked out a claw-like hand towards the rug. "That were it. The fire it would be flickering and flaring and casting shadows. And the killer 'e would think there were someone moving there in the corner of the room. And 'e would panic and up with the tantalus and 'url it. Same as 'im in the Bible did with the inkpot at the Devil."

Swindle, Appleby reflected, did Martin Luther too

much honor. Nevertheless his suggestion hinted unlooked-for imaginative powers. It conjured up a real picture of something which might have happened in this sinister room. . . . Appleby looked down at the remains of the tantalus. "There's not enough glass," he said.

"What's that?" Hyland was startled.

"It's made to hold three decanters. There's about enough glass there to reconstitute two."

"Perhaps one had been broken long ago."

"That it had not!" Swindle was suddenly indignant. "Three there was, as 'twas fit and proper there should be."

Hyland slapped his white-gloved hand on the table. "The weapon!" he exclaimed. "The blow might have been given with just such a thing as a decanter. It mightn't even break if it was the heavy square sort."

"It's a possibility." Appleby considered this for a moment. "But why should he make off with it? Remember he didn't simply hit Sir Oliver and bolt in a panic. He was here for long enough after his deed to permit of all the burning of the arms. And then, for whatever reason, to hurl the tantalus. Would he then pick up again the decanter he had committed the crime with, and carry it away with him? I don't see that."

"I think I do." And Hyland, always suggestible, nodded with conviction. "Panic overcame him, not at first, but slowly. And then he threw the tantalus for the reason Swindle suggests. In the confusion of that moment he might well think of the third decanter as incriminating—fingerprints on it, for instance. Indeed, there's a rational motive in that."

"So there is." Appleby nodded. And as he did so the litter of crystal on the floor gleamed like spilt diamonds. "Hyland," he said, "do you know I may have seen the fellow—decanter and all?"

7

Had Appleby wanted Inspector Hyland out of the way (and it is not inconceivable that he did) he could not have done better than retail at this point his encounter with the slumbering man with the glittering object at his feet. Instantly Hyland's picture of a dark domestic tragedy went by the board and he addressed himself with all his energies to organising a hunt for this prowler in the environs of Sherris. Whereupon Appleby decided that, unearthly as was the hour, he would endeavour to introduce himself to the family. And Swindle, approached on this, thought it possible that Mr Sebastian Dromio might be still available.

And presently Appleby was shown into the library, a gloomy room full of ancient books arrayed behind latticed doors, and suggesting that some eccentric Dromio had been fond of reading perhaps a couple of hundred years ago. At the moment it contained a Dromio who seemed fond of drinking, for Sebastian sat before the cheerless fireplace plying himself from a syphon and a half-empty bottle of whisky. He received Appleby matter-of-factly and without enquiry as to his status. "Nasty thing," he said. "Hard on the women. But then young Oliver never was the thoughtful sort. Have a spot."

Because he was no longer a policeman Appleby had a spot. "Who's the heir?" he enquired.

"To the title, you mean? Dashed if I know much about that sort of thing. If it dodges backwards I suppose it comes to me. But probably it just fades out. I must ask some fellow at the club." Sebastian looked sharply at Appleby and appeared to see that he found this ignorance surprising. "Never enquired," he said, "because I was just not interested. No money nowadays in a handle to your name. And it's money I'd like to see—particularly after this mess, which is likely to give the last blow to the family business. Young Oliver couldn't have got himself killed at a more awkward moment. Forgive my talking like this. No use, you know, putting too fine a point upon matters in an affair of this sort."

"Not at all," agreed Appleby. "So you don't stand to gain by what has happened, Mr Dromio?"

Upon this, at least, Sebastian did for a moment seem to feel that a finer point might have been put. But he shook his head confidently. "Quite the other way. I've been holding things together for years and filling my own modest nose-bag on the strength of it. But I'm dashed if I see myself doing it any longer. Have to retire to lodgings in Cheltenham—that sort of thing." Sebastian picked up the bottle. "And the simplest comforts are so deuced expensive these days. Take whisky." And Sebastian took whisky. "Or take—"

"I think it would be better to take care." And Appleby pointed frankly to the bottle. "The police, you know. I was one of them myself—"

"A policeman!" Sebastian Dromio was startled. "I thought you might be the under—the doctor, that is to say."

Appleby shook his head, not at all offended at having been taken for some one sent to measure the body. "I know their ways, and presently they'll be back badgering you again. So it would be just as well to keep a clear head."

A fleeting gleam as of sharp calculation passed over Sebastian Dromio's face. Then he looked impressed. "Well," he said, "thanks for the tip. And I won't take more than two fingers." He tilted the bottle. "Not that they have anything on me."

"Of course not. But they'll ask some nasty questions. By the way, what were you doing when this thing happened?"

"Doing? Mucking about the grounds with a cigar, I'd say. Warm night. A deuced disagreeable old woman came to dinner. Name of Gollifer. But I looked in on the drawingroom in a civil way round about half-past eleven and found her gone. We took a stroll in the garden and got the news as we came back. Nasty thing. Hard on the women."

Appleby nodded. "But then," he asked, "young Oliver never was the thoughtful sort, was he?"

Sebastian Dromio frowned, as if finding this observation dimly familiar. "Thoughtful?" he said. "Selfish, trivial chap. Vain as an eighteen-year-old lad buying his first ties in the Burlington Arcade. Not that I don't go there myself. Little shop half-way up."

"What was Sir Oliver doing in America?"

"Trying to marry money, as far as I could find out. Project had my blessing, I must admit. Girl with pots of it and lost her head to him entirely. Family was the difficulty. Merchants in Amsterdam long before the Dromios came to England. And a bit particular, as Americans of that sort are apt to be. Made enquiries, no doubt, and found that Oliver was a bit of a black-guard, poor chap. You know, he treated Lucy—" Sebastian, who had suddenly flushed darkly, checked himself. "Mustn't speak ill of the dead. Have a spot, doctor?"

"Thank you, no. Inspector Hyland tells me that when you rang him up you said something about a fire—some fire that occurred here long ago."

"Did I do that?" Sebastian was startled and crafty. "Well, there was a fire, and a mystery of sorts, when Oliver was a baby. But I must have been a bit upset to talk rot like that. More the sort of thing the women would say."

"No doubt. And of course this crime is likely to be the consequence of troubles much more recent than that." Appleby paused. "Money, I should say."

"Money?" Sebastian's voice was sharp. "What d'you mean by that? Only effect of Oliver's death, I tell you, will be to see what money there is fly out at the window."

"He was the head of the firm, I suppose?"

"Of course he was."

"But you had more or less to manage it for him?"

"I've done it for years. Deuced intricate, I can tell you."

"The money is intricate? You mean you are about

the only person who has been seeing his way through it?"

"Well, yes, I suppose that's so." Sebastian smiled uneasily. "I say, colonel, what about a spot?"

"No, thank you." Appleby was unimpressed by this sudden dignity conferred upon him. "Had Sir Oliver been showing any curiosity to see his way through it as well? If he was thinking of getting married, and the lady's family was of consequence, they might want to know—"

"Dash it all!" Sebastian Dromio lurched to his feet, and Appleby saw that he was older than he had supposed. "Do you know, I don't believe Kate and young Lucy have gone to bed? Ought to go in, I think, and do what I can." And Sebastian moved towards the door.

Appleby picked up the whisky bottle. "I think," he said gravely, "you'd better have another spot first. And, if you like, I'll go in instead."

Sebastian sat down again. "Deuced kind of you. No, I can pour it out for myself, my dear chap. Straight along the corridor and the drawingroom's on the right." And as Appleby reached the door he raised his glass and stared at him with a glassy eye. "Chin-chin!" he called.

Two ladies sat in the drawingroom. They appeared to be listening to the tick of the clock, which stood at twenty minutes to two. And when Appleby entered they looked at him in some surprise.

This was natural enough. The intrusion, he thought, was not decent, and would scarcely have been so in a fully accredited officer. He had better tell the simple truth.

106

"My name is Appleby and I have been brought here by Inspector Hyland because I used to be at Scotland Yard and responsible for such enquiries as must unfortunately be made here. May I come in?"

The elder lady bowed and with a hand which trembled slightly pointed to a chair. The younger lady looked at him fixedly and suddenly her eyes widened. "Did you marry Judith Raven?" she asked.

"Yes—nearly twelve months ago."

"Mama"—and the younger lady turned to the elder—"this is very odd. Here, for the first time, is somebody who may well discover the truth. And you have asked him to sit down."

"Lucy, dear, I don't know what you mean." Lady Dromio's voice was plaintive, vague—but her eye upon Appleby was appraising nevertheless. "Would you prefer me to stand up?"

"The gentleman has a great reputation. He is clever at finding out about all sorts of abominable things. Do you really want him around the place?"

Lady Dromio flushed. "You are unkind," she said.

"We go in for foul secrets." Lucy Dromio turned an expressionless face to Appleby, and he suddenly saw that quite recently this young woman's whole being had been overthrown. "I was speaking of it only this afternoon, when I went for a walk with a clergyman."

There was a silence, Lucy Dromio apparently judging this an effective speech by itself. And she looked at Appleby out of a sort of mocking misery which he found himself disliking very much. "Would that be Mr Greengrave?" he asked gently.

"Yes, it was he. Mama, I told him that we camped outside the cupboard with the family skeleton, and that you took your pleasure in leaning forward and making the door creak. But how was I to know that it would fly open to-night?"

The young lady, Appleby thought, should write mediocre novels. She would then probably not be a nuisance again. As it was, she had to give this sort of little quirk to grave matters. "You had no idea," he asked her, "that Sir Oliver Dromio might be killed?"

"I threatened to kill him."

"When in conversation with a clergyman?"

"No. Later this evening. Not long before it really did happen."

"I see. Would that, Miss Dromio, have been as the result of the painful emotional scene that took place after dinner in this room?"

Lucy Dromio caught her breath sharply. Lady Dromio reached out for a crumpled object which might have been a fragment of embroidery. The clock ticked. Then the elder lady spoke. "Was some calamity expected?" she asked. "Was there a spy?"

"I cannot say. But certainly there was no police spy. The police knew nothing until Mr Dromio telephoned."

Lucy Dromio had gone very pale and she was looking at Appleby as if he must indeed have prescience in abominable things. "Then how do you know that in this room—"

"Because of that rose." And Appleby pointed to a little heap of twisted and shredded petals on a table. "It is what a woman does when her unhappiness—her despair—is very great. And, had it been done before dinner, the debris would probably have been cleared away when servants went through the room."

Rather unsteadily, Lucy Dromio laughed. "Mama," she said, "did I not tell you? Everything is crumbling about us. Oliver is dead. And the secret of Sherris is on its last legs—or perhaps I should say bones."

Lady Dromio drew herself up and turned to Appleby. "Our misfortune has been heavy, sir, and my daughter is overwrought. Perhaps—"

And Appleby stood up. Suddenly Lucy Dromio sprang across the room, picked up the torn petals in her cupped hand and sent them over him in a little shower. "Rose leaves, when the rose is dead," she cried, "are heaped for the beloved's bed." She ran to the door and paused by it for a moment. "A rose is a rose," she called. "A rose is a rose is a rose." She was gone.

Appleby brushed rose-leaves from his hair. "You say, Lady Dromio, that your daughter is overwrought. She appears to seize upon the remark as a cue, and goes off like mad Ophelia with snatches of song. Casually, one would say she is acting a part. And yet she is, obviously, greatly upset. Can you tell me if there is anything that she is trying to conceal?"

"I don't think I can."

"But this evening, and in this room, there *was* some distressing scene? And Miss Dromio's talk of a family skeleton in the cupboard, and of the door creaking as it stirred, has some meaning?"

"There are things that I must tell you." Lady Dromio took up her fragment of embroidery and turned to a basket beside her. For a moment her hand hovered irresolutely between two contrasting shades of silk, and she was silent. "What I must tell you is this." And Lady Dromio's hand went decisively down on one skein. "Three sons were born to me when Oliver came. Now Oliver is dead, and it will be thought that I am childless—that I have only Lucy. It will be thought that the property should go to Sebastian. But now I must tell you something which I have told nobody. There is no reason to suppose that my other sons are not alive."

"The children who were thought to have perished in a fire?"

"Yes, Mr Appleby." And Lady Dromio inclined her head. "My own boys. And they are still alive and may come back to me."

"And it is your knowledge of this that Miss Lucy has referred to as a skeleton in the cupboard?"

"Lucy knows nothing of it. Nobody does. But she feels that I have always been . . . waiting."

"I see." But Appleby looked at Lady Dromio doubtfully, not at all sure of what light had in fact come to him. So far, extreme reticence had marked the Dromios. And now this story—which nobody knew—was pitched at him. Was there something odd in that? The story itself was certainly odd. Its simplest explanation was merely that this old lady was mad. The world is full of crazy old souls who believe that dead sons are alive and coming back to them. And yet, if Hyland was to be believed, there really had been some mystery attaching to that fatal fire forty years ago. Was it possible that Lady Dromio's persuasion had at least some basis in fact?

"My *eldest* boy may come back."

"I beg your pardon?" Appleby was startled out of his speculations.

"My husband was mad, Mr Appleby. Until just before he died it was a thing not commonly known. But he was mad and violent. When the three boys were born he was like a man demented. It is said that he tossed them about the room until it was not known which was which. And hard upon that there was the fire. We cannot tell that it was really Oliver who was rescued. My husband was indifferent to the matter. He was only concerned that he should have one son and not three."

"Lady Dromio, do I understand you to mean that under cover of this fire he had two of the infants smuggled away?"

"Yes—just that. It was very rash and unkind. But then, as I have said, he was mad."

"I do not at all see how he could have contrived such a thing." Appleby hesitated. "Are you quite, quite sure that the shock of losing the two children did not—"

"Send me mad myself?" Lady Dromio was now working composedly at her embroidery. "That, of course, is the natural thing to think. I might have comforted myself with the—the fantasy that my children were really alive, after all. Is that not it?"

"Some such possibility does occur to me. You see, I find it hard to understand how, even under cover of a big fire, two infants could be spirited away. There would have to be remains—what were definitely the remains of two human children—before the coroner who must have investigated the accident would be satisfied."

"But there were. That was what puzzled me."

"Puzzled you?"

"Yes. You see, I knew that none of my babies had died. I knew it because I knew that my husband had caused the fire."

"Did it follow?"

"Somehow it did—quite certainly. He was mad,

and he had done something very wicked. But he had not killed his own children."

"Or any children?"

Lady Dromio was silent. "It was my great fear. For years there was this fear as well as my uncertainty and sorrow. And then at last my mind was relieved—thanks to Grubb." Lady Dromio paused. "Grubb was the garden boy and they had arrested him for starting the fire. Since I knew that my husband had done it I had of course to insist that they let Grubb go. When my husband died I reinstated him, although by now he hated the family. It seemed the honest thing to do. Honesty is sometimes the best policy—just as it says in the book."

"No doubt. But you haven't yet told me how you knew it was your husband who started the fire."

"I just knew."

Appleby, who had felt his interest in Lady Dromio's statement growing, was suddenly exasperated. "But you must see—" he began.

"Yes, I do see. And what you want comes later. But I only came by it through just knowing; otherwise I shouldn't have been looking for it, and I shouldn't have noticed Grubb. There was a cottage where my husband used to lodge a gamekeeper; it is on the edge of the park. And I came to notice that young Grubb kept watching that way and staring at it. He still does. He is head gardener now, you know—and, I fear, a very lazy and dishonest man; I have had to dissuade Oliver more than once from dismissing him. Well, it was like this. Grubb would stand in front of this cottage and behave in a very odd way. It was a sort of play-acting. And one day I understood it—quite in a flash. He was imitating my dead husband.

He was imitating his manner of acting when a sudden idea would come to him. I couldn't think why. But now I believe I know. He was trying to puzzle out something that had come to my husband, once, standing just there. So I began to inquire."

Lady Dromio, prompted perhaps by some instinct for drama, paused to match her silks. Appleby waited silently. He had no doubt now that from this straggling narrative something of substance was going to emerge.

"I remembered that the cottage had been empty from just about the time of the fire; when I was up and about again the gamekeeper and his family were gone. And what I eventually found out was this. The man's wife had given birth to twins a few days before my own children came. The doctor who had delivered them was certain that they would not live. And then the whole family disappeared. My husband told the doctor a little later that he had sent them all off to the woman's mother, where they would be better cared for. And nobody, of course, was the least curious when they never came back. Don't you think, Mr Appleby, that what really happened is clear? My husband had this sudden wicked inspiration. He simply waited until these infants were dead and substituted their bodies for two of his own children whom he persuaded the gamekeeper and his wife to take away. I had no difficulty in understanding that this was what had happened. But I found it very difficult to decide what to do. My husband had been mad and that frightened me. I was afraid that it might all be supposed as—as you think, and that I might be taken for mad, too. I couldn't bring myself to have the horrible thing opened up and a search made. I put it off from day to day and week to week, hoping that I might find real evidence, something that I could take with confidence to lawyers and people like that. But I didn't find any real evidence."

"Never?"

"Not for a very long time. And as the months went by it seemed more and more hopeless to bring such a strange story forward. For it is strange, is it not?"

Appleby nodded. "Yes," he said soberly. "As strange as anything I have ever heard."

"Only something did turn up at last. But by that time I had adopted Lucy—I thought somehow it would help me along—and Oliver had begun going to school. I was very ignorant of the world and of affairs. I did not know what trouble I might start if somewhere I found two boys with an obscure claim to be Oliver's brothers. And yet I wanted my children very much."

"That was natural." Lady Dromio, Appleby could see, had hardened with the years, and now her character had a strength which had been lacking to her in the period she described. Yet there was something affecting in the rather helpless simplicity with which she told her story. "But will you tell me now just what was the evidence you finally found?"

"I read a novel about detectives and that gave me an idea. It seemed that there really were rather low but clever people whom one could employ to find things out without any necessity of really explaining oneself. I bought some nasty newspaper and found one of these people advertising. I went to see him, which was very horrid. I think he mostly lurked about hotels, peering through keyholes because of divorces and things like that." Lady Dromio paused and looked at Appleby vaguely, as if wondering who or what he might be. "Not," she added hurriedly, "at all the sort of person one would associate with the police. But quite able all the same. He found out two things. The first was this: that someone with our gamekeeper's name had taken his wife and two infant children to America about a fortnight after the fire. And the second thing—"

"One moment, Lady Dromio. Had you asked this fellow to discover whether something of that sort had, or had not, happened?"

"No—I had said nothing about children. I simply gave the gamekeeper's name and said I thought he might have emigrated. But the second thing this man discovered was even more important. I had to pay a great deal for it—no doubt because there were solicitors' clerks and rather superior people like that to bribe. In the few months before his death my husband had sent very considerable sums of money to somebody whom I recognised as an old university acquaintance of his, a rather eccentric doctor in New York. So, you see, at last I had something on which I could definitely act."

"And you acted?"

Lady Dromio laid down her embroidery, crossed the room, and wrapped a fine shawl around herself; it had the effect of making her look very much older. "I found I couldn't. It was something too unknown and big. I could mean nothing to those distant children, and something had grown up obscurely within me to make me fear them. I had a foreboding of disaster should they—my own children—return to Sherris."

There was silence. On the mantelpiece the little silver clock ticked its way doggedly through the small hours; on the floor the shredded rose petals lay. Appleby looked searchingly at Lady Dromio. "And that is all?"

"No—no, it is not. I have always known that one day I would do something. And I did—forty years after all the unhappiness began. Oliver was in America. On a sudden impulse I wrote to him, telling him everything and giving him that New York doctor's name. After that I heard nothing from him—although he usually wrote regular letters when away—except when he once rather urgently sent for money. I was much worried, thinking the shock might have been very great. Only sometimes I wonder whether that particular letter reached him, for he was moving about a good deal and was sometimes careless about his mail."

"You would have been glad to know that the letter had, in fact, missed him?"

"Yes, Mr Appleby. The letter was a mistake. If he was to hear the story he should have heard it face to face."

"I rather agree with you. And you have heard nothing to suggest that he had contacted those unknown brothers?"

"Nothing whatever. And I have now told you everything." Lady Dromio once more applied herself to her embroidery.

Appleby looked at her seriously. "Everything? What of your son's plan to marry? Had he advanced far with that?"

"I suppose Sebastian has told you of his pursuing an heiress. But I cannot say how far it had gone. At the time of his ceasing writing he was still very reticent."

"His plan must have upset your adopted daughter?"

Lady Dromio's vaguest manner returned. "I don't understand you at all."

"A few minutes ago Miss Lucy volunteered the information that she had threatened to kill Sir Oliver. Can you substantiate that?"

"Certainly not. I have nothing to say about it at all."

"Was Miss Lucy in love with your son?"

"Really, I hardly think—" Lady Dromio's voice faltered. "Yes," she whispered, "I think she was."

"Please forgive this question. Was Sir Oliver a man scrupulous in matters of sexual relationship?"

"No!" The word came unexpectedly and almost explosively. "He was . . . rather horrible in such things."

"Thank you." Appleby picked a final rose petal from his shoulder and dropped it in a waste-paper basket. Had there run, he was wondering, some deep current of emotion—and that by no means one of affection—between the dead man and his mother? Had the unsatisfactory Oliver been in some obscure way rejected in favor of the mere idea of those other sons of whom Lady Dromio had been robbed? Appleby was silent for a moment. "Do you think," he asked, "that Sir Oliver had made Miss Lucy his mistress?"

But at this Lady Dromio suddenly raised oddly helpless hands. "Go away!" she exclaimed. "You must please go away. I have told you everything—everything that is mine to tell. And I belong to a generation that—that did not discuss such things."

And Appleby withdrew. It was true that he had been told a lot—indeed that a complex and astonishing, if fragmentary, story had been pitched at him. And it was not a story that sounded to him like an invention. There seemed every possibility that Hyland had been right; that the death of Sir Oliver Dromio was in some devious way the issue of that forty-year-old fire.

But one thing, he realised, he had not been told— the story of the torn and shredded rose.

8

In the corridor Appleby bumped into Sebastian Dromio, and at the same time became aware of uproar somewhere outside: shouts, pounding feet and a succession of blood-curdling yells.

"Whash that?" Sebastian was grasping a tumbler and it was evident that he had been far from taking Appleby's advice on keeping a clear head. "Whash shishit?" Sebastian's hand trembled and he stared at Appleby with a wild and wavering surmise.

"I have no idea—but I'm going to find out."

"Shtop. It's those damned villagers. Shoshialists, colonel. Think we're dagoes. Always have, confound them. Heard about this beashtly affair and come to burn down the house. Polish no good; call out the military at once."

"I hardly think it's as bad as that, Mr Dromio. In fact there's no reason why you shouldn't go to bed."

Sebastian shook his head. Finding that it continued to shake after the negative nature of his gesture

119

was clear, he looked first puzzled and then alarmed; presently however he succeeded in putting up a hand and stopping it. "Die with my bootsh on. All Dromios prepared to die with their bootsh on ever shinch they had any. Defend our women to the lasht. Shoot at shight." And Sebastian clutched Appleby by the lapel of his coat.

The shouting renewed itself. Appleby shook himself free. "All right," he said, "shoot away. But I'm going out."

"Shoot?" Sebastian looked immensely surprised. "Dam good notion, colonel. Teach them who we are." And with surprising dexterity Sebastian Dromio whipped out a revolver and fired it through the nearest window, shattering a large sheet of glass.

"You can't do that!" Appleby grabbed at the revolver; Sebastian dodged, turned and ran. Appleby pursued him, swearing. Sebastian blundered down the corridor, whipped into a vestibule, threw open a door and disappeared into darkness. Appleby followed him with misgiving but at his utmost speed, and found himself on a terrace bathed in moonlight. Twenty yards away stood Hyland, all gleaming buttons and peaked and braided cap. Appleby gave him a shout—and as he did so saw the cap rise some inches in air and go spinning to the ground; there followed a second shattering report close by his ear. Sebastian gave a yell, vaulted a balustrade, and was lost in impenetrable shadow.

Hyland came forward, dusting his cap. "Appleby, is that you? And what the devil was that?"

"Almost another sudden death. Your Sebastian Dromio's tight, and he's got a gun."

"Don't call him my Sebastian Dromio." Hyland

was aggrieved. "Have you got a gun?"

"Have I got a tank or a jeep? Don't be an ass."

"No more have I—or any of us. But the fellow must be stopped. What does he think he's doing anyway?"

"Defending his women to the last. Thinks he's in the thick of a peasant revolt. My God!—there he goes again."

A third revolver shot had rung out in the gardens below. And, farther away, men were still shouting. Appleby got on the balustrade. "Are these your men making that fool noise? That's what upset Dromio—and I'm afraid it's going to keep on doing it. Couldn't you call them off?"

"Call them off? Dash it, man, they've got the murderer cornered."

"I don't believe it for a moment. And, even so, need they behave like a pack of dogs after a fox?"

"Hounds, Appleby—for heaven's sake." Hyland was outraged.

"It will be Dromio who has got them cornered, if you ask me. Even if there's been no damage so far, your local constabulary may still show a death roll of three. Pretty stiff—even if they are clearing up a grim crime of retribution. Come on." Appleby dropped into darkness.

"What are you going to do?"

"Jump on Dromio's back and rub his nose in the mud. Come on, I tell you."

Hyland came on, landing heavily in a freshly manured flower-bed. He got to his feet, breathing heavily, and both men ran. As they did so a fourth shot rang out and there was a brief startled silence. A fifth shot followed—and from somewhere a man's voice rose in a sharp cry of pain. Hyland stopped. "He's got one."

"But listen."

The cry of pain was repeated, and then, turned into a stream of lurid curses. "All's well," said Appleby. "Only an arm or a leg. You can't think up all that if you've got it in the tummy."

"But he's got a sixth shot in the locker." Hyland was running. "There they are. Hy, you men, there—lie down, scatter!"

A voice came back out of the darkness. "He's here, sir—somewhere among those hedges. But he seems to be armed."

"Nothing of the sort. It's another fellow altogether who has the gun. Lie down, the whole lot of you. He has one more shot to go. Then you can rush him as soon as he shows himself."

Appleby, crouched in the shadow of a patch of shrubbery, peered ahead. Two tall hedges came together at a right-angle straight in front of him, and disposed round these, like men besieging a house, there could just be discerned a number of helmeted forms, now sheltering behind what cover they could find. Appleby moved cautiously up to the nearest of these. "Just what is this, anyway?"

"I don't know what I can say, sir. One of our men came upon the fellow wandering in the park. He was the man we were told to get, all right, for he was waving a decanter the same as if he intended to brain somebody. Dead drunk, he looked. But when we closed on him he put on a fair turn of speed and got the shelter of these hedges. And somehow we can't get at him. And now some fool's turned up with a gun. . . . There he goes!"

Just so, Appleby thought, might a whaler cry "There she blows!" And following the constable's finger where it pointed above the dark line of the hedge he saw, momentarily glinting in the moonlight, that crystal decanter which ought to be lying shivered like its companions in Sir Oliver Dromio's study. Three times it waved in air and then vanished; its disappearance was followed by a wild yell of derision and defiance. "Come on," yelled a raucous voice; "come on, you bastards and let me bash the whole bloody lot of you! Call yourselves coppers? Yah!"

Appleby sighed. His expectations of enlightenment from this grotesque episode were meagre. He listened carefully. "Hyland," he called, "do you know, I think I hear that fellow Dromio going right down the drive?"

It was true. As the taunting presence beyond the hedge fell silent it was possible to hear Sebastian's voice receding into distance. He was calling upon an imaginary corps of Dromio cadets to drive the threatening *Jacquerie* off the estate. His sixth shot, however, he appeared to be saving up still.

"All right, men—forward you go." And Hyland advanced upon the system of hedges before him, waving his cane. The effect, Appleby thought, was rather like a travesty of some battle-piece by Lady Butler.

"Yah, muckers!" The jeering voice rose again. "Come on, the whole blurry gang. I'll make bleeding 'ermits of the lot of yer."

Undeterred by this mysterious threat, the local constabulary advanced. With cat-like tread, Appleby murmured to himself—and indeed it was a Gilbertian moment. There were angry exclamations, mutters of bafflement. "Can't make it out, sir," somebody called. "Seems like a little garden with this hedge all round."

"Come into the garden, you bleeding Mauds!" The decanter was erected again and circled—rather like Excalibur waving above the surface of the lake. It disappeared and the voice broke into uproarious song. "For I'm the king of the carsle," it sang, "And you're—" The traditional words appeared altogether inadequate to the feelings of the singer; he extemporised after a fashion that made Hyland breathe hard as he listened.

There was a sudden shout of triumph. "Here you are, sir, I've found a gap."

The constabulary converged upon this rallying-cry and were presently piling through a narrow opening in the hedge. Appleby followed. He was in time to hear shouts of bewilderment and alarm. "Can't make it out, sir." "Seems to be hedge wherever you turn, like." "No sight of him, sir." "Them little paths all over the place."

"Hyland," called Appleby, "do you know where we are?"

"Yes, I do. We're in a damned maze."

"Yah—muts! Will yer walk into my parlour, you blurry bluebottles? I'll fix yer! I'm a coming at yer!" With very considerable dramatic effect, the voice sank to a gloating stage-whisper. "I'm a-coming at you bleeders with a blurry rusty knife. Where will it get yer, mate? Arsk Haristotle. That's what I advise you. Arsk Haristotle and the 'ermits."

Appleby lit a cigarette. All around him constables blundered and swore. It seemed that only two or three of them had flashlights, and into the narrow canons of the maze the moonlight cast no gleam.

124

"Hyland," Appleby called again, "you know how these places are commonly made? As soon as you get to the centre there's a direct path straight out. Why doesn't the fellow simply make off?"

But the fellow showed no intention of that; he was plainly enjoying himself enormously. "Nah, then," he cried, "I'm a-coming after the first of you. Let's 'ope it's your boss, mates. No more wife and kids for 'im. Listen, will yer?"

Everybody listened. The sound with which they were regaled was definitely displeasing, being nothing less than the whetting of some iron implement upon stone. From somewhere outside the maze the constable who had been winged by Sebastian Dromio swore softly as a comrade administered first-aid. Then there was absolute silence—a silence through which there could presently be heard a soft rustling, as of somebody creeping on his belly over fallen leaves. Appleby could hear a young constable near him breathing with unnatural haste. Here and there lights flickered. But the forces of the law had precipitated themselves so gallantly into the intricacies of the maze that all were now isolated and no one man able to help another.

For seconds the silence was absolute. Then there was a spine-chilling scream, a dull thud, an ebbing succession of dull, deep sobs. Appleby could hear men gasp around him; Hyland, the commander who had led his forces into a fatal trap, was grinding his teeth beyond a barrier of hedge. The sobs grew fainter. Then imperceptibly they grew again in volume and altered in tone; presently they made a distinguishable laughter which welled to a wild mocking delight. "That tickled yer!" called the voice. "That sent yer running home to yer mothers."

Appleby chuckled. "Him all the time—and just treating us to a little play. Hyland, do you think it any good trying to track this rustic Minotaur through his labyrinth?"

"I can't say that I do."

"Quite so—and moreover we are wasting our time. The fellow can be no more than a grotesque flourish somewhere on the outer margin of the case."

"'Ere—'oo are you calling names?" The gloating voice was abruptly injured.

"Come along, men." Appleby's words carried clearly across the maze. "Find your way out and make your way back to the house. There's nothing of any interest to us here."

"That's right, sir." From somewhere in the darkness a constable of nimbler wit than his fellows took up Appleby's words. "Nothing here, I reckon, but a kid from the village having a game with us."

"I tell yer I've got an 'orrible knife! I tell yer I'm going to spoil all yer 'igh 'opes of romance! D'yer 'ear, you blurry bluebottles?" Anxiety to reinstate himself dominated the unseen lurker's tones.

"Been to too many picture shows, I reckon," said another constable. "Here's the exit, boys. Make for my voice."

"'Ere, wait a bit—you can't do this to me!" From the recesses of the maze there came a sound of hurrying feet and laboured breathing. "Yer can't leave me all alone 'ere in the dark, lads; not after wot I seen to-night. 'Tain't Christian—you arsk parson. Nor 'tain't the law neither. Ain't yer policemen?"

The body of men thus invoked had by this time extricated itself from the maze. "That's right," called

Hyland briskly. "Straight up to the terrace."

"Don't I 'elp pay yer bleeding wages? I demands protection—that's wot I do." The voice modulated from indignation to pathos. "Don't even a mucking gardener 'ave 'is rights? 'Ere I am."

Appleby turned round in time to see a lurching figure break from the cover of the maze and advance unsteadily but rapidly towards the retreating constabulary. In one hand he swung a crystal decanter, quite empty. Here was undoubtedly the fellow whom he had encountered earlier that night, a queer terror in his eyes. Appleby halted. "Are you Grubb the gardener?" he asked.

"That's me, sir." Grubb raised his free hand and gave a deferential tug at a forelock.

"I thought so. Well, good-night to you."

"Good-night to me? *Me*—wot's seen such 'orrors as you wouldn't believe?" Grubb was very drunk; he had just passed from extreme belligerence to some ecstacy of fraternal feeling; it was plain that this cavalier treatment hurt him very much. "Don't be 'ard of 'eart, sir. Take me along of you, and 'ear what I 'as to say."

"If you want to tell us something you may come up to the house. But hurry along. We have very little time to waste."

At this Grubb took a constable's arm and moved amiably forward. The hunt had come to the tamest of ends. Up a long flagged path between beech-hedges the forces of Hyland advanced, majestic and measured, conscious of duty laudibly discharged. The moon, as if to dignify the scene yet further, emerged from its clouds; the lawn was silvered; the bold arabesques of the hippogriff cast their shadows across it like a gaping and carious mouth. And into this the party marched.

"Halt!"

The word rang out so commandingly that, as if on a parade ground, everybody stood stock still. Some peered into the shadows. Others, with a nicer ear, apprehensively eyed the moon. Appleby, sceptical of any supernatural intervention on the captured Grubb's behalf, scanned the hippogriff. And, sure enough, on one of them the diminished figure of a man perilously swayed. In one hand he held a revolver. For a badly intoxicated man Sebastian Dromio had achieved a remarkable climb.

"Back to your hovels!" Sebastian's weapon circled in air. "Not to be intimidated by a mob of beashty peasants, believe me."

"Whose yer calling a pheasant?" Grubb was again abruptly truculent. Swaying slightly on his feet, and slowly swinging the decanter—of which nobody had thought to relieve him—he stared vacantly upwards. "Who are yer, anyway?" he called.

"I am Shir Shebastian Dromio." The answer came slurred but promptly from the hippogriff. "I am defending my property—deuced great property just come to me from my desheasted nephew. Not going to stand for any nonsense from peasants. Got a gun. Shoot at shight. Shoot one of you now. Picking my man." And Sebastian pointed his weapon with an unsteady but dangerous hand.

"Property!" Grubb raised his voice scornfully. "A bleeding Jack on the bean-stalk—that's what yer are."

"I tell you I am Shir—"

"You're nothing but a blurry nigger up a gumtree." Grubb brandished his decanter and favoured the heavens with an unfocused stare. "Send the police after yer, that's what I'll do. Friends of mine, they are. And what yer doing to that mucking 'orse anyway?" And Grubb pointed a wavering finger at the hippogriff. Suddenly his body stiffened and his voice changed; his eye had at last fixed itself on the relevant object overhead. "Gawd—if it ain't Mr Dromio! I knows yer"—the voice was shrill—"I knows yer 'orrible family crime! I seen—"

Sebastian Dromio's arm stiffened and his weapon spurted fire; a moment later his figure had swayed, spun, toppled from its crazy perch. What followed was a loud splash. The curve of Sebastian's fall had taken him into the lily-pond.

"Well, I'm blessed." Hyland found his voice. "A couple of you men haul Mr Dromio out. As likely as not he's very little the worse."

And so it proved. They hauled him from the pond, green with duckweed and shivering. Hyland looked at him distastefully. "It might be worse," he said. "He might have done something pretty nasty with that gun."

"He has, sir." It was a constable who spoke soberly from a little distance away. "Grubb is quite dead. That bullet got him through the heart."

9

The body of Sir Oliver Dromio still lay on the bearskin rug. The body of Grubb the gardener had been brought into the study, too—this social indecorum being justified, Appleby supposed, by the convenience of having a single depository for corpses. Would there be any more to follow? Hyland, at least, appeared not to think so. He was drinking whisky with the air of a man who prepares for bed. "Thank goodness," he said, "that that's that."

Appleby too helped himself to whisky. There was only a drain left in the bottle. Sebastian Dromio had consumed the greater part of it earlier—and hence, it was to be supposed, his undoing and present languishing in whatever dungeon Hyland had assigned him.

"I was pretty sure it was a family affair. And now—well, there you are." Hyland nodded sagely. "Grubb must actually have seen him do it."

Appleby set down his glass. "You are convinced

that Sebastian Dromio killed his nephew?"

"Of course I am. It stands to reason. We all heard Grubb begin to denounce him, and then he fired and stopped his mouth."

"You think that Sebastian up on his hippogriff was acting from calculation? I don't see that Grubb's denunciation—whatever it was going to be—could have been absolutely incriminating. It was no more, after all, than one drunkard's bawling about another. Whereas the actual shooting of Grubb was a plain and confessed crime in itself. It will be argued in court that he had an insensate notion that he was defending the place from pillage. But on the score of Grubb he has no chance of getting off. Apparently the shooting was mere drunken stupidity."

"But, dash it all, you heard what Grubb said."

Appleby smiled. "I kept on hearing what Grubb said. He was chucking words about in a very wild and unedifying way. And I don't assert that his accusation may not have substance. I merely assert that it is not in itself evidence of a very impressive sort. However, I'll agree that Sebastian is a suspect. He had substantial control of the family finances, and if Sir Oliver came home and demanded an account of them he may have judged it the simplest thing to hit him hard on the head. But there's a great deal that such a hypothesis just doesn't begin to touch."

Hyland put down his glass briskly. "No doubt," he said, "one or two points are not quite clear."

"For instance, pitching the body into a fire. And pitching the tantalus into a corner of the study. And Sir Oliver sending Swindle a telegram to open the study on the quiet—one doesn't see why an intention to bring Sebastian to account should require that. Still, the Sebastian hypothesis has one great attraction. Sebastian himself is not a hypothesis. He's a fact."

"What the dickens do you mean by that?"

"The late Sir Oliver's brothers are a hypothesis. They may have substance and they may not. Their mother found some evidence that they survived the fire and were smuggled away. In that case the probability is that they are still alive to-day. There is a further possibility that Sir Oliver contacted them when in America." And Appleby gave some account of his interview with Lady Dromio.

Hyland was impressed. "It's a deuced queer tale," he said.

"Almost too queer. And rather thrust at me, too. But consider it. Did Sir Oliver bring one, or both, of those brothers home? It would be the natural thing to do. And it almost explains the first mystery—that telegram to Swindle. These brothers are middle-aged Americans. We don't know what provision was made for their up-bringing, but it may have been not very substantial. They might be quite simple people, interested in this queer discovery about themselves, but awkward and shy. Oliver might propose to introduce them to Sherris in some unobtrusive way; to take them quietly in of an evening and let them see what they thought of it. That would explain his instruction to Swindle."

"It wouldn't quite explain his being killed."

"That's true enough. But imagine something like this. Just one of those brothers comes across to have a look—and so far as Oliver is concerned he is altogether an unknown quantity. They walk round the place in the dusk and this disinherited brother begins to realise what a grand place it is. They go into the study, have a drink or two, and Oliver begins to take quite the wrong line. Perhaps he lets out an old story that nobody really knew which of the three infants alone appeared to survive—so that not he, Oliver, but actually this disinherited brother may be the true heir. And at that his brother may have been moved to make some substantial demand upon the estate. Upon that they may have quarrelled—"

"And the long-lost brother taken a fatal swipe at him?" Hyland shook his head. "It's a bit far-fetched, if you ask me."

"Of course it is. But then so was this brother— fetched from forty years back and from lord knows where in the backwoods of America. We may suppose that the whole queer discovery had sent him a bit off his head. The fire which had been the instrument of his father's abominable plot would rather obsess him, no doubt. And in the thoroughly crazy state that follows upon homicide it gave him some odd emotional satisfaction to start a fire in the study and pitch his murdered brother into it."

"What about that tantalus?"

"We bring in the second long-lost brother. Both came back with Oliver. Both were in this room. The quarrel was general. One or other of them killed Oliver, and then they fell out between themselves. One pitched the tantalus at the other; there was the most frightful crash; and at that they came to a sense of their danger and bolted. They are on their way back to America by now. By next week they will be back to the common round of selling insurance or peddling vacuum-cleaners."

Hyland sighed. "Do you always go to work this

133

way? And do your powers of belief keep pace with those of your imagination?"

"I would rather not believe in the long-lost brothers at all. As I say, they may be phantoms— mere ghosts."

"Then they may turn up at any time." And Hyland glanced at the clock. "Half-past two in the morning is no bad hour for supernatural appearances."

"And an awkward time to get at ordinary flesh and blood. But there is more of that to be got at. For instance, what about the woman who came to dinner?"

"Mrs Gollifer?" Hyland shook his head. "I can't see that she's very likely to come in. Simply an acquaintance who came and went. And the evening begins to be abnormal, surely, only when Sir Oliver and whoever it may have been arrive home and step through that window."

"I think not. The evening began to get out of hand not in this study but in the drawingroom. There was a row there. Quite possibly it was an altogether independent row—or revelation."

"We could do with a bit of revelation ourselves." Hyland, his confidence in the guilt of Sebastian Dromio now shaken, glanced gloomily at the two shrouded bodies. "I wish they'd come and take these things away."

"The person who was particularly upset was the girl—Lucy Dromio. It would be interesting to know a little more about her. Do you think Sherris runs to any more old retainers besides Swindle and the late Grubb? An aged crone, long ago familiar with the nursery and schoolroom, would be a most desirable acquaintance. I don't think one will get much from

Lady Dromio—and from Miss Lucy herself still less. Of course, about a girl brought up in such a situation one can make a guess. The wonderful little Oliver turned her head—and she quite failed to screw it straight again when she grew up."

"Bother guesses. I never heard anything less like useful police work in my life." Hyland checked himself. "Sorry, my dear chap. Feeling a bit out of my depth, to tell the truth. So guess away. But I suggest we keep it till breakfast. I'd uncommonly relish a few hours' sleep."

The study door opened and a heavy-eyed constable put his head into the room. "Reverend Mr Greengrave," he said. "He's just been seeing the ladies."

Hyland groaned. "This is as interminable," he muttered, "as one of those beastly mystery thrillers in a cinema. No let-up at all. Show him in."

Mr Greengrave, too, was heavy-eyed, as if alternate driving and slumbering in moonlight had not quite cleared his head of either the Landorian periods or the Falernian potations of Canon Newton. He glanced from the living to the dead—both the dead —and his jaw sagged. "A chair," said Mr Greengrave. "A chair and a glass of water, if you please. You see, it keeps on happening."

The constable and Hyland brought forward what was required. "Keeps on happening?" said Hyland. "I don't understand you."

"I scarcely understand myself. The night has taken upon itself a habit—well, a habit of duplication. I am not in error"—and Mr Greengrave took a wary glance towards the fireplace—"in supposing that

135

there are two bodies in this room?"

"There are certainly two. Mr Sebastian Dromio has killed the gardener, I am sorry to say." Hyland, somewhat uncertain in the presence of the clergy, announced this with something of the air of a superior servant announcing disaster to the second-best dinner service. "He shot him while under the influence of drink."

"Drink?" Mr Greengrave gulped hastily at his glass of water. "I have often thought that if only the bishop would encourage the practice of total abstention within the diocese—" He stopped. "Would that be a man named Grubb?"

"That's the man. He worked here as a lad, it seems, in Sir Romeo's time. I suppose, sir, you'd like to look at the bodies?" Hyland spoke a little more briskly, as if passing to what he took for a routine professional procedure.

"Thank you. It will no doubt be proper to do so presently. Let us pray."

"I beg your pardon?"

"Let us pray."

Hyland, much confused, looked round for a suitable object by or upon which to kneel. Then he compromised by assuming the attitude generally judged proper at the more solemn moments of the burial service. Mr Greengrave prayed—and rose very much a different man. "This is altogether shocking," he said. "As an unresolved mystery it is not to be borne. The women of the family are altogether overwhelmed. For their sakes I hope that the truth, however distressing, may be found at once. I have myself a communication to make. Sit down."

Obediently Appleby and Hyland sat down.

"I saw Sir Oliver. And I saw his brother too. They were driving together in a car."

Appleby spoke for the first time. "You knew, then, that Sir Oliver had a brother living?"

"Certainly not. But Lady Dromio has just told me her story, and now I know it must have been a brother. At the time, and for reasons which our earlier encounter to-night have made known to you, I supposed my eyes to be playing tricks on me. In a sense it is something of a relief to know that what I saw was—um—veridical. The two men were uncommonly like each other—a most striking family resemblance. But then I suppose they were what are called uniovular twins—or triplets, I should say." Mr Greengrave paused on this, a little proud of his command of a scientific vocabulary. "Clearly they were driving home to Sherris together. And clearly it was with this brother that Sebastian—the wretched Sebastian, as I fear we must say—saw Sir Oliver earlier in the day."

"That what?" Hyland almost jumped from his chair.

"It is a circumstance which Lady Dromio has not been able to bring herself to communicate to you. You must forgive her. It is not unnatural—nor, I venture to think, altogether improper—that it is to her spiritual adviser that a woman will first choose to reveal a matter of this sort." Mr Greengrave, who until this night had never with Lady Dromio achieved very much in the way of spiritual admonition, spoke not without a modest triumph. "Sebastian knew that Oliver was back in England. He caught a glimpse of him lunching with a stranger in London to-day—or rather I should say yesterday. He did not actually see the stranger's features, but there is a strong inference, surely, that it was one of the missing brothers. Sebastian appears obscurely to have felt that his nephew's return was likely to occasion some crisis in the family's affairs, and so he hurried down here at once."

"And what did he do when he got here?" Hyland was once more alert. "That's the question, if you ask me."

Mr Greengrave shook his head. "At the moment," he said, "I for my part ask no questions. Rather, I have further information to give. Or, better, I have a speculation." He frowned. "Or, better still, I have an intuition strongly supported by subsequent reflection. It may be that I ought to have taxed Lady Dromio with the matter at once. At a moment of bereavement, however, such things are difficult. I have half a mind to ask Canon Newton to come over. He has great confidence and address. He faces the most distressing pastoral tasks with what I can only term aplomb. Only I have a notion that, at the moment, he will be—um—particularly fast asleep."

"Perhaps," said Appleby, "it will not be too distressing to you to confide this intuition to *us*?"

"I believe I am bound to do so. Although in all probability my discovery is unconnected with Sir Oliver's death."

"To say nothing of Grubb's. We mustn't forget him."

Somewhat unexpectedly, Mr Greengrave robustly laughed. "To Grubb himself," he said, "it doesn't at all matter if we do. He will be adequately borne in mind elsewhere. But about my discovery let there be no beating about the bush. I believe Lucy Dromio to be the daughter of a lady who, I am told, came to dinner here yesterday evening. Her name is Mrs Gollifer."

"I see." Appleby looked thoughtfully at the dying and still sinister embers in the great fireplace. "And does your intuition extend to the girl's father?"

"Dear me, no. On that I have no information whatever."

Hyland stirred impatiently. "But have you any information at all? Or is it just a feeling inside?"

"I can only describe it as a sharp visual perception. I was driving home earlier to-night, and Miss Dromio was much in my mind. Suddenly her image rose vividly before me—and at the same time that of Mrs Gollifer, whom I had never connected with her in any way. I realised at once that they are mother and daughter. And the realisation is the more curious in that they are not really at all like each other. I doubt whether an excellent photograph of each would remotely hint anything of the sort."

"Very interesting—very interesting, indeed." Hyland glanced over at Appleby with an expression suggesting profound gloom. "But as evidence—"

"It's not offered as evidence." Appleby had sat forward and was looking at Mr Greengrave attentively. "Was this before you saw Sir Oliver and the stranger we suppose to be his brother?"

Mr Greengrave nodded. "It was some little time before. As a matter of fact I took those two men to be something in the nature of a hallucination, and the experience tended somewhat to shake my confidence in this earlier visual experience. But I have no doubt of it now. Very strange as it must seem, Mrs Gollifer is the mother of Lucy Dromio."

139

Hyland shook his head. "Really, sir, your conviction seems to me most unreasonable. For instance, why mother? Might she not be the girl's aunt?"

"I quite understand your misgivings." Mr Greengrave was unperturbed. "But I believe it will turn out as I say."

"And what is known of this Mrs Gollifer?" Appleby addressed the two men equally. "Is her husband alive? Has she children? Is she an intimate friend here?"

"Her husband died many years ago." It was Hyland who replied. "He was one of the largest landowners in these parts. There is one son, a Mr Geoffrey Gollifer, who inherited the estates. Mrs Gollifer now lives on one of the smaller of the family properties not many miles away. Whether she has been much in the way of visiting here I don't at all know."

"I have an impression that she is a very old friend of Lady Dromio's." Mr Greengrave had risen, crossed the room, and was standing composedly over the shrouded bodies by the fireplace. "That she comes here often I do not know. Rather less often, I imagine, than the degree of intimacy existing between the two women would suggest."

"And her moral character?"

Mr Greengrave smiled. "Really, Mr Appleby, she is rather too old to have a moral character—at least in the sense which you probably imply. She is not, of course, one of my parishioners, and I am only slightly acquainted with her. I would hazard that she is a woman of high principle."

Hyland, his hands deep in his pockets, sighed with a resigned impatience. "Does that not suggest its being unlikely that she should have to farm out an illegitimate daughter on Lady Dromio?"

Mr Greengrave took a turn about the room. "Assume," he said, "that my intuition in this matter is correct—although I grant that you do very right to question it. The illegitimacy of the child by no means necessarily follows. To begin with, I have the impression that Lucy Dromio is by some years older than Geoffrey Gollifer. Thus if the late Mr Gollifer were not her father—and it is hard to imagine that he can have been so—it is yet possible that she is legitimate. She may be the legitimate daughter of Mrs Gollifer and some man unknown to us."

Appleby too had risen and was looking out of the window. Hyland's bodyguard—whether with licence or not—had departed, and the terrace was empty under a fitful moonlight. He turned round. "You say that the late Mr Gollifer was a land-owner? He would be the old-fashioned territorial magnate with his wealth pretty well entirely locked up that way?"

"Just that, I imagine." Hyland yawned. "Though I don't see—"

"Then we have a very queer situation indeed. Mr Greengrave's suggestion is virtually this: that Mrs Gollifer's marriage—her known marriage—may have been bigamous. It is this Geoffrey Gollifer who is illegitimate. And he is at present in the enjoyment of estates which are likely enough entailed upon his father's legitimate heirs male. The situation has the makings of a melodrama of the most orthodox sort."

"And is obviously quite intimately connected with the deaths of Sir Oliver Dromio and the man Grubb." Hyland was reduced to irony. "Mr Greengrave has been privileged to see a vision in the midst of great darkness, and at once our problem becomes crystal clear."

"If true, it certainly makes our problem more complicated. But that is all to the good. With police work, it is only in the very simplest cases that failure can be excused. The unknown body in the river, the robbery in the dark lane—"

"Yes, to be sure." Hyland made an impatient gesture. "The queerer a case, the more there should be to get hold of. But here we are heading for having a lot too much. Mr Greengrave has formed rather an irrational conviction and you, my dear Appleby, have built upon it one of a number of possible flights of fancy. But even if what you say is true all along the line it appears to me to give us not a single and more complicated case but two cases with no more than an accidental connection. Think of that brother—or of those brothers—brought back from America. Half an hour ago you were for having them right in the forefront of the investigation. But what earthly connection can they have with the hypothetical bigamy of Mrs Gollifer?"

"One possibility is surely not at all difficult to grasp." Appleby took another turn about the room. "It attracts me too—just because I am reluctant to have those brothers back from the shades at all."

Hyland shook his head. "They're back all right. Mr Greengrave here saw two Dromios driving in a car, not one."

"But I don't think you have any confidence in the other thing he saw?"

"Well, no—I haven't. But that wasn't really seeing, was it?"

"Here was Mr Greengrave driving through the

dusk. His mind was active but his senses somewhat abstracted. I am myself inclined to give more weight to his sudden inward perception about Mrs Gollifer and Lucy Dromio than I am to the two men of similar appearance whom he actually believed himself to see. He was sitting behind a wind-screen—and so, too, presumably, was whatever he saw. You yourself must often have observed that a mere defect in a sheet of glass will momentarily produce the appearance of two identical objects where there is, in fact, but one."

Hyland threw back his head in despair. "Really, my dear fellow, this exceeds all bounds. First you build up a most ingenious story on the basis of there having been two, and perhaps three, Dromio brothers in this room. And now you talk of a defect in a sheet of glass. Be serious, for heaven's sake."

"But Mr Appleby is to be commended." Mr Greengrave spoke with mild confidence. "It is plain to me that in such an affair as this there must be a stage at which nothing is more useful than a facility and fertility in hypothesis. Canon Newton said something of the sort to me only this evening. Only he was speaking—or I think he was speaking—of investigation in the field of the higher physics."

Hyland clasped his head in his hands. "Where were we?" he asked. "Just tell me that."

"I was going to say that the American brothers are still conceivably shades—convenient shades who have been wished on us for the purpose of obscuring something else." Appleby paused. "This matter of Mrs Gollifer's bigamous marriage may be the core of the whole affair. Even if the American brothers are a fact, and were about the place, this may still be true.

And we mustn't forget that more has been destroyed than two lives. A rose has been destroyed as well."

"A rose?" said Mr Greengrave blankly.

"Yes. A rose is a rose is a rose. And in the presence of Mrs Gollifer. It was after that that Sir Oliver died."

"It was after a good many other things as well." Hyland was sarcastic. "And who destroyed this rose, anyway?"

"Lucy Dromio. I attach some importance to it as indicating a mental state."

"I see no sense in that. A flower may be idly plucked to pieces by any petulant girl . . . Who the devil is that?"

Again there had been a knock at the study door. It opened to reveal not a constable but the corpse-like face of Swindle. Swindle looked balefully at the three men and then peered despondently at the clock. "No baths before breakfast," he said.

Hyland stared at him. "What's that you say?"

"Breakfast we can manage, though there won't be no heggs. But a bath you can't 'ave—not without a new boiler."

"We don't want baths and we don't want breakfast either. We're going away presently to get some sleep. Now, don't come disturbing us again."

"As you say—hofficer." Swindle's was a malignant snarl. "I just 'as to know. And what of the dead?"

"The dead? They don't need baths or breakfast either." Hyland checked himself, aware of the peculiar impropriety of this witticism in the presence of Mr Greengrave. "And now, go away, my man. Go to bed."

"Bed? With 'er ladyship choosing to keep open 'ouse all night? There's company in the drawingroom

144

now." Swindle paused. "Gentlefolk," he added witheringly.

"You mean to say that Lady Dromio has visitors at this hour—at three o'clock in the morning?"

"Mrs Gollifer come back—and young Mr Gollifer come with 'er. I daresay they might like to 'ave Mr Greengrave in, if 'e cares to go along. But they'll 'ave 'ad enough of the constabulary."

"The Gollifers haven't had the constabulary at all. You can give them my compliments and say I'd be glad to see them. By the way, isn't Dr Hubbard supposed to be coming?"

"Dr 'Ubbard be out still delivering some drab of her folly. And what be the use of it, I ask? Wickedness behind a hedge, travail in a hovel—and then it all come to that." And Swindle pointed at the shrouded form of Grubb. "Birth, copulation, death," he said, and slammed the door.

Mr Greengrave shook his head. "Do you know, I seem to have heard that depressing summary of human existence before? But no doubt the unfortunate old man has been much shaken by these sad events."

"Very odd about the Gollifers." Hyland frowned at the ashes fluttering in the great fireplace. "Can somebody have rung them up? And why should they come straight along in the middle of the night?"

"For the sake of what used to be called the Unity of Time." Appleby moved towards the door. "The Dromios' tragedy has its roots forty years back—or so we are asked to believe. But, as with some classical drama, its action is to be compressed within the space of twenty-four hours."

Hyland laughed shortly. "You think we shall have a

tangle like this cleared up by ten o'clock to-night?"

"It seems not impossible. But, of course, we must keep moving; and I greatly doubt our getting to bed." Appleby turned to Mr Greengrave. "At the moment I think we might tackle the Gollifers—constabulary and all."

10

Lady Dromio, it appeared, had made no attempt to go to bed before the arrival of the Gollifers; she now sat on one side of the empty fireplace in the same deep crimson gown which she had worn earlier that evening. And opposite sat Mrs Gollifer—a woman of the same age and somewhat statelier presence, wrapped in a flowing cloak of white velvet. Between the two stood Geoffrey Gollifer, a handsome young man now so sunk in sombre thought that it was some seconds before he became aware of the three men who had entered the drawingroom.

There was a moment's silence as the door closed behind them. What, Appleby wondered, had been passing in this room? Had these people been sitting in a stricken silence? Was there some good understanding among them, and had they been engaged in rapid conference—planning an attitude, a story? Or was each an uneasy enigma to the others? Or was there here merely a bereaved and bewildered woman with two sympathising friends? To some of these questions, at least, it should be possible to arrive at an answer now.

But it was Lady Dromio who took the initiative. "Inspector Hyland," she said sharply, "where is my brother-in-law? Swindle has a fantastic story of his having shot a policeman. I am very much distressed."

"Very naturally, Lady Dromio. And I am sorry that you should have further occasion for sorrow. But it is unfortunately true that Mr Sebastian Dromio has acted in a very rash manner." Hyland, a monument of caution, was giving nothing away. And now he turned swiftly to Mrs Gollifer. "What brought you back?" he asked.

The question was unprepared for; in the little silence succeeding it Mrs Gollifer could be heard catching her breath. "I was afraid—" she began.

"Better ask me why I came back." Geoffrey Gollifer spoke without taking his eyes from the floor— but commandingly nevertheless. "And I'll tell you at once."

Hyland shook his head. "You misunderstand me, Mr Gollifer. Your mother is here for the second time to-night. It is about that that I inquire."

"So am I."

"Geoffrey!" Mrs Gollifer had sprung to her feet— and there was, Appleby judged, nothing theatrical in the action. This woman had heard something which dumbfounded her. Whatever conference had been going on a few minutes before had not comprehended this signal fact.

"Do I understand you to mean, Mr Gollifer—"

"Yes, you do, man. Don't beat about the bush. I

148

was here, and I was seen—otherwise I would keep quiet about it, no doubt."

Hyland had produced a notebook. "May I ask upon whom you called?"

Geoffrey Gollifer laughed harshly. "Well," he said, "I may tell you later on. But you may take it that I was here, and that I cleared out hastily, and that—for good or ill—somebody who knows me saw me doing so. . . . I suppose you have a pretty good notion of the hour at which Sir Oliver died?"

Hyland was silent. But Appleby spoke. "Between eleven and eleven-thirty, Mr Gollifer."

Geoffrey Gollifer nodded. "Poor devil," he said. "Didn't expect him to come to quite that end. Sudden too, I suppose. Hardly knew it was happening, so to speak."

"Quite so." Appleby, despite a protesting mutter from Hyland, was disposed to be conversational. "He was hit hard on the head from behind."

"Was he, indeed?" The young man's tone was heavily ironical. "Well, he deserved it, I dare say."

"Geoffrey, how can you?" Mrs Gollifer advanced towards her son. "How can you speak so before Oliver's mother? And what madness has come over you? Of course you were not here earlier to-night? Didn't you tell me—"

"Be quiet, mother." Geoffrey Gollifer turned back to Appleby. "We might as well have the truth, mightn't we?"

"Most certainly—if we can get it." Appleby paused. "And you assert part of it to be this: that you were here earlier to-night and were then unfortunately observed and identified as you hurried away from what may be called the scene of the crime?"

"That's it."

"Did you commit the crime?"

Geoffrey Gollifer hesitated. "There wouldn't appear to be much motive, would there?" he asked.

"None at all, that I can see." Appleby spoke with matter-of-fact conviction. "But there well may have been."

"Exactly—there well may have been." An obscurely growing excitement was in Geoffrey Gollifer's tone. "Anyway, I was seen here. Begin with that."

"Perhaps you will tell us who this witness is? Then we can call him in."

"Certainly. Send for him right away. It was Sir Oliver's gardener—a fellow of the name of Grubb."

Hyland, who had been listening to all this in silence, dropped his notebook wearily on a table. "Mr Gollifer," he said, "do you, or do you not, know that this man Grubb is dead?"

"Dead?" Geoffrey Gollifer raised his eyebrows with every appearance of amazement. "How the deuce can he be dead?"

"Lady Dromio here appears not to be apprised of it, and I am sorry to shock her. But the fact must already be pretty widely known in the household, and I think it possible that you are already aware of it. Only a little time ago Mr Sebastian Dromio—with what motive or justification we need not now inquire —shot Grubb dead."

With a little cry Lady Dromio fell back in her chair. But Geoffrey Gollifer took no notice. "Heavens!" he cried, "—then I might have kept quiet and got away with it."

Mrs Gollifer had crossed to Lady Dromio and was

holding her hands in hers. But now she turned to her son and made as if to take him by the shoulders. "Geoffrey, are you crazy? You could not possibly—"

"I killed him." Geoffrey Gollifer's voice was suddenly strident. "I killed Oliver Dromio. And I now confess the crime, being troubled in my conscience."

There was a moment's stupefied silence. Then Hyland took a step forward. "Geoffrey Gollifer," he began seriously, "I arrest—"

"And now—stand back!" As he spoke the young man whipped a revolver from his pocket, vaulted a sofa, threw open a French window with a crash, and disappeared into darkness. "Keep still!" His voice came again, quiet and full of menace. "I have you covered. I killed Oliver Dromio. I shall pay for it in my own way."

"Mr Gollifer, this is folly." Appleby spoke, and as he did so walked quietly to the sofa and sat down on it. "But if you must shoot yourself I would suggest that you retire to some remote corner of the grounds —so much consideration your mother surely deserves. Not that you propose to shoot yourself yet—nor us either, I hope. You want to tell us the story—the story of why you killed Sir Oliver Dromio. Why not come in and sit down?"

"I killed him because of a girl. I heard that he had probably come home and I motored over. There was a light in the study. I called to him from the terrace just on eleven o'clock. We quarrelled. Finally he turned away from me contemptuously and I struck at him from behind with the butt-end of this revolver. As I came away I was seen by the man Grubb, who appeared to be spying or skulking on the terrace."

"You say all this was over a girl?"

151

"She was my mistress—a girl in a London night-club. Dromio took her from me. Have you got that down? It's the whole story."

"Mr Gollifer, please listen." Appleby's voice was very much in earnest. "You may have killed Sir Oliver. I cannot tell. But you altogether miscalculate the consequences of what you now propose to do. Shooting yourself now, with this abrupt confession on your lips, will not cut short a single inquiry. No magistrate and no officer of police would rest on your story. And the girl of whom you speak is a transparent fiction. The truth—the real truth—will have to come out. Your mother—and everybody concerned—will have to face it. It will be manly in you to face it too. So please come back and talk sense. And put away that gun. There has been enough folly with such things already to-night."

There was a long silence. Lady Dromio wept quietly. Beside her, Mrs Gollifer sat perfectly still. Mr Greengrave had left the room. Through the open window there came the sound of a motor-car approaching the house. "Dr Hubbard," Hyland said. And again silence fell.

"Here I am." Geoffrey Gollifer was in the room again, the revolver trailing idly in his hand. "And no doubt you are right. But it is pleasant for nobody—this story of why I really killed Oliver Dromio."

"I think," Appleby said quietly, "that we had better hear your mother first."

"My son's confession is wholly false." Mrs Gollifer spoke at once. "Question him on details of the crime, and you will find that he cannot give information which the real murderer would be bound to have."

Hyland, whose eyelids were heavy and drooping, roused himself at this. "There may be something in that," he said. "Unless"—he glanced suspiciously from mother to son—"unless the two of you are up to some pretty deep game. Mr Gollifer—just how did you leave the body?"

"I left it where it fell." There was not a moment's hesitation in Geoffrey Gollifer's reply. "Lying there on the terrace."

"Nonsense!" Appleby spoke quickly. "You dragged it into the study—didn't you?"

"I did not."

"You see? Geoffrey is talking at random." Mrs Gollifer leant forward. "His whole story is only designed to conceal some very terrible secret which I know is bound to come out."

Appleby inclined his head. "That there is such a secret I am quite willing to believe. But if you, Mrs Gollifer, know that it is bound to come out, it seems likely that your son knows too. Suppose he did not, in fact, kill Sir Oliver. Is he not more likely to be shielding a person than a secret? Now, who is the person whom it is most likely he should wish to shield?"

"It is a secret, I tell you—and a secret Geoffrey did not even know until some time after this horrible murder had happened. It must have been nearly midnight when his car overtook me as I was driving home."

"I am afraid I don't understand that at all, Mrs Gollifer. It would appear that you took leave of Lady Dromio before eleven o'clock. How, then, can you still have been on your road home at nearly midnight?"

"Because I lingered here in the grounds." Mrs Gollifer had hesitated only for an instant. "I was extremely agitated, as you will presently understand. I lingered for some time before getting into my car and driving away. Geoffrey overtook me and recognised the car—"

"Overtook you! Where then, was he coming from?"

"I was coming from here." Geoffrey Gollifer interrupted harshly. "I was coming from Sherris after killing Dromio."

"He overtook me and stopped." Mrs Gollifer pressed desperately on. "I was so distressed—almost prostrated, indeed—that concealment was impossible. Moreover I knew that my secret was a secret no longer, and that Geoffrey must know of it soon. Because Lucy knew."

"Lucy had learnt that she was your daughter?"

Mrs Gollifer paled. She looked at Appleby with dilated eyes. "It is impossible!" she said hoarsely. "It is impossible that you should know that."

"Nevertheless, we do know it. Long ago, Mrs Gollifer, you committed—what must have been as difficult as it is uncommon in your rank of society—the crime of bigamy. It is Miss Lucy, and not Mr Gollifer here, who is your legitimate child."

"You have discovered the truth. It was in India, and when I was a girl, that I married. The marriage was secret at the time, because certain property of my own might have been forfeited had it been made public. And then the man whom I had married proved degenerate and wholly bad. I ran away from him—and presently found that I was with child. Kate—Lady Dromio, here—befriended me; my

154

daughter was born without the knowledge of my relatives, and adopted into this house. I regarded it as a chapter in my life wholly closed, and later I married the man whose name Geoffrey bears."

"You mean," said Hyland grimly, "that you went through a form of marriage with the late Mr Gollifer."

"That is what I mean. But of all this Geoffrey knew nothing until I told him the story to-night—and after poor Oliver had been killed."

"But why to-night? What prompted this sudden confession to your son? It was news of the most serious moment to him. Quite conceivably his tenure of the Gollifer properties is invalidated by these long-concealed facts."

"I had lived with the deception too long." Mrs Gollifer was now composed. "And moreover I saw the possibility of a very dreadful complication approaching."

Appleby looked up suddenly. "What was that?"

Mrs Gollifer hesitated; it was her first moment, it might have seemed, of real indecision. "That is where Sir Oliver comes in," she said. "It introduces something that Geoffrey does not even yet know. And that is very important. For this further information might indeed suggest a motive for Geoffrey's killing Oliver." Mrs Gollifer paused. Then she turned to her son. "Geoffrey," she said, "you are frantically resolved to take this crime upon yourself. But I challenge you. There is something I know about Oliver Dromio which might almost excuse the killing of him. But you do not know it; you have had no opportunity to learn it yet. Name it to these men, if you can."

"Oliver Dromio was blackmailing you. He had learnt the truth about Lucy, although I cannot tell how. He had been threatening to reveal the truth, and so extorting money from you for a long time."

Abruptly, composure left Mrs Gollifer; it was as if her face fell quite suddenly into the tragic lines of age. "You knew!" she whispered. "Then all that living lie was in vain."

Geoffrey Gollifer nodded sombrely. "I knew—but it was only an hour or so before Dromio's death that the knowledge came to me. I went home to find my passport. Very wrongly, I rummaged among your papers—" He paused. "And almost at the same hour your reserve had broken down here at Sherris and—for some reason—you had told Lucy the truth."

There was silence in Lady Dromio's drawingroom. Appleby, bending down, picked a single crumbled rose petal from the carpet. "A rose is a rose," he said —and looked at the petal as if it yet had some secret to reveal. "A rose is a rose is a rose."

"I told Lucy that she was my daughter. I told Kate that her son knew the story; I told her that I had been forced to pay him money." Mrs Gollifer spoke tonelessly now. "I had not intended to speak. But—quite suddenly—it seemed to me that anything was better than those lived and acted and spoken lies. Lucy was horrified. I had not realised before that she loved Oliver so much."

Geoffrey Gollifer made a sudden movement where he sat. Hyland, apprehensive of the revolver, sprang towards him. But the young man was sitting immobile and pale again. "It was to be expected that Lucy would be upset," he said quietly.

156

"And Kate was, for the time, completely overthrown. I realised that I had done wrong—that once again I had done wrong. I ought to have struggled to take both secrets—of Lucy's birth and Oliver's blackmail—to the grave with me. Meanwhile, there was nothing to do but go home. I said good-bye and then for what seemed an eternity wandered the grounds here. Then I did go home—and was overtaken by Geoffrey, as I have said. I was constrained to tell him the truth—part of the truth— and he immediately insisted that we return to Sherris. But that he had only an hour or so before learnt everything—learnt more than I could bear to tell him now—of that I had no idea."

"So now it is all tolerably clear." Geoffrey Gollifer looked first at the clock and then at Hyland. "It must be very satisfactory for you to get this affair straightened out within a few hours of its happening."

"Straightened out!" Hyland flared into sudden exasperation. "I have never met such an abominable tangle of lies and deceptions in my life. You claim to have killed Sir Oliver. Yet you say that the body—"

"There are certainly one or two points that are a shade obscure." It was Appleby who interrupted. "But I do not see that we need seriously quarrel with Mr Gollifer's claim to be the murderer of the dead man—of one of the dead men. He had just discovered the fact of his own illegitimacy. No doubt he has been proud of his birth and proud of his possessions, so the discovery might very well unbalance him for a time. But there was more than that. He made the simultaneous discovery that the secret of his birth was being exploited by Sir Oliver Dromio to extort money from his mother. Here, surely, is a very sufficient motive for a crime of passion. We might well rest on it. And yet there is a further fact to be considered. Mr Gollifer had made another discovery. Lucy Dromio, Lady Dromio's adopted daughter, was his half-sister. And here there is a reasonable question to ask. Was it simply the fact of Sir Oliver's blackmailing her that prompted Mrs Gollifer, in this room earlier to-night, to tell Lucy Dromio the truth of the matter? Here was a secret which had been kept for years— and plainly it had been the intention to keep it for ever. What prompted Mrs Gollifer to reveal to Lucy that they were mother and daughter? Mrs Gollifer, in explanation, has spoken of seeing the possibility of a very dreadful complication approaching, but she has avoided elucidating this. I think she must see that her motive leads us to a fact enormously strengthening the case against her son. She had reason to believe her son to be in love with Lucy. And the growth of a love-affair between these two children of the same mother—between her two children—would appear very terrible to her. All the horror of incest would attach itself to the idea. Panic seized her and she told the truth." Appleby paused and then turned to Geoffrey Gollifer. "I think," he asked gravely, "that you had formed such an attachment for Miss Dromio?"

"I told you that the quarrel was over a girl." Geoffrey looked up with haggard eyes. "And it was Lucy, of course. What else should persuade me to kill the brute?"

"Very well. Your story is so far emended that the girl becomes not somebody in a night-club but Miss Dromio, whom you had just discovered to be your half-sister. Let us, please, have what further emendations are necessary. You arrived on the terrace and through the open study window you called upon Sir Oliver to come out and face you. What then?"

Geoffrey Gollifer passed a hand over his forehead; he knit his brows in what might have been an effort either of calculation or memory. "Do you want it *verbatim*?" he asked.

"We should like the most exact account you can give."

"There wasn't much said. I went straight to the point. I said, 'Dromio, you've been blackmailing my mother.' He said, 'Then has she split?'—or not exactly that, for he applied a filthy term to her. I said, 'No, I found your letter.' He cursed and then laughed. 'That bungling first shot,' he said. 'I knew it might bring trouble.'"

Appleby nodded. "I see. In fact, what you found among your mother's things was the first letter demanding money that he wrote?"

"Yes. There was only the one letter. After writing it he no doubt realised that it was poor technique."

"Uncommonly so. And what happened then?"

"I said, 'You've been blackmailing my mother about Lucy's birth, and at the same time you've been letting Lucy fall in love with you. You're not fit to live.' He said, 'You'd have liked Lucy to be in love with you? Well, your precious discovery has cooked that goose. Unless you're not too particular in such things. After all, we can all keep quiet. You can have your bride—or ought I to say your sister? I've done with her.'"

Geoffrey Gollifer paused. There were beads of sweat on his brow. Every eye in the room was intently fixed upon him.

"When he said that"—Hyland's voice was pitched

low—"did you understand him to mean—"

"Yes, I did. He meant that Lucy had been his mistress. I don't believe it now. It is just the sort of foul lie that the brute would tell. But at the time I believed it. He saw I did, and he turned away with a laugh. That laugh did it. I brought out my revolver. But I realised I mustn't make a row. So I hit him on the back of the head as he was about to step back into the study. And the blow killed him, as I meant it to do."

Hyland stood up. "And that is the whole truth, at last?"

"It is the whole truth."

"It is a lie!"

They all swung round. Standing in the doorway, pale as the long white gown she wore, was Lucy Dromio. Hyland moved towards her. "Miss Dromio, I think it would be better—"

"It cannot be other than a lie. Mr Gollifer can have had no such conversation with Oliver and then killed him. It is impossible."

Lady Dromio too had risen. "Lucy, Lucy," she cried, "—it is all too horribly true. Oliver was wicked. He was a wicked, wicked son. If only the others had come back to me! Oliver was wicked, and poor Mary's son was tried and taunted by him beyond endurance. But we can do nothing to help Geoffrey now. To deny the truth is useless. All we can do is to try to comfort your—your mother, my dear."

"This is idle talk, mama." Lucy's voice was at once hard and full of indefinable emotion. "I repeat that Mr Gollifer's story is a lie—though told to what purpose, I do not know. I stood here—you none of you

160

saw me—and heard him tell his story. Out on the terrace, he says, he quarrelled with Oliver and killed him. It is impossible."

There was a moment's silence—the girl's words carrying a queer, bewildered conviction through the room. And it was Geoffrey Gollifer who spoke. "Lucy," he cried, "this is useless! Nothing can come of it but trouble to yourself. As for me, let them hang me if they will. I quarrelled with him, as any decent man would have done. I killed him with a rash blow—"

"You did neither—or I would kill you now." Suddenly Lucy Dromio's voice was simply passionate. "Who were you—queer half-brother though you are—to say what should stand between Oliver and me? And why must you now tell these meaningless lies?"

Appleby stepped forward. "Miss Dromio," he said quietly, "it is time to speak out. You declare that Mr Gollifer here cannot have quarrelled with and killed Sir Oliver. Why not?"

For a moment Lucy Dromio hesitated. She made a gesture that was at once helpless, baffled and strangely joyful. "Because," she said, "it is not Oliver who has been killed. It is a man strangely like him— but Oliver himself it is not."

With a low moan, Lady Dromio dropped insensible to the floor. And at the same moment Geoffrey Gollifer, with a cry which might have been either of rage or despair, leapt for the window and vanished into the night.

11

"And just when we had it all taped!" Hyland angrily paced the library to which he and Appleby had retired; he gave a vicious shove with his foot at certain mouldering folios of patristic learning which protruded from a lower shelf.

"Well, you know, there had been triplets." Appleby was mildly reasonable. "And there was some evidence that one at least of them had been about. So perhaps we ought to have thought that the body was not really Sir Oliver's at all." Appleby stared at the ranged books, obviously a man profoundly dissatisfied.

"It's almost incredible." Hyland came to a halt before the fireplace. "Dash it all, the corpse is in Sir Oliver's clothes—the very clothes he sailed in."

Appleby smiled. "Come, come, my dear chap. Corpses have been found in other people's clothes before now. The question is—how long had this fellow been in Sir Oliver's shoes?"

"In his shoes?" The small hours were making Hyland heavy-witted.

"Is this a brother who travelled back from America as Sir Oliver? Or did he only become Sir Oliver, so to speak, after he was killed out there on the terrace, or in the study? You know, Hyland, there are a great many possibilities in this."

"I don't deny it. Too many possibilities by a long way. But at least that young fellow Gollifer—" Hyland broke off and groaned. "They haven't found him. He's got clean away. Lord, Lord, if there won't be a row about that!"

"Nonsense. The Chief Constable thinks the world of you, my dear fellow. But you were saying?"

"At least that young fellow Gollifer is a shocking liar. It is impossible that he should have killed the wrong brother by mistake. The conversation he reports himself as engaging in could not conceivably have taken place with a stranger from America—and one who would have, presumably, an unmistakable American accent."

"That is true. But Gollifer may have conversed with one man and killed another—unwittingly, no doubt. He would still necessarily be a liar, but only as to the detail of what took place. He could not immediately have hit out at the man he talked to and quarrelled with. That is the bit he may be inventing."

"But why ever should he invent just that?"

"To give his crime the appearance of a decent spontaneity. Dromio said something filthy, laughed, turned away—and instantly young Gollifer hit out at him. Suppose actually he let Dromio return unharmed to the study; suppose he then prowled about a bit, screwing himself up; suppose he finally crept into the study and attacked the man he took to be his enemy from behind. It makes a much nastier picture —particularly for a jury."

"I suppose that's true." Hyland was dubious. "But —dash it all!—if he killed the wrong man, that wrong man had changed into the right man's clothes."

"Yes—or was subsequently shoved into them. And then he was shoved into a most unnecessarily lighted fire. It must be admitted that the case has its obscure side."

"You couldn't express it better." Hyland breathed heavily. "I may say that I have been involved in melodrama before. Melodrama does occasionally turn up in real life. But real life with two intertwined melodramas really is a bit thick. Sir Oliver had long-lost brothers. Now Geoffrey Gollifer turns out to have a long-lost half-sister. And all these people are mixed up we just don't know how."

Appleby was filling a pipe. "Quite so," he said. "And moreover what may be called the nomenclature is distinctly confusing. The girl called Lucy Dromio is really Lucy We-don't-know-what. The young man going by the name of Geoffrey Gollifer has, I suppose, legally no name at all. His mother is Mrs We-don't-know-what. The dead man is almost certainly a Dromio, and his Christian name may be Oliver."

"Oliver?" Hyland looked blank.

"Certainly." Appleby struck a match. "For it isn't known which two of the triplets were spirited away, and which was left to be the heir. But if we agree to continue calling Oliver the man who grew up with that name here, then the man who has been killed would appear to be either Jaques or Orlando Dro-mio. But in America, almost certainly, he has always gone under another name. Of course when one does get melodramas intertwining one must expect little complications of this sort."

"We'll stick to the names under which these people have commonly gone." Hyland was dogged. "And we'll work on your supposition that Geoffrey Gollifer crept into the study some time after the row he has described to us and killed the wrong man."

"Then where is the right man now?"

"Sir Oliver? Heaven knows. Perhaps he was never here at all. Perhaps both long-lost brothers were here. Perhaps it was they who were seen by Mr Greengrave from his car; perhaps it was they who were heard by the footman talking in the study." Hyland checked himself and made an impatient gesture. "But no! that's impossible. Only the real Sir Oliver could have taken and replied to Geoffrey Gollifer's points during that row on the terrace. Unless, of course, Gollifer is inventing that too. By Jove—do you know I believe that may be it? There was no row. Gollifer simply crept in and killed the man he took for Sir Oliver without a word. All the rest is simply his invention to set a better face on the matter—to show him as almost intolerably provoked."

"It's a possibility." Appleby frowned. "But what about the telegram received by Swindle? Do you remember how it was signed—with a sort of confidential pet name of Sir Oliver's? That suggests that the real man at least meant to come down to Sherris. And, on the whole, we are safer assuming that he did."

Hyland nodded; he walked to the mantelpiece and

peered despondently at a clock. "It's nice to be safe somewhere. And at least we can be certain of one thing: we've got a murder on our hands. It's not much, but it's something."

"Two murders, surely. Don't forget Grubb."

Hyland groaned. "Now, what sense was there in that? Was he really going to let out something important about Sebastian Dromio? And did Sebastian Dromio really kill him of deliberate purpose? Could a man who was absolutely roaring tight be said to do such a thing?"

"If he was roaring tight."

Hyland sat down heavily. "Now, you don't mean to suggest—"

"Definitely I do. Grubb was hopelessly drunk, if you like. But Sebastian Dromio is a different matter. At a guess I'd say he was playing rather a deep game."

"Deep? It's certainly likely to land him in a six-foot drop." Hyland laughed without pleasure. "But that he also killed Sir Oliver—"

"Not Sir Oliver. Say a Dromio unknown. And it is, as you say, a possibility. So is the supposition that Geoffrey Gollifer did it. But there are difficulties in either case. If Gollifer's mind worked so swiftly to think up extenuating fairy-tales why was he so dead set on confessing from the first?"

"Because he knew Grubb had seen him and, not knowing that Grubb was dead, he believed it to be all up anyway. And the fact that he has bolted—"

"Is uncommonly odd. He was anxious to give himself up; to take upon himself Sir Oliver's murder. That looked much as if he were endeavouring to shield someone. But as soon as he heard that the

166

dead man was not Sir Oliver he repented of his rashness. And at that, supposing—quite wrongly—that he had hopelessly incriminated himself by his confession, he cut and ran for it. Why?"

Hyland shook his head. "Heaven knows. But this is clear. If he was indeed shielding somebody he was shielding either the actual murderer or a person whom he believed—but in fact wrongly—to be the murderer. Now, take it that he genuinely supposed the dead man to be Sir Oliver Dromio, whom might he have believed to be the criminal?"

"His mother, who had been blackmailed by Oliver. Or his half-sister—as he now knew Lucy to be— since she had just been terribly disillusioned about the character of Oliver, whom she passionately loved. Hardly an unknown brother from America. Geoffrey Gollifer could have no motive to shield a stranger." Appleby paused. "But although Geoffrey Gollifer has thrust himself so violently into the picture he is not really the person of prime importance at the moment. Where is Sir Oliver Dromio? It is reasonable to believe that he was here to-night. Where has he gone? And what did he do?"

"Well, he didn't get himself killed, worse luck to him. We were properly had for suckers over that."

"I suppose we were had? I mean, it has genuinely turned out not to be Sir Oliver's body? It was the first identification which was mistaken, and not this second one?"

Hyland fiddled gloomily with his gloves; he had been carrying them round all night. "Not a doubt of it. There's not a soul who believes it to be Sir Oliver's body now. I can see it's not myself."

"Well, that appears conclusive. I was thinking, you

know, that death can play tricks with the looks of a man. And, once the notion of 'indistinguishable triplet brother' got floating round, mere suggestion—"

"No doubt. But suggestion was working all the other way. Sir Oliver was expected home. His voice was heard from his study. Presently in that study a body was found dressed in his clothes. And the boy was uncommonly like him. Notice what happened. The body was found by servants, and it was Swindle, a dim-eyed old creature, who first went hurrying round announcing the death of Sir Oliver. Then Sebastian Dromio had a look. He was, of course, more or less intimately acquainted with his nephew but, like everybody else, he hadn't seen him—except fleetingly, earlier in the day—for a good many months. Moreover he probably didn't care a damn for him—and that's important. The only person who did care was Lady Dromio, who insisted in going in, it seems, although at that time in a state of collapse, and who accepted the body as her son's—I mean as Sir Oliver's. Lucy Dromio they didn't at that time let have a look. After that there was myself, who used to see Sir Oliver about Sherris Magna, and there was that young ass of a doctor, who was so proud of having sat next him at a dinner table."

"I see." And Appleby chuckled. "We ought to have thought, you know. As soon as the triplet business floated up we ought to have thought."

"No doubt. But the point is this. The deception— for clearly we must call it that—was discovered by someone who wasn't thinking at all. The family doctor arrived—this old fellow Hubbard, who had been out at a confinement. He was taken straight to the study and the sergeant whom I left there stripped the sheet from the body. Hubbard said, 'That's not Sir Oliver.' And at that moment there was a stir in the hall. It was Mr Greengrave coming out of the drawingroom where we were having it out with young Gollifer. Hubbard behaved very sensibly. 'Greengrave,' he called, 'come in here.' And Greengrave went in. Remember that he hadn't earlier accepted my invitation to view the body. So he looked at it for the first time now, and without Hubbard's saying another word to him. 'That must be one of the brothers,' he said; 'it's not Sir Oliver at all.'"

"Pretty." And Appleby puffed thoughtfully at his pipe. "Your melodrama could hardly give you a more pat curtain to the second act. Do you know that before we left the study ourselves I had a look at the terrace and noticed that your sentry-going constable was gone?"

"What the dickens do you mean?" Hyland was startled.

"The question is: did your servant go too, after we did? Did he find his vigil with those two bodies a little drear and did he slip out—like the primadonna, you know, to recruit his flagging energies with bottled stout? What I mean is this. Were there a few minutes during which people operating from the terrace might have substituted a second body for the first?"

Upon Hyland, jaded and baffled, the effect of this diabolical suggestion was electric. He sprang to his feet, his face suffused with blood, strode to the door and flung it open. "Morris," he bellowed—and

Sherris Hall rang to his voice—"Morris, come here at once!"

Appleby moved to a window and peered out. Quite soon it would be dawn.

Sergeant Morris appeared startled. Presumably he was not accustomed to being bellowed at. "Sir," he said, "did I hear you call?"

"Certainly you did. When Mr Appleby and I went to the drawingroom I left you in the study with the bodies. Have you left that room between then and now?"

"I stepped into the hall."

"And why the—" Hyland checked himself. "What made you do that, Morris?"

"I thought I heard the ambulance, sir. We've been expecting it for some time now. So I stepped out to inquire and found that it was Dr Hubbard. The butler was just admitting him as I came into the hall. I had your instructions that he was at once to view the body—the two bodies, for that matter—so I took him back to the study. And, after that, I didn't myself leave it."

"Good—very good, indeed." Hyland directed a triumphant glance at Appleby. "In other words, you can scarcely have been out of the room a couple of minutes all told. Is that right?"

"Well, no. I can't just say that, sir. You see, the first thing Dr Hubbard had to do was to make a telephone call about the case he had just left. There was a good deal of difficulty in getting through. So I waited."

"I see." Hyland's weary voice trembled with suppressed irritation. "And is it too much to ask how long you waited?"

Morris considered. "Well, sir, it might have been a matter of ten minutes, all things considered."

Hyland's self-control broke down. "Hell and damnation!" he cried. At this moment the library door opened to reveal Mr Greengrave. Beside him was a figure of equal gravity who was presumably Dr Hubbard. The two men paused doubtfully, Hyland's exclamation ringing in their ears, and made as if to withdraw.

But Appleby beckoned them into the room. "It will be clear to you," he said to Dr Hubbard, "that we are the police. It might be called a conference. Please sit down."

Mr Greengrave looked with mild reproach at Hyland. Dr Hubbard glanced round the room. "I hope," he asked drily, "that all goes smoothly?"

"I am beginning to feel that it does." Appleby knocked out his pipe. "But for whom? There is quite a question there."

Hyland registered his disapproval of this pleasantry with something between a groan and a growl.

"Has somebody's plan been going forward very nicely step by step? What was agitating Inspector Hyland and myself when you came in was this. Is it possible, Dr Hubbard, that you and the police surgeon examined different bodies?"

"Different bodies? But of course we did. The man Grubb—"

"We are not thinking of that. It is with the other body that we are concerned. First, you see, a number of people declare that it is Sir Oliver Dromio's, and later a number of people declare that it is

171

not. Might both groups be right? Could there have been a substitution in the mean time? At the moment, I cannot make sense of the case on any other basis. And we have just stumbled upon a fatal ten minutes when something of the sort could have taken place."

Dr Hubbard raised his eyebrows. "The inference from that would be that both Sir Oliver Dromio and a brother are now dead. And somebody has concerned himself with juggling with the bodies. Have you any notion as to who this person might be?"

"Well, there were triplets, as you know. So it might be the third brother."

With a grotesquely theatrical gesture, Hyland flung despairing arms in air. "Madness!" he cried. "The whole thing is a nightmare. Three identical brothers creeping round the place with each other's dead bodies! It's like a drunken hallucination."

Mr Greengrave looked up quickly. "Dear me!" he said. "I hope it's nothing like that."

"It is worse." Dr Hubbard spoke drily again. "It is a hopeless cast into the darkness of what appears to be a singularly impenetrable crime."

Appleby shook his head. "Say a complicated crime —and for that reason the less likely to be impenetrable. But I confess that the discrepant identifications trouble me. The notion that one body may have been substituted for another similarly injured body while Sergeant Martin here was out of the room is admittedly but one possibility among many—"

"But surely it is extremely far-fetched." Mr Greengrave spoke with sudden conviction. "Consider the burning of the hands and arms. That a second body—"

"Not a bit of it, sir." Rather surprisingly, Sergeant Morris had abruptly interrupted. "What do you do when you want to pass off one boy as another during a conjuring trick? Why, give each of them an Eton collar and a big black patch over one eye. The similarities, as you might say, distract the eye from the differences. Not that I hold with the substituting idea myself."

"Don't you, now?" Hyland turned to his subordinate without enthusiasm. "Perhaps there is some idea you do hold with?"

"Well, yes—there is. It appears to me like this, sir. Sir Oliver Dromio came upon somebody extraordinarily like himself. I think something's been said about a brother."

Appleby nodded. "Two," he said. "Conceivably he had a choice between two."

"Thank you, sir. Well, if it was a brother the thing becomes even more horrible. Sir Oliver, I reckon, wanted to fade out quietly. Money difficulties, perhaps—or it might be women. Now, if you want to quit and no questions asked, the best way to go about it is to leave your own body behind you."

Dr Hubbard looked at Hyland. "This man," he said with faint malice, "talks sense."

"Moreover, sir, if you are feeling kindly towards anybody—say a mistress or somebody like that— you can do them a bit of good in the insurance line. Well, that is what Sir Oliver Dromio did. He found this long-lost brother and realised that the two of them were as like as two peas. So he brought him here quietly, killed him, changed clothes with him, and disappeared. Nobody is going to search for Sir Oliver, because here is Sir Oliver dead. And this ex-

173

plains the strange business about the fire, and the burnt arms and hands. Nobody who got suspicious-like would ever take the corpse's finger-prints and compare them with any which might be found preserved on possessions of Sir Oliver's. Because the corpse, you see, no longer has fingers to take prints from. It was a clever plan—very clever, indeed."

"Only it didn't work." Mr Greengrave was looking at this subordinate policeman with frank admiration. "Or rather it worked at first—until it so happened that Dr Hubbard and I detected the imposture."

"Quite so, sir. But then there's the question—Did you? Of course Sir Oliver Dromio's plan has failed thus far: that suspicion is now aroused and he will be hunted for. Still, whose body does lie in the study there? Suppose that property and such-like were to turn on the answer. Can't you see a barrister making a good case for its being really Sir Oliver's, and the first identification the right one? Though of course one would want to know about the teeth."

"The teeth?" asked Mr Greengrave innocently.

"Certainly, sir. If the body still has any of its own teeth then Sir Oliver's dentist could say conclusively whether the body is Sir Oliver's or not."

"How very interesting." Mr Greengrave turned to Dr Hubbard. "Perhaps," he suggested, "you can say something about the teeth?"

"I'm not a dentist. But the body as I examined it there has teeth—very good teeth which have received comparatively little dental attention."

"Even a little would serve. Not that I haven't heard of corpses having had a dentist at them by way of disguise." Morris grew expansive. "Whole rows of

174

another man's stoppings copied all at one go. I've heard—"

"You've heard a great deal of balderdash, it seems to me." Hyland appeared still to hold his subordinate in disfavour. "Not," he added magnanimously, "that you haven't been talking a good deal of sense. In fact, your explanation is the best and simplest we yet have. I think I may say that something of the sort has been forming itself in my own mind."

"Capital!" said Dr Hubbard. "It is reassuring to see a consensus of professional opinion beginning to form upon so perplexed a matter. But here are three policemen, and so far only two voices." He turned to Appleby. "Perhaps you, sir, have some other view of the problem?"

"I cannot see the truth." Appleby spoke with a sudden energy which was startling. "I cannot see the truth because I cannot see, first of all, what was designed to appear the truth. In what persuasion was it designed that we should rest? Where does the criminal hope we stand now? Does his plan depend on our accepting that body as Sir Oliver's? Or is it a plan subtler than that: does it depend on our penetrating to a deception as we have just, in fact, done? Does he hope that we are now saying, 'Why, this is not Sir Oliver's body after all!'—and are we still simply following a lead that has been given us? Is it indeed true that matters are still going smoothly for some person unknown or unsuspected?" Appleby paused and smiled. "Such a huddle of questions, I am afraid, is hardly helpful. Nor is this simple statement: that I cannot get away from the downright queerness of that fire."

"Talking of fire—" began Mr Greengrave.

"The fire," said Hyland, "is to some extent covered by Morris's theory. But I agree that there is something queer about it, all the same. One seems to smell a rat."

"Talking of smelling—" said Mr Greengrave.

"And now, what is to be done?" Fatigue had blunted Hyland's hearing or his manners. "Perhaps if we went back—" He paused, a fresh thought seeming to strike him. "By the way, Morris, whom did you leave along there in the study?"

"Leave, sir?" Morris stared. "Why, you shouted in so urgent a way that I doubled straight along here without calling anybody."

Hyland's lips moved. But he was interrupted, successfully this time, by Mr Greengrave. "What I wanted to remark," said Mr Greengrave, "is that I rather think I smell fire. Quite powerfully so, indeed."

It was true. The room was imperceptibly filling with an acrid smoke—and from somewhere outside there came in ominous crescendo a dry, crackling sound. With an oath Hyland leapt to the door and flung it open. It gave upon a long corridor. The farther end of this was already a blinding screen of flame. Sherris Hall was burning.

12

Momentarily the flames vanished behind a wall of dense black smoke; the wall billowed, broke, rolled down the corridor towards them in a suffocating wave; the wave eddied, whirled, receded; behind them half-open windows were rattling as if shaken by a giant hand; the corridor was clear again and the screen of flame brighter than before. Fiery tongues lapped at air, or ran low along the floor like questing hounds. Beyond was a dull roaring sound, strangely hollow, as if this were some inverted cataract of burning waters running into space. For a second's interval they stood watching; then they heard above the inhuman racket a high, screaming voice call for aid.

Hyland sprang down the corridor. His silver buttons glittered as if molten; he still clutched the crumpled finery of his best white gloves. Almost immediately he was back again. He started to curse; thought better of it; compressed his lips against some suddenly apprehended pain. Dr Hubbard took him by the arm. "No good," he said. "We must get round by the terrace."

They turned, ran through the library, tugged at heavy curtains before a French window. As they did so the lights went out. Darkness and the flicker of the advancing flames were for a moment at interplay around them. Then they were out upon the terrace in the last hour of a summer night.

A faint grey light was on the lawn and somewhere beyond it a single blackcap still sang; in the east low clouds lay across a sky of apple-green and rose. Sweeping up the drive came the unhurrying headlights of a car; perhaps it was the ambulance for which Sergeant Morris had waited in vain. They turned. The house too was peaceful and sleeping. It rose above them here in a faintly perceptible warmth of mellow brick, and if a first pall of smoke already hung fatally over it this was as yet invisible against the darkened zenith. Undisturbed, the blackcap tried another phrase.

The delusive calm held only for a moment; it was broken, queerly, by a crash and tinkle of falling glass; almost immediately above them a single tongue of flame shot into the sky. Voices were calling; windows could be heard thrown up; a police whistle shrilled in short urgent blasts. And than all these sounds were drowned beneath the clangor of a great bell. Someone in the stables had given the alarm.

"It seems localised so far." Hyland had taken charge. "Morris, collar someone who can check over the household as we get them out. Assemble everybody on the lawn. Doctor, make for the nearest telephone and make sure of the Fire Service. Mr

Greengrave, find the ladies and keep an eye on them. Appleby, we'll get out those bodies even if we sizzle for it."

They parted and the two men ran along the terrace and rounded a corner. At once they saw both the centre of the fire and the extent to which it had already spread. From the study windows shot great tongues of fire. Already the blaze had reached two floors up, and the crash of rafters could be heard. "Old," said Hyland; "panelled, wasn't it? Go up like a tinder-box."

Appleby nodded. "No go, I'm afraid. And, after all, better the quick than the dead. Servants in the attics is the likeliest danger. Better get through as much of the house as we can."

"Very well." But Hyland hesitated, his eye lingering on what was now the fiery inferno of Sir Oliver Dromio's study. "Didn't you say something about a plan going forward step by step? This looks to me like a little more of it."

"It certainly doesn't look like mere coincidence. Still, there was that great fire someone pitched the body in. It might have started some mischief in the chimney. Or smouldering fragments of clothing—"

"Fiddlesticks! Morris was in that study not much more than half an hour ago. And look at the fire now! A four-gallon drum of petrol is the likeliest explanation I can see. . . . It looks as if everyone were being got out all right."

They were now before a side-entrance to the house in a wing as yet remote from the fire; through this, shepherded by policemen, was passing a huddle of servants in various states of undress. As they looked Mr Greengrave appeared with Lady Dromio on his arm; in an effort to set an example of composure they walked with a studied formality and rather as if going in to dinner; behind them came Mrs Gollifer, assisting some hysterical girl. A moment later Dr Hubbard appeared, followed by a policeman; both were as black as chimney-sweeps, and as they hurried forward they brought with them a smell of acrid smoke and singed cloth. Dr Hubbard shook his head. "No good," he called. "Only a couple of telephones in the place and neither could be got at, try as we would. A fatal piece of parsimony, I am afraid. The nearest is at Hodsoll's farm, and a constable has gone to it. But not much of Sherris will be left by the time the Brigade gets here."

Hyland nodded. "But we have plenty of men, sir, and at least we can organise something. The first question is whether everybody is out." He glanced at the group collecting round him. "Where is Miss Dromio?"

"Gone round to the back courtyard, sir." It was the footman Robert who spoke. "There's a groom there and she'll be all right. Wants to see the dogs safe, I reckon."

"That won't do." Hyland in such a crisis as this had the merit of entirely knowing his own mind. "I'll have everybody here on this lawn, and nowhere else." He turned to a constable. "Go with this fellow and bring them both round." Again his eye circled the group before him. By now the fire was sweeping into the nearer parts of the house; windows were cracking and flame leaping through; a flicker of dull crimson light began to play upon the circle of pale faces in the grey of dawn. Hyland frowned as if in some effort of recollection.

"Sebastian Dromio," said Appleby quietly.

"Great heavens—we locked him up!" Several times in the course of the night's adventures Hyland had been dismayed, but not to the extent he was now. "Surely—"

"Then let us hope," said Appleby mildly, "that somebody has thought to unlock him. His character is unamiable, I don't doubt, and he has Grubb's blood on his hands, at least. Still, it wouldn't look well."

"Where the devil is Morris? It was Morris—"

As if in answer to Hyland's question there was a crash of glass from a direction now almost entirely obscured in smoke; the smoke swirled apart and revealed a ruddy glare from amid which staggered Sergeant Morris, stooping under the weight of an inert body across his shoulders. He dumped his burden on the grass almost at Hyland's feet. "It's Mr Dromio," he said. "And that only leaves the butler."

"The old fellow Swindle? Can't he be got out?"

Morris shook his head—both soberly and painfully, for his face was seared and scorched. "I'm afraid not, sir. He wasn't in his bedroom, and it seems he probably continued to sit up. He has a little basement room right under where the worst of the blaze is now. Without the firemen here there's just no getting near it."

In a momentary silence they stared at what was now the full-scale conflagration before them. This time, Appleby thought, more was going to go up than a mere nursery wing; it looked indeed as if within a couple of hours Sherris Hall would be an empty shell. A chain of men was being organised to bucket water from the lily pond, and one fire-hose had been brought round from the offices and brought into operation. But all this was as nothing before the blaze; the house was like some vast Tartarean monster wounded and in a hundred places gushing fire. Blast upon blast of hot air caught at the breath as one watched and already on the lawn there lay a coating of fine gray ash flecked here and there with soot. The glow of the flames rose as if to meet and answer the sunrise, now blood-red in the east. It was as if beacon were calling to beacon across the shires.

"Madness."

They started and turned. Sebastian Dromio had struggled weakly to his knees and was staring at the blazing house. "Madness," he repeated, and his voice although hoarse was wholly sober. "My brother did it once. I knew very well it was he. He fired the place in madness, and in madness he died. But which of us has done it now?"

"Which of you, indeed?" Hyland looked down grimly at the old man. "Which of you—and why?"

"Where is Lucy?" With a further effort Sebastian Dromio staggered to his feet and looked about him.

"Miss Dromio is safe enough. She has been saving the dogs. The only possible casualty is the butler. We are afraid that he must have perished."

"Swindle?" Sebastian relaxed and sat down again. "Let the surly old brute roast; he might as well get used to what it feels like." Upon this untimely pleasantry Sebastian chuckled—and the chuckle turned to a cracked and evil laughter. Suddenly he checked himself. "You say Lucy is safe? She ought to be here. I don't like it."

"No more do I." As Hyland spoke he caught sight of Robert approaching with a pale-faced groom. "You, there! Why isn't Miss Dromio with you?"

"It seems she went back, sir." Robert was agitated. "The fire didn't seem near her own room, and she ventured back for something."

This time Hyland wasted no time on swearing. "Where is the room?"

"There, sir." Robert pointed. And as he did so—and for all the world like a *coup de théâtre*—Lucy Dromio appeared. At a first-floor window—but high above their heads, because of the loftiness of the lower rooms—she stood looking down, and with what appeared to be perfect calm. But, even as they watched, the darkness behind her was shot with livid flame. Through the window she must come, or the fire would take her.

Once that night Appleby had circled Sherris Hall with an inquiring eye. He darted forward now—and was fleetingly aware as he did so that with surprising strength Sebastian Dromio was hurrying forward too. "Stay still!" he shouted—and saw the girl nod as if, above the roar of the fire, she had heard and understood. He turned and ran towards that wing of the house which alone was now untouched by the fire. Here was the billiard-room; he broke into it by pitching himself through a window bodily; tore from the table the canvas covering that shrouded it and raced back to the spot beneath Lucy Dromio's window. He called out and men hurried towards him. In the same moment he caught a glimpse of Sebastian.

Only five minutes before Sebastian had been carried from the burning building helpless and apparently insensible; now he was stumbling up a wrought-iron spiral staircase which led to the flat roof of what appeared to be a conservatory or palmhouse.

183

A constable was endeavouring to overtake him. But surprise had given him a good start and, even as Appleby looked, he gained the roof, stumbled across it, and climbed crazily out upon the abacus of an adjoining column. He was now above the level of Lucy's window and his intention was clear. Treading upon a narrow cornice which here ran between the first and second floors, he proposed to sidle out to a point directly above her. The plan could only be futile, for even were he to succeed in this hazardous scramble he would be hopelessly cut off from the girl by the overhang of the projection upon which he stood.

So much Appleby saw without pausing to admire; the queer revelation inherent in Sebastian's unexpected conduct must be matter for future meditation. The great canvas sheet was stretched out taut by willing arms. Lucy eyed it carefully from above, still composed. Appleby gave the word and she jumped, coming down with her full skirt blown about her head, grotesquely like some gay advertisement for the intimacies of feminine attire. For a moment she lay on the sheet, winded and gasping. Then she scrambled off it. "Sebastian," she panted, "—quickly!"

They raced along the side of the house. A window belching flame forced them to a circuit, and now heavy wafts of smoke made it hard to see what was happening above. "There he is!" The man next to Appleby threw up his arm and pointed. In the next instant there was a single cry, the swift impression of a body hurtling through space, a dull impact—inexpressibly horrible—straight before them. Hyland ran forward, pale before this fresh disaster. "More than thirty feet," he said. "Not a hope."

But Sebastian Dromio was alive. He opened his eyes upon Lucy kneeling beside him. "Dam' *Jacquerie*," he whispered. "Trying to burn the place down. Took my gun to them and cleared them out. Glad to see you all right, my dear. Had an idea"—he paused and his breath was laboured—"had an idea you'd got into a pickle. If Oliver—" Some spasm shook Sebastian Dromio's broken body. "If Oliver—" His eyes closed and his head fell back. He was placed on a stretcher and carried to the shelter of the waiting ambulance.

And now across the still and empty countryside, over which light mists were beginning to stir in level shafts of sunshine, came an urgent jangle of bells. Making as much noise as if all Oxford Street had to be cleared before them, the two fire-engines from Sherris Magna were hurrying to the scene.

At last, Appleby thought, it might be possible to reflect on the events of the night. With the arrival of the fire-engines everybody was organised and busy. Indeed, nearly everybody was happy too. The rescue of Lucy Dromio and the heroic if crazy conduct of Sebastian had marked a turning-point. For the time people appeared to forget the earlier horrors and mysteries to which this conflagration was a sequel; instead they gave themselves to united effort against the impersonal force of the flames. Appleby passed a bucket—he had slipped into the line of men working from the lily pond—and saw Hyland blessedly busy organising matters some thirty yards away. Another fire-engine, an emergency tender, an ambulance and a mobile canteen had arrived from a neighbouring town; several car-loads of sight-seers were already parked beyond the lawn; nearby, and under the eye of a watchful constable who could apparently be spared for the purpose, a line of children from neighbouring cottages watched the blaze with delight and awe. Somebody had found Lady Dromio a garden chair. Mr Greengrave, not without a wistful glance at the manipulating here of a hose and there of a ladder, was discoursing to her apparently in his professional character. Mrs Gollifer stood a little apart, gazing quietly at the flames.

Appleby gazed too. What was the meaning of them? To what end had this devouring monster been let loose upon Sherris? Was it conceivable that the fire was an accident? A sheer coincidence it could scarcely be. But in Sir Oliver's study there had been no fire kindled for many months; that evening one had been kindled either for fantastic or for obscurely practical motives; into that fire a body had been pitched, and out of it the same body had been hauled. These circumstances did suggest the possibility of accident—perhaps of some smouldering ember having been kicked unwittingly into a corner. It was not possible, then, positively to assert that the blaze was the consequence of design. But it did look uncommonly like it.

Long ago there had been a fire at Sherris. If Lady Dromio was to be believed, that fire had been the consequence of design—and of design equally fantastic and wicked. Sir Romeo Dromio through some queer freak of mind had resented the three sons who came to him at a birth; for two he had substituted dead bodies; and the third he had then rescued from a disaster of his own contriving. That third son had lived to be Sir Oliver Dromio, and it was impossible to say that his father was not a madman. Was there madness in this second lurid act of the Dromio drama? Appleby thought that there was. Sir Romeo's crime—for it was that—had been freakish and unscrupulous; and that was the complexion which this crime might finally be seen to wear, too. A superstructure of guile upon a foundation of insanity. An elaborate and intricate construction mirroring a fertile but unbalanced mind, rather like a scientific contrivance by Heath Robinson... But this, Appleby thought, was prophecy, not detection. He swung another bucket along the line. Just what had this fire been calculated to conceal or destroy? And, conversely, what had it revealed?

Sebastian Dromio was a selfish and callous old man: this there was required no conflagration to show. But Sebastian Dromio had risked his life in an effort to save Lucy, and perhaps there was revelation in that. Indeed, had he conceivably taken such a risk twice that night? Among the mere impressions which the affair had brought him none, Appleby found, was stronger than this: that Sebastian Dromio had been playing a part—and playing it with very sufficient skill. If he had been uneasy under interrogation his uneasiness had not really lain precisely where it had appeared to lie; and if he had drunk much he had yet appeared to drink far more.

What had Grubb the gardener seen in the neighbourhood of Sir Oliver Dromio's study that night? That he had seen Sebastian was not unlikely—and at some moment when Sebastian would rather not have been observed. But was that why Grubb had died from that apparently irresponsible shot from Sebastian's hand? Or had Grubb seen something else as

187

well—or at least had Sebastian believed him to have done this? Had Grubb known too much about Lucy Dromio—Lucy who had declared that she might kill her foster-brother Oliver? Was Sebastian's aim to shield this one person for whom he cared?

But it was not enough to ask what Grubb had seen near Sir Oliver's study; one must ask too what he was doing there. And here was something characteristic of the case. Every question brought another in its train; and as soon as one concentrated upon one aspect of the affair one was uneasily conscious of others which had drifted out of focus. . . .

Appleby looked about him. The firemen were bent upon saving the two extreme wings of the mansion, and its centre, abandoned to destruction, was now from top to bottom compact of fire. The dawn had brought a breeze; under its influence an interplay of smoke and flame chequered the advancing daylight and gave an effect of confusion—almost of the phantasmagoric—to the scene. A group of men, red-eyed and begrimed, stood with mugs oddly poised beside the canteen; above them on their lofty pedestals the Dromio hippogriffs appeared to take motion and curvet and prance in air; dogs had collected in surprising number and their barking mingled with the throb of engines, the crackle of the fire and the hiss of steam.

Where lay the heart of the case? Huddled up in its incident within a few hours, it yet when brought under review appeared to sprawl away in more directions than it was easy to follow. Yet some nexus there must be; some point, perhaps quite tiny, at which the beginnings of precise revelation lay . . . As Appleby made this obvious reflection he suffered an odd experience.

It was rather like the experience which Mr Greengrave had described as befalling him in his car. Appleby saw something; was aware of a compelling visual image. And this image, he obscurely knew, was vital to the matter; it ought to lead to some precise point at which enquiry might begin. . . . Appleby frowned. For the image was simply that of Lucy Dromio, falling or floating down from her window, with her dress blown back like the petals of a windswept flower. It could not be called an erotic vision, yet markedly it was an anatomical one. And urgently but in vain it recalled some word—some vital word —which had been spoken, Appleby knew not by whom, that night.

He shook his head, dismissing this mere vagary of mind. The house is burning, he told himself doggedly, in order to conceal the truth about a dead body now consumed to ashes within it. But this is the second time that fire has been evoked for such a purpose—the second within a few hours. Somebody was killed. His body was so disposed upon a fire that the arms and hands were virtually destroyed. The body was then identified. And hard upon its identification there was more fire and it was destroyed *in toto*. From these facts certain conclusions were surely clear. The body had been partly burnt in the first instance because without burning the desired identification would not have been made. And now it had been wholly destroyed because, even when made, that identification would not have held for long. Nor had it. That the body was not Sir Oliver Dromio's had in fact been discovered at a very brief interval before this ghastly bonfire. And Appleby looked grimly at the flames. They were too late. This large act of destruction was in vain.

But was it? The body had been identified as Sir Oliver Dromio's—and by witnesses who included Sir Oliver Dromio's mother. Later other witnesses had come forward who were of a contrary opinion. And now there was no further opportunity of determining between them. Except the teeth—thought Appleby, following the thought of the admirable Sergeant Morris. Freakish amateur criminals with a strain of madness commonly do not think of little matters like that. The fire might burn on . . .

The fire might burn on. Nevertheless Appleby swung the next bucket with a will. As he did so he was aware of a stab of pain. He looked down at his hands and found them begrimed and blistered. And that of course might be it. That the body had gone into the fire to destroy finger-prints was a false cast. There was a far more immediate give-away to be avoided by the criminal. The features of that identical triplet had been virtually indistinguishable from those of his brother Sir Oliver. But his hands had been different; they had been the hands—the wholly undisguisable hands—of a laboring man.

Here, then, was a reasonable hypothesis forming —forming by the very light, as it were, of the blazing pyre that was now Sherris Hall. The plot was Sir Oliver Dromio's, and it turned upon several factors. First, that he was of criminal mind—and this the peculiarly nasty blackmail in which he had engaged documented convincingly enough. Secondly, that he was sufficiently crazy to envisage following murder with arson, and this at the not inconsiderable risk of incinerating his mother and his foster-sister. Thirdly, that some difficulty or combination of difficulties came upon him just at the time of his discovering that he was one of three identical brothers. It was a fantastic discovery, Appleby reflected, and might well lead the mind of the man who made it to some construction of answering fantasticalness. What then had Sir Oliver done? He had lured one of those new-found brothers to Sherris and into his study. And there he had killed him, changed clothes, kindled a fire with which to destroy the tell-tale hands, raised an alarm before there was risk of the body being too pervasively burnt. Then when he knew that the body had been discovered and a first identification had been made he returned and started the major confla-gration which should ensure that closer scrutiny would not reveal the truth. And now he had van-ished, confident that none would inconveniently look for Sir Oliver Dromio among the living again. Only he was mistaken. Dr Hubbard's swift realisation that the body was actually another's had spoilt the plan.

But why, then, had Geoffrey Gollifer told so strange a tale? Why had he declared, and with such a labour of circumstantial detail, that he had called Oliver Dromio from his study, quarrelled with him, and killed him there and then? He appeared not an imaginative youth, and of such an impassioned flight of fancy only one explanation seemed possible. Geof-frey Gollifer was shielding someone with whom his emotions were deeply engaged.

Appleby continued to pass the buckets. This par-ticular amateur effort in which he had joined clearly possessed not the slightest utility. It would be alto-gether more sensible to stop and gather round the mobile canteen for whatever creature comforts the modern technique of fire-fighting provided. And yet perhaps this exercise had its utility. Did it not stimulate the brain?

Whom, then, was the young man Gollifer shielding? The real Sir Oliver, whom he knew to have killed a brother hitherto unknown? This was evidently impossible. Gollifer might not positively wish his enemy to the scaffold, but it was altogether unlikely that at deadly personal risk he should endeavour to save him from it. Gollifer, then, had indeed believed that it was the real and unquestioned Sir Oliver who was killed. He was shielding the person whom he believed guilty of that killing. His mother and Lucy Dromio were the likely people. But here, surely, Sebastian Dromio came in again. Sebastian had no demonstrable feeling for Mrs Gollifer. But for Lucy he had shown devotion enough. If he too, then, were shielding somebody; if he had killed Grubb because he feared some impending revelation—

Appleby paused and mopped his brow, feeling as one who has entered the last lap of a race. Lucy Dromio could have had no part in the killing; that she should, hard upon the revelation of that evening, have acted in any sense as Oliver's accomplice was a thing wholly incredible. But if Geoffrey Gollifer was shielding her, and Sebastian was shielding her, and there was something against her which Grubb could have said; if it could by several people be believed that she had been involved, then surely in some way she must have been sufficiently close to the affair to have at least something to tell. Here was a case—almost a complete case—and perhaps there were particulars in which she could confirm it. Appleby glanced round him, wondering where she might be. And as he did so he saw her.

But again it was with the inward eye. Perhaps his sight, dazzled with the flames, was predisposed to play him tricks. There, with almost hallucinatory vividness, and strangely carrying with her the feeling of a misgiving, of a warning, was Lucy Dromio falling into the waiting canvas, a brief vision of silk-clad legs and thighs, of billowing white draperies blown about her head. It had no meaning; it could have none; its quality as of a threatening obsession was a mere freak of the mind, a reflex of some buried interest of the sensual man . . . Appleby passed one more bucket and fell out of line. For some time he had been tired. Now he was depressed.

13

Mrs Gollifer stood immobile by the lily pond. In her long evening gown and white cloak she might have been a statue of Hera, posed to look fixedly towards the dawn. Whatever life this stately woman had contrived to build for herself upon a basis of deception and lies was now over. She was a confessed bigamist—a squalid crime, reflected Appleby, commonly associated with the lower classes. Her son, whether truly or not, was a confessed murderer. Her daughter had been in love with a man who was blackmailing her over that daughter's existence; and this relationship had now been revealed to a girl who was wholly unprepared to make any emotional response to it. Mrs Gollifer's position might be called tragic. In addition to which she must be feeling a fool.

Appleby grabbed a second mug of coffee and approached her. "I am afraid," he said, "that you must be exhausted. Try this."

She took the mug and thanked him. "Mr Appleby, is it not?" she asked. "Speak if you have a mind to."

"It would seem that there is not much chance of saving the house."

"Nobody will regret it. Kate, it is true, will miss her embroidery task of the moment, and there may be difficulty in remembering the title of the novel she will want replaced. It is about a large hotel. But more than one writer, I have been told, has essayed the theme."

Oddly, the woman spoke with something of the accent of that daughter who had grown up orphaned and unacknowledged; here was the same disguise of hard talk. "Is Lady Dromio, then, so unfeeling?" Appleby asked. "She would seem to have taken some risk for you long ago."

"In accepting Lucy? It was her whim. Later she tired of it and I do not think Lucy has been happy. And Kate would not be logical about it. She was used to me as a friend and she would not exchange me for Lucy. She must have both. Of course I ought to have lived far away and known nothing of Sherris. But the position of the Gollifer estate made that difficult, and to watch my daughter growing up was a temptation into which it was easy to fall."

"Had you no misgivings over your son Geoffrey?"

"You talk idly. Remorse and horror have never left me from the first day. But Geoffrey's danger—the danger he stood in with regard to Lucy—I became aware of only lately. It was doubtless what drove me to speak last night. We used to speak of Geoffrey and Lucy as growing up almost like brother and sister. It was a foolish irony."

"It was a wicked one."

Mrs Gollifer glanced at Appleby with a flicker of surprise and what was perhaps respect. She inclined her head. "I could see that Lucy was very much in love with Oliver. When Oliver turned out bad—a worthless man growing middle-aged—the security there seemed to be in this was mingled with pain. But when Oliver came upon the truth of Lucy's birth and basely proposed to make money out of it the painfulness became intolerable."

"I can well believe it. You would have gladly killed him, I should imagine."

Mrs Gollifer smiled—and although a drawn smile it was genuine. "You have been a police-detective, have you not, Mr Appleby? I suppose that every trail must be pursued."

"Assuredly it must."

"I do not think I had any impulse to kill Oliver Dromio. Of course the impulse may have been there in what they call the subconscious mind."

"We won't trouble ourselves about that."

"But I saw that I must in a sense kill Oliver; I must kill him in Lucy's mind. But then where might she come to stand in regard to Geoffrey, her own half-brother who had fallen in love with her? It appeared to me that nothing would serve except the truth all round."

"It is an excellent maxim of conduct, in a general way. But here it would seem to have precipitated disasters enough."

"Did it do that? Has anything that I have done or said had influence upon the events of this horrible night?" Mrs Gollifer glanced from the lily pond to Appleby, and there was swift intelligence in her gaze. "Geoffrey's was an independent discovery; it would

196

appear that he rummaged among papers that were no business of his and came upon the truth that way. And only coincidence—or might it be telepathy?—brought this about on the same evening that I told the truth here."

"And a further coincidence brought Sir Oliver and we don't know which of his new-found brothers."

"There was rather more than coincidence there. It was the sense that Oliver was returning and bringing the problem of Lucy with him that made me speak when I did."

"I see." There were shouts and Appleby looked at the blazing house. Some roof or wall was about to crash and the firemen were being ordered back. "Does it still hold, Mrs Gollifer, that nothing will serve except the truth all round?"

"It may be that there are matters on which I shall be silent. But I do not think I shall ever tell a lie again."

"If that is so," said Appleby gravely, "you will make an altogether uncommon witness, and I should be sorry to lose the opportunity of questioning you."

"You may question me."

"Do you believe that your son—" Appleby checked himself. "Do you still know more about this business than you have yet told?"

For the first time Mrs Gollifer hesitated. "There is something," she said; "something very small—far smaller than I would wish. I had thought not to speak of it until my solicitor was with me, for it is something that might help Geoffrey in the terrible position in which he has placed himself. But now I think I will tell you, for you seem a very fair sort of man."

There was a sudden childishness in this that was

moving. "I certainly have no case," Appleby said, "to which I wish to twist the facts. Every possibility I take up leads me only to misgiving."

"What I have to tell is this: Geoffrey is confused about my own part in the events of the night. He thinks that I insisted on concealing something from him. It is not so, but he is convinced of it. That is important, is it not, Mr Appleby?"

"It may be very important indeed." Appleby pitied the urgent impulse of hope in the woman's voice. "Can you be more precise in the matter?"

"When I eventually drove away from here I was still very agitated. I was still in that condition when Geoffrey overtook me and made me stop. He saw how it was—although he was agitated himself—and the first words he spoke were very strange. 'It's all right,' he said, 'but we must square the fellow who grabbed you.'"

"I see." Appleby tested the words on his ear, and it seemed to him that Mrs Gollifer spoke them in all sincerity. "That was certainly strange. And your son's remark had no meaning for you?"

"None whatever. And the thing was so urgently said! Remember what had happened so far. I had revealed to Lucy that I was her mother, and to both Lucy and Kate that Oliver had been blackmailing me. I saw that those two revelations should not have been made together; that the shock of them had overthrown Lucy entirely. I was filled with remorse and for a time, as you know, I wandered about the gardens here. But nothing else occurred. And so, you see, the unaccountability of Geoffrey's words frightened me."

"Mrs Gollifer, let us be very careful. You say those

words were these: *It's all right, but we must square the fellow who grabbed you.* Now, you were agitated, and you may have a little twisted your recollection. I put it to you that what your son said may have been something like this: *It's all right, for I have settled the fellow who had you in his clutches.*"

Mrs Gollifer drew in her breath sharply and there was a second's silence. "No!" she said—and her voice held a quiet intelligence which was impressive. "That would be an altogether unnatural turn of phrase. But you are very ingenious."

"Only as a barrister would be ingenious with you in the witness-box. He would certainly endeavour to twist the thing into some such sense."

"It is unnatural. He would have said: *I have settled Oliver.* And my recollection, I assure you, Mr Appleby, is wholly accurate."

"Very well. And you are sure the words do not now—as they did not then—convey anything to you? There was no sense in which any fellow had grabbed you?"

"None whatever. I was immediately at a loss. I told Geoffrey that I had no idea what he meant. And from that moment confidence disappeared between us. He seems to have felt that I was concealing something, and that I was in danger." Mrs Gollifer paused. "Nothing has been heard of Geoffrey since he—since he escaped?"

"Nothing at all. But the police have been rather preoccupied, as you see. . . . Do you know anything about Grubb, the dead gardener here?"

"About Grubb?" Mrs Gollifer looked startled. "I knew him by sight very well, but I don't think I ever spoke to him."

"I wonder if there is anybody who was in his confidence, or particularly well acquainted with him?"

"There are always several other gardeners. But it is the red-faced lad over there—I believe his name is William—who was commonly to be seen working with him."

"Then I think it is to William that I must go and talk now."

At first William was not conversable. He stood looking at Appleby open-mouthed—and so very red was his face that it was possible to wonder whether his words were simply vaporising as they left his lips. But it was clear that William enjoyed the fire. He enjoyed seeing his employers' house utterly destroyed; he also enjoyed his own unsparing efforts to extinguish the blaze. "You'd better come and have a mug of cocoa," Appleby said. William's mouth opened wider; he mopped his sweaty brow with an equally sweaty forearm and looked at Appleby with mingled wonder and distrust. That anyone should approach him with this affable proposition was obvious cause for suspicion. Nevertheless William did throw down his bucket and accompany Appleby to the canteen.

"I suppose," said Appleby, "that you would know a good deal about Grubb and his ways?"

"Old Grubb," said William.

This was encouraging. It could not perhaps be called very communicative, but plainly there was considerable achievement in having brought William to the point of articulate speech. "Did he," Appleby asked, "drink much as a regular thing?"

"Old Grubb," said William.

Just as William was enjoying the fire, so had William enjoyed Grubb. This much was clear from his tone, which was of connoisseurship rather than of affection or admiration. So might a man speak of a vintage, characterful but unendearing, of which the last bottle has recently disappeared from the cellar. There was silence while William swilled cocoa. It was as if, by some act of retrospective gustation possible to the initiate, he was recalling the tang of that bottle to his palate. "Old Grubb," he presently repeated once more. He knit his brows—bunching them much as he might bunch his muscles to propel a heavy barrow up a bank. Some supreme effort, Appleby could feel, was being made to snare the well-nigh indefinable in words. "Old Grubb," said William, coming down with decision on a much deeper note. "'E were a one."

"And drank?"

"When 'e weren't drinking 'e were thieving. Thieving liquor yesterday, thieving terbaccer to-day. And to-morrow? Thieving worms, most like, from his neighbour's winding-sheet."

"I see. And was he a friendly man?"

"'E were a man always chewing over ill turns done 'im long ago." William once launched, proved to be a person of some intellectual power. "And 'e relished a conundrum. There be a cottage in park with a legend to it. 'Tis where a keeper and his family disappeared from, sudden-like, long ago. Grubb 'e would stand along afore it as if 'e would thieve a secret from the place."

"That is very interesting. But now about his thieving. It would appear as if some time yesterday he slipped into Sir Oliver's study and made off with a

201

decanter of spirits. If I supposed that some time last night he made his way to the terrace with the idea of replacing the empty decanter would that be more or less in accordance with his way of going about such things?"

"Old Grubb never went out of 'is way to meet trouble. Like enough 'e'd take the decanter back."

"A little later he was still very drunk, and he was very abusive—"

"'E 'ad a dirty mind, 'ad old Grubb." William supplied this information again with his air of disinterested connoisseurship. "Fair likely to stop the devils in their 'owling, 'e is, once 'e gets started on women."

"No doubt. But the point is this: when Grubb was abusive was he also inclined to be violent? Would he be likely to attack anybody?"

William slowly but emphatically waved his large red face in air behind his cocoa mug—a gesture designed as a comprehensive negative. "Talked big, 'e did—talked big and 'orrible. But old Grubb were chicken-hearted. Wouldn't so much as throw a pint pot at you if you was to talk filthy about his grandmother."

"I see." Grubb, Appleby supposed, had not actually evinced a special veneration for this relative, and William's phrase was illustrative merely. "You don't think he might have killed Sir Oliver?"

William's eyes rounded. He thought for some time and then spoke. "Old Grubb!" he said.

This time Appleby understood that his suggestion was thrown entirely out of court. He turned to other matters. "If a man wanted three or four gallons of petrol what would be his quickest way here of getting hold of it?"

William looked about him. "From fire-engines," he hazarded.

"I don't mean that. I mean last night. Suppose you had been standing on the terrace there, close by the study windows, and you had suddenly wanted petrol. What would you have done about it?"

William set down his mug and made a jerking motion with his thumb. Then he set off for the burning house with as much resolution as if proposing to immolate himself. Appleby followed. Every now and then William turned his head as if to give encouragement; the effect was rather as of a deep-red lantern intermittently flashed against a background of the brighter glow of the flames. Firemen began to shout at them, for they appeared to be making for the short flight of steps which led to the terrace, where debris was now dangerously falling. But at the last moment William turned aside and led the way to what was apparently a tool-shed, ingeniously concealed on the lower level. He thrust his hand beneath some sacking on the window-sill and drew out a key. "'E did always keep 'un there," he said, and unlocked the door. The place held a miscellaneous collection of tools at one end and at the other a motor-mower and several tins of petrol. William examined these with slow care and then turned upon Appleby reproachfully. "Not a drop gone," he said. "It be all here as 'twere when I put mower away yesterday."

"We can't always strike lucky first time." Appleby picked up a couple of tins. "But we can get these out of the way. A spark might get this place any moment."

203

They carried the tins to safety. Appleby looked about him. "Well," he asked pertinaciously, "where else?"

"Motor houses at back."

"But they will be burning, will they not?"

William shook his head. "They be right back from house by spinney." William's complexion and interest were alike fading and the long trudge round the burning house was made in silence. It was, however, rewarded. Three sides of the courtyard upon which they came were burning. But the fourth, a detached building across a broad flagged space, was intact. From a small store-room here, with the word "Inflammable" painted in white letters on the door, Lady Dromio's chauffeur and a fireman were engaged in removing a quantity of petrol in two-gallon tins. In order to do this the chauffeur had been about to run to his cottage for the key when he discovered that the place had been broken into and four tins of petrol removed.

Appleby left William to help and returned thoughtfully to the front of the house. It was sufficiently clear that the last probability of the fire's having been an accident had vanished.

In full daylight the scene had become less spectacular. Smoke and steam were now more evident than flame and of the idle spectators a number could be observed preparing to depart. Nevertheless a crisis was yet to come, for of the main structure a greater part of the roof was still standing, and when this came down it was expected that much of the weakened walls would come down too. Appleby made no effort to join again in the fire-fighting. He saw that the ambulance was still on the drive and walked across to it. Dr Hubbard, who was pulling on his gloves, looked up as he did so. "Ah," he said drily, "another professional man in search of a victim. For my own part, I am just about to hand over to Ferris."

"Ferris?" asked Appleby.

"The young police surgeon whom you met, I think, earlier in the affair."

"Yes, of course." Appleby frowned, conscious that something stirred obscurely and vainly in his mind. "How is Mr Sebastian Dromio?"

"His condition may perhaps best be expressed by saying that Ferris can do him no harm. He is conscious, however, and you may talk to him if you like."

"Good." Appleby was about to turn away to the ambulance when a thought struck him. "Would it be true to say that Dr Ferris could have done him little harm before his fall either? He looked a sick man to me."

Dr Hubbard nodded. "You have an eye for man's mortality, Mr Appleby. And I don't doubt that better doctors than either Ferris or myself have given Sebastian Dromio over. He had a few months to live. Now he has a few hours. You yourself have from twenty-five to thirty years if you keep your weight down. Good morning."

Appleby, his sympathies veering sharply to young Dr Ferris, watched him go. Then he squeezed into the ambulance. Sebastian Dromio lay under a blanket, drowsy but sufficiently aware of what was going on around him. His eye rested on Appleby and he looked faintly puzzled. "Ah," he murmured, "the colonel—the inquiring colonel who would have weaned me from the bottle. Good morning to you."

"Good morning, Mr Dromio. Are you prepared to die?"

Sebastian Dromio looked considerably surprised. "Damn it," he said, "the fellow's a parson. Took him for a military man." He glanced at Appleby warily. "You an Anglican?" he asked.

"Yes."

"Pity—a great pity." A fleeting expression of cunning crossed Sebastian's ashen features. "Happen to be a devout Catholic myself. Sorry you can't be of use to me. Good-bye."

"You are dying, you know. And I think I can mention it without gross inhumanity because you have known for months that it is so. Now, what can you do about it? I think it likely that your life on the whole has been disagreeable and useless. Well, now, what about your death? Can we put our heads together and turn it to some reasonable account?"

"Fellow doesn't sound like a parson." Sebastian turned his head painfully to get a better view of Appleby. "By God!" he said, "it's the undertaker. Well, as I used to tell them at board meetings, business methods are deuced keen nowadays. But it's useless, my good fellow. As it happens, I am under arrest by the local police, and I don't doubt they will have their own man. Obliged to you, all the same."

"I'm not interested in your funeral. But it would worry me to see a nice girl hanged."

Sebastian closed his eyes. When they opened again it was as if nervous intensity had flooded back to them for some crisis. "Talk," he said. "Be quick about it."

"Confess that you killed your nephew, Oliver. I, for one, won't blame you. He was always worthless.

And now it has turned out that he was a bit of a rat."

"I knew there was something damned queer in the air. Did you say a rat? I rather like you. You seem to have good taste. Interested in wine?"

"I was saying that it would be a pity to see a nice girl hanged. So why not confess you killed Oliver?"

"But I didn't kill Oliver."

"They why did you kill Grubb?"

"Because—" Sebastian hesitated. "Grubb?" he asked. "Did I kill Grubb?"

"You know you did. And there's a chance of people's thinking it was because he was going to give you away. He did call out that he had seen you prowling round. But he was going to call out that he had seen something else. And then you shot him. You had seen the possibility of the emergency's coming, and you had feigned drunk on the chance it might be useful. But let me get back to the main point. You are going to die. So why not confess?"

"But surely—"

"You are going to die, you know. Perhaps within a couple of hours."

"Then get a pen and paper." A light sweat had broken out on Sebastian Dromio's brow. "And get a couple of witnesses too."

"Very well." Appleby rose. "But just a moment. It won't do to get the story wrong, or to make a muck of it. We'd better run over the true facts first and then see just what we ought to say."

"That's right. Got to see that we bally well fox 'em." Sebastian began to laugh; then he checked himself at some spasm of pain. "Better hurry," he said. "Quite right about that couple of hours. Deuced discerning fellow, colonel. Obliged to you."

Appleby leant forward. "Then, just how much do you know for certain? What did you hear? What did you see?"

"Not so much as Grubb did, I'm afraid. Can't think what the fellow was doing, slinking around like that."

"He was doing no more than propose to return a half-empty decanter to the study. Later, and when he was scared, he drank the rest of it."

"Well, I was scared too. You see, I heard her say she'd do it."

"You heard Lucy say she would kill Oliver?"

Sebastian nodded painfully. "Haven't got the exact words, but that was the sense of it. Told you there was something damned queer in the air. Something between the women. I kept away most of the evening. Couldn't stick it. Had a shock earlier, you know, seeing Oliver like that in a restaurant. Nerved myself to join them once of twice and just didn't make it. I was hesitating on the terrace just outside the drawingroom window when she said it."

"I see. But you know more than that?"

"I took another turn on the terrace later, and strolled down into the garden. As I came up a flight of steps there was this fellow Grubb grabbing at Lucy and saying 'So it was you, was it?'—or something like that. She broke away from him and ran down the terrace. There was horror on her face, poor girl. I didn't understand it. I went on through the rest of the evening—or night, rather—in a dazed, automatic sort of way. But, of course, I realised in the end. At the moment I did not more than go up to Grubb with the idea of ordering him away. Fellow took one look at me and bolted into darkness."

"What time was this?"

Sebastian shook his head. "It would be after eleven, I should say. It wasn't until half-past eleven that I went into the drawingroom. Can't think what I said—except that I mentioned having seen Mrs Gollifer in the garden, which was true enough. Rather imagine I gave a fancy picture of seeing Grubb too; probably I wanted to see how Lucy would take it. I just knew there were queer things happening. It wasn't until Swindle told us that Oliver had been killed that it all came together in my mind."

"Did you at any time become aware of anybody else on the terrace or in the grounds—for instance, Geoffrey Gollifer?"

"Didn't set eyes on a soul. But I did have an irrational feeling there were other folk about."

"Now, Mr Dromio, this is very important. Apart from what you have told me, have you any other reason whatever for associating your niece Lucy with Oliver's death?"

"That's the whole story. And bad enough, colonel. First she threatened it and then Grubb caught her. My one idea after that was to see how I could help. And now you've solved the problem. So bring in those witnesses quick."

"I don't think we need hurry, Mr Dromio."

"Haven't you told me I am going to die? In two hours, didn't you say?"

"I see now that there would be no point in your confessing."

Sebastian Dromio by some gigantic effort stirred his limbs. His features contorted in agony. "The confession!" he whispered hoarsely. "I must make the confession."

Appleby rose. "I will see what can be done," he

said, and slipped from the ambulance. As he closed the door Sebastian Dromio was making rather horrible noises in his throat.

And almost immediately Appleby ran into Hyland, who stared at him in astonishment. "Good heavens!" he cried. "Are you hurt? You're as pale as a sheet."

Appleby laughed rather unsteadily. "Did you ever read of those hard-boiled detectives in American crime stories who will do any unspeakable thing to get what they want?"

"Well, yes." Hyland spoke reluctantly. "I suppose I have."

"I've been trying it out. And I rather think I made the grade."

Hyland shook his head. "I can't think what you're talking about. But I'm going to have a word with Sebastian Dromio. They say he's conscious still."

"I wouldn't do that." And Appleby laid a hand on Hyland's arm and led him away. "The poor chap is very confused in his mind. And I rather think he might confuse you too."

14

The Chief Constable had arrived without his breakfast—a fact showing that the destruction of Sherris Hall was a matter of importance in the county. Hyland hurried off to him with the nervous haste of one who has a good deal to explain, and Appleby was again left to his own resources. He sought out Lucy Dromio and found her in company with Mrs Gollifer. Mother and daughter, both tall figures in white, were pacing the lawn together, and it appeared to Appleby as if confidence was establishing itself between them. But now Mrs Gollifer walked away at some call from Lady Dromio and Appleby joined Lucy.

"You know," he asked, "that by a strange coincidence Mr Greengrave last night discerned the fact of your relationship? As I stood watching you both walking here I almost persuaded myself that I could have done so too. You have the same figure."

Lucy looked at him wearily. "Is that a matter of

professional interest, Mr Appleby, or is it merely a compliment?"

"It is very interesting to me. You have the same figure and you are both dressed in white.... Did you know that two people were watching when Grubb grabbed you last night?"

The girl caught her breath sharply. "Do you suspect me of really having killed someone I thought was Oliver?"

"That you did so is not impossible. You loved Oliver and he had treated you badly. And so, although your love still seemed great, there might be a smouldering resentment underneath it. Then you learnt that he was a blackguard; that he had been making money out of the secret of your birth. I can hardly imagine anything more humiliating and wounding. You said that you felt like killing him. And not long afterwards you were grabbed by Grubb as you hurried, terrified, along the terrace in the dark. He said, 'So it was you, was it?' Am I right?"

"You are wrong. He said, 'So it is you, is it?' In the circumstances there is a very great difference between these two questions."

"I agree. But what had you been doing when he came upon you?"

Lucy looked Appleby straight in the eyes. "If I had been killing Oliver, or one whom I took for Oliver, I would have told you so by this time. Do you think I would shelter behind Geoffrey's absurd confession?"

"Perhaps I shall be able to answer that question soon. Do you think, then, that Geoffrey Gollifer is endeavouring to shield you?"

"No, I don't think he is." Lucy shook her head. "It is puzzling and obscure, but somehow I feel that that is not what was in his mind."

"You are quite right. What he was thinking to do was to shield his mother."

"My mother."

Appleby inclined his head. "Your mother—who seems to me, if I may say so, rather a remarkable woman. Geoffrey Gollifer was one of two people who saw Grubb grab you. He mistook you for your mother. And when your mother naturally failed to understand a reference he made to the incident he concluded that she was not being open with him. But he was resolved to shield her—to keep her entirely out of the affair."

Lucy made a weary gesture. "That is merely to shift suspicion from Geoffrey to our mother. But at least it means that he could not himself have killed the man whose body was found."

"Not necessarily. He may simply have felt that if your mother was to be suspected the situation was intolerable and he was bound to confess what he had actually done. I may say there has been another offer of confession. And this definitely to shield you. Did you know how devoted to you was Mr Sebastian Dromio?"

"I scarcely did until his heroic attempt to rescue me."

"He heard you speak of killing Oliver. And he too saw Grubb seize you on the terrace. He saw your terror. Later he decided that Grubb held the secret of your having committed the crime. So he killed Grubb. And now, when he is dying, he wants to confess that it was he who was guilty of the first killing."

Lucy sat down suddenly on a low stone balustrade and buried her face in her hands. "It is very horrible," she said in a stifled voice.

"And from my point of view it is very complicated." Appleby spoke emphatically. "My experience in crime is considerable. But never have I faced so complicated a case, or one so bewilderingly huddled up both in space and time. We cannot undo what has been done. I myself cannot seek other than the full truth and the subsequent action of the law. But we can perhaps prevent further error, further confusion and complication, the horror of indefinite and ramifying distrust, unresolved suspicion and doubt. But frankness is required—and among others from you. Why have you not told us of your meeting with Grubb?"

Lucy looked up. "Simply because I failed—stupidly, I don't doubt—to see it as relevant. I was pacing the terrace—in terror and horror, as you say. But that was simply because I was weak enough to feel that I could not support my personal predicament as revealed by my mother's story. It had no connection with anything I had either seen or suspected of a crime. I saw nothing. I suspected nothing. I was walking the terrace, wholly abstracted and absorbed, when this fellow grabbed me and asked his question. I took it for mere drunken impertinence, and even now I do not believe that it was anything else. He had been troublesome before. I shook him off and walked, or ran, on. And that seemed an end of the matter."

"You ought to have divulged these facts, nevertheless. If they are as you represent them we have arrived at a badly needed simplification. You yourself know nothing of the crime. Sebastian Dromio knows no more than he has told. There is nothing to challenge your mother's story that she was merely lingering in the garden. Your brother Geoffrey's story is hard to believe, since with anyone other than Sir Oliver it seems impossible that he should have held such a conversation as he claims."

"Then you do believe that it was the first identification that was mistaken, and that the body was not Oliver's at all?"

"I believe something a good deal odder—or rather the only satisfactory hypothesis that I can at present see is a good deal odder." Appleby paused. "The facts seem to require this: that Sir Oliver was not involved at all."

Lucy stared at him as if he had taken leave of his senses. "I don't understand you."

"I scarcely understand myself. It would appear overwhelmingly likely that the first flurried identification was the mistaken one, and that when the body is recovered from the ruins of this fire the dental evidence will prove it to be not Sir Oliver's. But already I possess evidence that Sir Oliver was not, in fact, the murderer. And the inference from these things is, I say, odd. Somebody, it seems, has killed one of the long-lost Dromio brothers and endeavoured to pass off the body as Oliver's. That somebody, I believe, was not Sir Oliver himself. But as Mr Greengrave did almost certainly see two brothers there is a presumption that the somebody was himself a brother. In other words, one long-lost brother killed the other and dressed up the body as Sir Oliver's. And Sir Oliver does not appear in the affair at all. Or he appears only as a voice overheard by a servant, and in that there may very well have been some error. Sir Oliver may be in America still."

"But it's nonsense!" Lucy spoke between irritation and despair. "There's just no sense in it at all. It's all horror and no sense. And that makes it insupportable."

"It is certainly bewildering. I wish I had not settled to my own satisfaction that Sir Oliver cannot be the criminal. For in that lies what would be far the easiest line to take. Sir Oliver wanted to get-away into a new life, and no questions asked. So he took advantage of having discovered an identical brother, killed him, passed the body off as his own, and then fired the house before the impersonation or substitution was likely to be discovered. That is the only clear road one can see; abandon it and everything becomes mere bewilderment. But it has to be abandoned. Because Sir Oliver did not fire the house."

"However can you tell?"

"It is very simple. The person who started the fire needed a lot of petrol. If he had been familiar with the house, and had known of Grubb's habit with a certain key, he could have had it in no time from a little shed not twenty yards from the study. But he actually got his petrol from much farther away and from where a stranger would look for it—in a little store, clearly marked 'Inflammable,' round by the motor house."

"I see." Lucy was silent for a moment. "It certainly seems a point conclusive as far as it goes. I just wish I could believe you. I wish I could believe that Oliver was not—or is not—here, and involved. But somehow I can't do it. My heart—my instinct—tells me that—that he is lost. How lost, I don't know. But I have no doubt of the fact of it." Again she was silent. "You are right about the truth. The only thing now is to find it, whatever ruin it brings upon us. Is there any way that I can help you, Mr Appleby?"

"Just at present, I don't think there is. Unless you can tell me what it was that stirred queerly in my mind when you came tumbling out of your window. . . . By the way, why did you insist on returning to your room?"

Lucy hesitated. "It was extremely foolish. I ought to have reflected that it might endanger other people. I wanted my diary."

"I see." Appleby glanced curiously at the girl. "Well, a diary is something one may do a lot to preserve."

"It was not so in this case. I wanted to destroy it."

"To destroy it! But surely the fire would have done that in any case?"

"I wanted to destroy it myself." Lucy was silent for a moment. "Why should something stir in your mind when I tumbled out of window?"

"You shot down, all legs and streaming draperies, and the sight touched off some association in my mind that ought to have led me somewhere. Only the association just didn't establish itself in consciousness and now I can't get command of it."

"How very odd. And if you got the association it would help you with the mystery? Then we must certainly find it." Lucy raised her head and looked absently at the burning house. The flames, although less intense than formerly, cast a glow like a faint blush on her pale, finely cut features. "Would it be falling stone, a missile, a weapon?"

"No."

"A sack, a bundle, a body?"

"Not that either."

217

"You speak of streaming draperies. What about a parachute, a soldier, a weapon?"

"No."

Lucy frowned. "Look," she said, "I am all in white. What about *The Woman in White*? That's a mystery. Perhaps there is something relevant there."

Appleby shook his head. "Your suggestion is ingenious, but I think not."

"It must have been a very upside-down sort of spectacle. Ankles, legs?"

"No."

"And I came down on that canvas with a bump and a bounce. What about that? Bounce, ball, bullet?"

Appleby hesitated. "Bullet...bullet?" He shook his head. "It sets up an echo, so to speak. But it's not right."

"Then try again." Lucy was both determined and excited. "Bounce, bump, come down with a bump—what about the associations there? They are mildly indelicate but may be vital nevertheless. For instance—"

"Good Lord!" Appleby, who had sat down beside Lucy, sprang to his feet. "I knew that young doctor—Ferris, isn't it?—came in. Something he said that I just didn't catch on to."

"Have I helped, after all?"

Appleby paid no attention. He was pacing up and down so excitedly that Hyland, who came up at this moment, stared at him in astonishment. "And I believe I know what he meant!" he cried. "And the arms?" He stopped short and stared back at Hyland as if thunderstruck. "Is it possible—" He turned to Lucy. "Would you substantiate the statement that—

218

that Sir Oliver probably bought his ties in the Burlington Arcade?"

Hyland made a sound eloquent of despair. But Lucy considered the question quite seriously. "I'm afraid I don't know," she said. "But he certainly has a great many of them—or had."

"Are we to understand"—Hyland was heavily sarcastic—"that this fire has been contrived in order to destroy Sir Oliver Dromio's stock of sartorial accessories?"

Appleby shook his head soberly. "Nothing of that sort," he said. "But that fellow Ferris—do you think he can be found? For that's the next thing to do. And then we must get on the trans-Atlantic telephone—and be quick about it if we are to finish up today."

"Finish up today!" Hyland, smoke-blackened and irritated, exploded once more. "Are you telling us that you have this fantastic work of confusion in the bag?"

Appleby smiled. "I don't know about that. But I do see one correspondingly fantastic explanation, and I very much doubt whether any other is possible—although it upsets almost every thought I've had so far. . . . Have you missed any bodies round about this district lately?"

"Have we what?"

"Mislaid a corpse."

"Certainly not. Such a thing is unheard of."

"So much the worse."

"Mystery-mongering," said Hyland, "—sheer mystery-mongering." Lack of breakfast—as also perhaps the conversation of the Chief Constable—was fraying what remained of his nerves. "Chatter out of a melodrama. But at least the melodramatic part of this affair is behind us, praise God."

"Look out, there!"

"Stand back!"

A sudden sharp burst of voices made them turn round. A section of the rustic crowd which had pressed almost up to the terrace was being hastily shepherded further off, and a group of firemen were trundling away a ladder. For a series of ominous cracks and a fresh leap of flame told that the crisis of the fire had come, and even as they looked some vital beam went and a great part of what remained of the roof began to move. As it did so the ground trembled, from the back of the house came a crash and rumble of falling brick, and some fresh draught of air thus released upon the blaze sent great tongues of flame leaping once more about the ruin. Through every gaping aperture the incandescence could be seen to grow; for a moment all Sherris Hall glowed like a vast transparent crucible filled with a molten and intolerable gold. Blast upon blast of searing air beat across the lawn, as if the great house like a creature in its death agony were panting out its fiery and infernal life. Then the roof came down, sucked in as by a tortured and terminal respiration, and everywhere great sections of retaining wall were tumbling. A pall of smoke rose like a last inky excretion and hung over the house. The noises of combustion were cut off. The crowd was mute. It was like a sudden silent sequence in a rackety film.

The silence was broken by laughter. Somebody was hysterical. The sound was disconcerting, uncomfortable; the sound grew menacing, unnatural, mad; it was an insane and pealing mirth, an exultant threnody over the ashes of Sherris Hall.

They turned. On a little hill beyond the lily pond, intermittently obscured by drifts of smoke like some theatrical figure risen through a trap from the infernal regions, stood a tall man wildly posed with arms above his head. The arms waved in crazy ecstasy, the man's head was flung triumphantly back, his laughter rang out again like a paroxysm.

There were cries of astonishment, indignation, recognition. Hyland shouted. A couple of constables ran forward. The laughing man stopped, gave a queer wave of the left hand, turned and fled.

Lucy Dromio swayed on her feet. "Oliver!" she cried, and fainted in Hyland's arms.

15

It was a turn in the affair, Appleby felt, eminently deserving of a curtain—and even of tumultuous and sustained applause. The villain screeching with triumph over the burning ancestral home, the heroine fainting away, justice baffled and scurrying over a countryside in vain pursuit: all this on its level could not well be bettered. Hyland, who had no fancy for the limelight and greasepaint which was thus become so uncomfortably prominent in the mystery, had called for maps, motor-cycles and firearms, and was now seated at a little table comporting himself like some harassed major involved in inexplicable manoeuvres. Around him bewildered constables came and went, most of them smoke-blackened and with sweat pouring from beneath their helmets. In the middle distance the Chief Constable ominously paced the lawn; behind him could be felt the impalpable and appalling presence of critical coroners, censorious Grand Juries, outraged High Sheriffs and implacable Lords Lieutenant of the county. Hyland's hair was ruffled, so that he looked as if he had been tearing it; lacerated black braid depended from various parts of his person, so that he looked as if he had been tearing that, too; his silver buttons were missing or in mourning. As all this witnessed to the fact that he had borne a vigorous physical part in the action it was doubtless unjust that the total effect should be of undignified desperation and plain absurdity. But so it was. Appleby commiserated with his official colleague. At the same time he was conscious of those inglorious but comfortable sensations which Montaigne ascribes to that fortunate man who, from the security of solid earth, watches the vessel labouring on a stormy sea. But, definitely, an act had ended and the orchestra was shuffling into its pit. Like an exhausted spectator edging his way out to the bar, Appleby retired to a secluded corner of the gardens and set himself to think.

A fountain was playing and he paused, startled by so peaceful and undisturbed a thing. In the basin surrounding it suspended or darting goldfish were beginning to catch the slanting rays of the sun. At its centre stood an Apollo Sauroctonus in white marble; from the figure's outstretched left hand a fine spray of water fell, drenching the little lizard that climbed the tree-trunk hard by. A pretty conceit, Appleby reflected, to make a fountain so—and doubtless the idea had flashed upon some long vanished Dromio as he dutifully paced the Louvre and came upon the original. A lovely youth was this Apollo, although faintly epicene to a modern eye. Had such a one stood in the flesh before Praxiteles in his studio? Appleby shook his head. That was not the way of it.

223

Rather had the sculptor and his fellows labored long after those obscure conceptions and then, some generations later, the actuality was born and just such over-graceful lads were to be seen sauntering in the green Arcadian valleys. For always it is in the wake of art that life lumbers tardily on to fresh expressions. Yesterday's canvas is the girl's face of to-day; the son's fact had been but the father's fable. And with melodrama—

Appleby sat down on the fountain's brim, conscious that he was back at work. And at least this might be said: that when for practical reasons our imagination must become urgent and working we tend to impose upon reality something of a make-believe world potent with us during our impressionable years. So what, in the light of this, was the significance of that gesticulating figure with its satanic laughter as Sherris hall came finally tumbling down?

Lucy read modern poetry of the most sophisticated sort. Lady Dromio, intellectually unambitious, read streamlined novels about big hotels. Such books as Sir Oliver's study had contained—Appleby shook his head. Swindle's literary world, were it to be supposed that he at all possessed one, would much more closely answer to the diabolic figure whom Hyland's motor-cyclists were now pursuing. But, of course, it might not be a matter of chronology. It might be in geography that the significant point lay. . . .

Appleby stooped down and picked up a tiny flint. On the broad flat rim of the fountain on which he sat he scratched a serrated line roughly representing the eastern coast of North America. Then he drew the British Isles, so that a tiny Atlantic Ocean stretched between. From a bed near by he plucked three rosebuds—red, yellow and white. The red rose he pitched into England, the yellow and white into America. He looked at them for some time. Then he moved the red rose across the Atlantic and paused again. Then he brought red and white to England. This time he paused longer and looked enquiringly at the Apollo above him—but the Apollo continued to watch the little water-drenched lizard undisturbed. "An heiress," said Appleby aloud; he picked up a pebble and set it beside the yellow rose in America; shook his head and brought the white rose back to America as well. Start again. White and yellow in America, with the pebble too, but a little apart. Red rose in England... Again he brought the red rose across the Atlantic to join the yellow and white. For a long time he stared at them with absolute concentration. Then his hand went out in a flash; he picked up the yellow rose and flung it away. He paused again and then brought both remaining roses to England. He flung one of them away in turn, so that only a single rose remained. This rose he transferred to America, then rapidly to England and back, then finally to England again together with the pebble.... He swept them all away and scratched out the continents. He rose and nodded to the Apollo. "Obvious, my dear Watson," he murmured, and walked on.

Nevertheless he had not the air of a man whose problems are all behind him. Twice he restlessly paced the length of a gravel walk; he returned to the fountain and peered down at the fish. For a moment two or three would be clearly in focus; they would dart hither and thither and yet it would appear impossible that they should escape the eye; a moment later they would have vanished. He shook his head at them and frowned. "Geoffrey Gollifer," he said.

Water trickled down the back of the lizard and fell with a tiny continuous splash into the pool. There was no other sound. "Geoffrey Gollifer," said Appleby again and with a different inflection. The effect was rather that of a man who doubtfully rotates some troublesome fragment of a jig-saw. . . . "Yes," he said, "—Geoffrey Gollifer! Impossible to get away from it, much as I should like to. And that means—well, it means something like genius." He considered this. "Improvisation," he said. "That's the point of astonishment." He looked up and saw Mr Greengrave bearing down on him.

"Do I disturb you?" asked Mr Greengrave. "I am sure that you must have much on your mind."

Appleby smiled. "I came into this corner of the gardens to think. But I appear to have been soliloquising instead."

"It is sometimes helpful. And you and I, you will recall, first met upon a mutual confession of recitation and song—or perhaps I ought to say hymnology." Mr Greengrave shook his head. "Incredible that it should have been less than twelve hours ago."

"I agree that it is odd. I get the feeling of playing out a rapid theatrical piece before an invisible audience. No doubt my soliloquy was for their benefit."

"And now we are providing a dialogue for several goldfish, a lizard, and a heathen deity."

Appleby laughed. "Actually I have been thinking that this is an interval. There has been a big build up, a crashing climax, and now we are all set for the last act."

"The last act? I am sure I hope so." Mr Greengrave

had become serious. "The tragedy has spread far enough."

"It has been a complicated crime, but it has also been a bloody one. Grubb is dead. A man whom it is reasonable to suppose an unknown brother of the late Sir Oliver's is dead too. Somebody else, who may either be a second brother, or Sir Oliver himself—"

"Lucy is convinced it is Sir Oliver. She recognised him at once."

"How could she do so? He was standing at a distance, and the air was full of smoke."

Mr Greengrave nodded. "That is true. But she is convinced, nevertheless. I have questioned her myself. Apparently it was his wave—that final gesture as he turned and ran. It was, she says, Oliver's wave."

"Whoever it is, he is at large, and with a gallows, it may be, waiting for him. Geoffrey Gollifer is at large and in the same situation. It occurs to me to wonder about Swindle."

"The butler? I am afraid there can be no doubt as to his fate."

Appleby shook his head. "I don't know just what the evidence is. A few seconds after we had become aware of the fire you may remember something like a scream—"

"It had nothing to do with Swindle. Apparently it was Lady Dromio's maid, who had been got up to attend her mistress. And she was successfully extricated. All that is known of Swindle is that he was probably in his basement room. As his senses were defective and he was accustomed to an atmosphere of almost intolerable heat it is supposed that he became aware of the fire too late to save himself. And unfortunately nobody else thought of him."

"I wonder. You see, he might have been so uncommonly useful." Appleby paused. "However, we shall know more or less for certain when they get in among the ruins."

"They are already attempting that, although the heat must still be terrific. Lucy Dromio, by the way, has a theory connecting Swindle with the origin of the fire. What a strange girl she is! Disasters have accumulated around her, and yet she is able to indulge in an untimely pleasantry. She declares that Swindle's body will never be found."

"The dickens she does!" Appleby looked sharply at Mr Greengrave. "And why—"

"She gives it as her opinion that what has occurred is a case of spontaneous combustion. Swindle had drunk so much port that his flashpoint, so to speak, had sunk dangerously low. Eventually he simply went up in flame and nothing more will be seen of him."

Appleby shook his head. "I think it quite likely that a body has disappeared without trace. Unless I am completely out in the whole matter—which is only too likely, you may well say—that appears to be an essential inference to make. Only I don't think the disappearance has been exactly in the neighborhood of Sherris. I should guess at something like an accident on a lake or river. . . . Did any word ever come to Sherris, do you know, of Sir Oliver's having been involved in some serious accident?"

"I think not." Mr Greengrave peered absently at the darting goldfish. "For a good many weeks there had, it seems, been a complete absence of news."

Appleby nodded. "Yes, I suppose it would be so. It

almost follows, indeed, from the nature of his ties."

"I know very little about them. But they would appear, I am afraid, not always to be very moral."

"What's that?" Appleby stared in astonishment. "Oh, I see! I wasn't speaking, actually, of ties of that sort. I meant neckties."

"Neckties?" It was Mr Greengrave's turn to be perplexed. "I hardly see—"

"Ah—but then you don't wear them. It is not a field in which a clergyman need be at all knowledgeable. Nor could Apollo here have a word to say on the matter. Shall we go back and see what's happening?"

Mr Greengrave nodded emphatically. "I think," he said, "we better had."

Firemen and policemen were cautiously exploring the ruins. Bathed in sunshine, they still in places dully glowed; smoke hung over charred woodwork and tumbled brick; everywhere the windows gave upon queer emptiness or blue sky. The lawn was muddy and trampled, the flower-beds ravaged, the lily pond half drained away. All in all, Sherris showed forlorn as a deserted theatre littered with the debris of an audience gone home to bed.

Hyland still sat at his little table, an imaginary office disposed around him. "Well," Appleby asked, "are all those desperate characters still at large?"

"All? Dash it all, there are only two: Geoffrey Gollifer and Sir Oliver—if it is Sir Oliver. But two is bad enough."

"Might there not be three? There were three brothers, you know: two long-lost and one common-or-garden. And only one is certainly dead." Appleby shook his head. "Now, if there had been Dromio quintuplets matters would be really complicated."

"It's no time for levity." Hyland was harassed and morose. "You haven't heard the news. Sir Oliver—for I don't really see that it can be other than he—is behaving like a madman."

"I'm sure he is."

"A pyromaniac. This"—and Hyland waved a hand at the smoking ruins of Sherris—"is only a beginning of the mischief. From all accounts he's racing across country in a big car firing anything he can. Hay-ricks going up all over the place. Mad as a hatter. So what are you to make of that?"

"Well, of course, Oliver's father went more or less mad, didn't he? We rather gathered he died quietly insane. And it came on with his fantastic firing of his own nurseries, and substituting two children for his own. So I suppose this looks like history repeating itself, more or less? Sir Oliver learnt the truth while he was in America; his mother wrote and told him about it. Clearly it sent him quite balmy and he became obsessed with the idea of fire and substituted bodies himself. Then he hitched this obsession on to something else—the fact that he was in perhaps more than one uncomfortably tight spot. Blackguards often are. He brought home one of those long-lost brothers, hit him on the head, proposed to pass off his body as his own, and himself make a comfortable get-away to another identity, with no curiosity pursuing him. He managed all this, complete with a little loopy—but nevertheless practically useful—incineration in the study, burning away the evidence of his brother's work-coarsened hands. So far, there was a sort of fantastic rationality in his proceedings. But

230

then, as was almost inevitable, all this criminal excitement finally overthrew any vestiges of sanity and calculation, so that now he is wandering the country like a maniac firebrand. Is that right?"

Hyland nodded emphatically. "That's right. But it's uncommonly complicated."

"To be sure it is." Appleby sighed. "But not nearly so complicated as the truth."

It was at this moment that a constable approached. He was holding before him, rather in the manner of a servant who has been bidden to handle some repellent object, a single battered and muddy boot. He placed it on the table before Hyland. "Sergeant's orders, sir," he said, "that you were to see this."

Hyland eyed the object without enthusiasm. "Well," he demanded, "what of it—and where did you find it?"

"In a ditch, sir, about half-way down the main drive."

"And what the deuce were you doing in a ditch, man? Did you expect to find this madman lurking in it?"

"I wasn't in the ditch, sir." The constable spoke reproachfully. "I was just passing by, like, and my eye fell on it. So I thought I'd better show it up."

"Show yourself up, I should say. Ditches are full of old boots. What do you expect us to do? Fit it triumphantly to the vital footprints?" Hyland's frayed temper was making itself evident again.

"Well, sir, I did think it might be some sort of clue."

"Good Lord! Well, I dare say you acted very properly. And now"—and Hyland turned the constable's clue distastefully over—"take it away again. It's

231

nothing but an old boot abandoned by a tramp. Some mud sticking to it, and some feathers. It's no more a clue than is the nose on my face."

"Excuse me. I wonder if I might—?"

They turned in surprise. Mr Greengrave, who had been standing beside Appleby, was advancing and peering at the boot. Hyland picked it up and handed it to him with a sigh. "Yes, sir?" he asked patiently.

"I hope you will not—that is, I should hate to claim any power of observation in matters of this kind. But—well, yes, I am sure of it."

"We are glad to hear of anybody being sure of anything round about Sherris these days." Hyland, not venturing to glower at a clergyman, glowered at the unfortunate constable instead.

"You see, it is like this. Last night I happened to be planning out the heads of a sermon, and it occurred to me to wonder whether I might not judiciously animadvert upon certain minor misdemeanours which have been troubling the parish of late—"

"Well, sir, you will have more than minor misdemeanours to speak of, I'm afraid, next Sunday. And I hardly see—"

"The fact is that old Mrs Marple had missed a couple of her Khaki Campbells. And the feathers on this boot are from a Khaki Campbell. I think it not possible that I could mistake them. And I know of nobody else who keeps that particular sort of duck."

"But this is interesting." Appleby spoke decidedly. "Does Mrs Marple live near Sherris?"

"No. She lives at the other end of the parish, on the Sherris Magna road."

"Then it would be wise to visit her Khaki Campbells at once. Hyland, have you got a car? Your men have borrowed mine."

Hyland appeared to swallow with difficulty. "Of course I have a car. But do you really think—"

"Certainly I do. It may bring us no nearer to your criminal. But just conceivably it may confirm a hypothesis—in rather a grim way."

"You mean that you are beginning to get this affair clear?" Hyland's voice sounded incredulous but faintly hopeful.

"It comes clear in bits. Have you got a map?"

Hyland picked up a sheet from his table. "Here you are. Leave the main road at this fork, and Mrs Marple's is the first cottage with a patch of land on the right. You can't miss it."

"Thank you. And now have you got one of the whole country?"

This too was produced and Appleby studied it silently.

"Fellow has almost certainly got a car," Hyland said, "—and a powerful one too. But we have no description of it, and by the time a blaze is reported he may be fifty miles away. It's awkward."

"You think he will go driving about England, firing things indefinitely?"

"I'm sure he will. You'd know he was mad as a hatter just from that laugh we heard—let alone from the accounts of what he's up to now. Of course it can't last. He probably looks as much of a chimney-sweep as we do, and his manner will be strange. Quite soon he will be spotted, the car described, and then we shall have him within a couple of hours. But there will have been the deuce of a lot of damage meanwhile. And when I think that we let that young fellow Gollifer slip through our fingers too—"

"Never mind Geoffrey Gollifer. Stick to Dromio—whether One, Two, or Three. Just where has he been reported so far?"

"There, and then there." Hyland's finger ran over the map. "And this is Sherris here."

"It looks a random progress."

"Of course it's a random progress. Just where he goes is all the same to him. One piece of incendiarism is as satisfactory as another, no doubt."

Appleby shook his head. "In itself that may be true. Nevertheless the movements of our quarry are purposive and strictly controlled. He has set himself what, in the south of England, appears to me a formidable problem. Moreover, he is in a hurry. But fortunately we are not."

"Not in a hurry!" Hyland was impatient. "With a maniac roaming the—"

"The maniac is a very clever man." Appleby paused. "Cleverer than any criminal I have ever met before."

"Dear me!" It was Mr Greengrave who broke in. "That is a most interesting observation to hear you make. Indeed, it gives me an irrational and topsy-turvy sense of some distinction's having been conferred upon our neighbourhood. But a sadly sinister distinction, I fear."

"A very clever man," Appleby repeated, "and I don't think that we have much chance of grabbing him before the next stage of the affair. I don't know, however, that it is of the first importance. It simply means that the lawyers will have rather more to argue about before a jury. He no longer has a chance of getting clean away."

"You are confident," asked Mr Greengrave, "that the criminal will be taken? Is is not likely that one so demented will rather commit suicide?"

"I don't say it won't turn out rather that way." Appleby was preparing to jump into the car which Hyland had summoned. "Perhaps you would care to come along? Your introduction to Mrs Marple might be valuable."

"By all means." Mr Greengrave jumped eagerly at this proposition. "I am most interested to know what we shall find."

Appleby shook his head. "I think I can promise you," he replied, "that we shall find very little."

16

The summer day was flawless. Ahead, towards Sherris Magna, a few low clouds lay over the sea; elsewhere the sky was clear and a warm sunlight bathed ample pastures in which cattle paddled in their several pools of shade. Behind them wafts of smoke still hung above Sherris Hall. To their right, and in the middle distance beyond a broad valley, rose a single column of darker smoke.

Mr Greengrave leant forward to peer at this across Appleby as he drove. "I suppose—" he began doubtfully.

"Most certainly. And over the horizon there will be a little chain of such conflagrations. They are a manifesto, you see—a large writing on the sky such as they used to squirt out of aeroplanes." Appleby paused. "Yes, this too is a sort of advertising. It pays to advertise. In this case it even pays—or is designed to pay—a murderer. . . . But what about a little song?"

"I beg your pardon?" Mr Greengrave was startled.

"It is our habit, isn't it, when we drive?"

Mr Greengrave smiled. "But I am not at all sure—"

"And let it be something appropriate." Appleby pressed the accelerator and began to sing:

"Fire in the top bucket, fire in the main;
"It's fetch a bucket of water, gals, and put it out
    again.
"Fire in the fore-peak, fire down below..."

Mr Greengrave frowned, laughed, hesitated no longer; his deep voice joined in:

"Fire in the windlass, fire in the chain;
"It's fetch a bucket of water, gals, and put it out
    again.
"Fire up aloft, and fire down below,
"It's fetch a bucket of water, gals, there's fire
    down below."

Appleby nodded. "Yes," he said, "that's it. That's what our man has to find—fire down below."

Mr Greengrave returned to gravity. "He is almost sure to, I am afraid."

"I mean here and now. Fire down below—it is the remaining condition of his problem." Appleby was silent for a moment. "And I doubt whether they will catch him until he has fulfilled it. Even"—and he swung the wheel of the little car—"although they've borrowed my Bentley to make the better speed. Look here." He pointed to another smudge of smoke on the far horizon. "The mad Sir Oliver, son of the mad Sir Romeo, perpetrated a crime of calculation. He killed his brother and endeavoured to pass off the body as his own—thereby ensuring himself an unembarrassed withdrawal from various predicaments. But the excitement was too much for his sanity and he at once went as overtly mad as his fire-raising father. That is the picture."

Mr Greengrave considered. "The true picture?"

"Dear me, no. It is an ingenious picture, but what these fires actually illumine is a picture much more ingenious than that. Of their perpetrator I would be inclined to say"—Appleby paused—"well, that he is one whose fires true genius kindles. They are elements in a deep design. You might almost call them, with King Lear, thought-executing fires."

Mr Greengrave took a moment to reflect on this. "When you fall to sea-shanties and to—um—talking like the *Oxford Dictionary of Quotations*, does it mean—"

"Yes, I suppose it does. It means that I feel reasonably near getting home to a quiet dinner. . . . Is this where we turn off?"

"Yes—and then to the right." Mr Greengrave shook his head. "Surely it is a crime of an altogether uncommon perplexity?"

Appleby nodded. "In one sense crimes are usually simple enough. One comes quickly upon a clear motive, obvious opportunity, sufficient passion. Common sense carries one through. But if this were all—if there were not another factor constantly at work—criminology would hold very little of interest. But there is another factor, and one which constantly tends to surround the simplicities of crime with what psychologists might call secondary elaboration."

"They use the term of dreams."

"Quite so. And the secondary elaboration may come to occupy almost the whole picture. But it is secondary, nevertheless. And it proceeds . . . but perhaps I bore you?"

Mr Greengrave shook his head emphatically. "On the contrary, I find this strange territory extremely interesting. I only regret that Canon Newton is not with us. You would find his grasp remarkable—very remarkable, indeed."

"No doubt. But it is really not so very difficult. All that happens is this. A surprisingly high proportion of human beings harbor criminal impulses just below the threshold of their conscious life. As long as their environment is well-ordered they are themselves well-conducted. But confront them suddenly with a context of violence and the criminal strain may assert itself. It is thus that crime breeds crime—and often with an amazing speed. Moreover, there is this to be remarked. Criminal actions released in this way tend to be far more ingenious and bizarre than the initial crimes the shock of which prompts them. The initial crime is likely to be a matter of simple passion such as we can all without difficulty understand; the further crimes elaborated from it tend to the extravagance and fantasy—as also the ingenuity—of dreams. From all this there emerges a good working rule. Find the simplicities of the case—those elements in it which make simple sense in terms of the elementary human passions. Take this as a centre and dispose everything else as best you can round about it. Don't be seduced into taking as a centre any of the secondary elaboration, however obtrusive and startling it may appear. . . . Is that Mrs Marple's?"

"Yes. It will be best to stop just beyond the bridge." Mr Greengrave picked up his clerical straw hat and set it firmly on his head. "And all this leads you to certain conclusions in the present case?"

"I think I have got pretty well through the maze. But various things are still lacking. I am hoping for a little quick work by the New York police. And of course we must have the dentist whose importance Sergeant Morris spotted."

"You think the evidence of the dentist might expose the truth?"

Appleby chuckled as he brought the police-car to a halt. "Here is a mystery turning on incinerated bodies. Do you think it really likely that the villain left the dentist out of account?"

"Good heavens!" Mr Greengrave was startled. "You don't mean that some innocent man's life may be in danger simply because he once attended to Sir Oliver Dromio's teeth?"

"No, we can be pretty confident that the dentist is as safe as houses. . . . We had better go straight up to the cottage. Will you lead the way?"

Mr Greengrave, thus bidden, opened Mrs Marple's garden gate. Then he paused. "I think I understand enough of this affair to be distinctly depressed by what you have said. I mean as to finding the centre of the case at that point where simple human passion clearly appears. It is all going to end badly, I am afraid?"

"Yes, I am afraid it is."

They walked up a narrow path between untidy box hedges. Mr Greengrave shook his head. "When this tramp's boot was found, and you showed some interest in it, I must confess that my hopes rose. I thought it might prove that the whole horrible business was, after all, the work of some thieving ruffian from out-side—one about whom there would be no heart-breaks. But reason tells me that there can be very little possibility of that."

"There can be none at all, I am sorry to say. But the owner of the boot may have his grim place in the affair, and as he appears to have been among this woman's poultry it is just possible that we may find some trace of it. The signs of some physical struggle are what I have in mind."

"Dear me! I devoutly hope we are not going to come upon another body."

Appleby shook his head. "No," he said. "There is no chance of that."

Mrs Marple's hens were clucking in their yard; her cocks strutted here and there in indecisive promiscu-ity, crowing the while; her geese cackled from beyond a hedge; at the sight of strangers her children ran screaming into the cottage; with a fog-horn's per-sistence her cow provided a melancholic commentary from a byre; of two small muddy curs one yelped while the other snapped in well-drilled alternation. Then Mrs Marple, although herself invisible, began to shout—and at this, with laudable loyalty, all her dependent creatures redoubled their vociferations. To a deaf man, Appleby thought, the whole scene would suggest the deepest rural peace.

Mrs Marple appeared. She was a massively ud-dered woman smothered in soap-suds; she waddled forward surrounded by a waddling entourage of her Khaki Campbells; of these some made gobbling noises while others hissed; Mrs Marple gave over shouting and fell to gobbling, too. It presently appeared that these new articulations were expressions of civility addressed to Mr Greengrave. Mrs Marple dried her soapy arms on her apron, scattered the curs with two well-directed kicks, delivered a number of threatening remarks in the direction of the now silent cottage, and led the way to what she evidently regarded as the scene of an important crime. Three nights before, the sleeping quarters of the Khakis had been broken into and two of the birds removed. "Felony!" said Mrs Marple with a dramatic gobble. "Felony stalking my own 'earth and 'ome. 'Itlerism in the midst."

Appleby surveyed the scene with no very lively interest. "Are you much troubled by tramps?" He asked.

Mrs Marple nodded. "Tramps and 'ikers," she said, "and low-clarse picnickers out of cars. Felons and fornicators, the lot of 'em—and you can take my word for it."

"You get a good deal of motor traffic this way?"

"Motor traffic!" Mrs Marple stared down the empty road that skirted her domain. "It's my opinion the King 'imself don't look out on more cars and sherry-bangs nor we do. Come back to the 'igh-road this way, they do, arfter turning orf to Abbots' Posset, the same being a beauty-spot with good 'igh teas. I done 'igh teas myself at one time, as parson 'ere knows. But I gave it over on account of the felony. For, believe it or not, while wife and young would be 'ogging it in my parlour at 'arf-a-crown cut and come again, the man would be out behind an 'edge, a-nicking of one of the fowls. Shameful, I calls it. As I said to young Timmins the constable, all I arsks for is the rule of law."

"Quite right, Mrs Marple. And it is the rule of law that I am here to assert." Appleby nodded as impressively as he could. "Now, did you see anything of the man who you suppose took the two Khaki Campbells?"

"See him! 'Asn't 'e been lurking in spinney there these three days past—and the smell of the creatures nicely broiled a-wafting over to my own 'ungry little ones?"

Mr Greengrave took off his straw hat and mopped his forehead. "Dear me," he said, "you told me nothing of this. And here have I been suspecting young Ted Morrow."

"Ted Morrow!" Mrs Marple's scorn was massive. "As if I wouldn't 'ave gone arfter Ted Morrow with a broom-stick. But I told young Timmins— confidential-like, as is proper when felons is to be dealt with. And wot did Timmins do? Did he go into that spinney and beard the ruffian in his lair? 'E did nothing but make pretense of writing in his note-book and took 'imself orf to 'is supper."

"That sounds very bad." And Appleby shook his head. "So a tramp has been lurking in that spinney and devouring your poultry? Just when did you see him last?"

"Only last night I seen 'im. And money 'e must 'ave 'ad, for 'e were as drunk as a Lord 'igh Chancellor and ready to drop into a ditch."

"He would be making his way from the road there to his encampment in the spinney? Then I think we will first find his hide-out and then cast around. And we mustn't interrupt your wash-day further. I think it unlikely that you will be troubled by this particular tramp again."

Mrs Marple, having offered some further observations on felony and the rule of law, retreated to her domestic occasions. Appleby and Mr Greengrave searched the spinney. There was no doubt that a tramp had been sleeping there. There was no doubt that he had regaled himself on Khaki Campbells; the creatures' feathers and carcasses were a conclusive testimony. Appleby searched the whole spinney with extraordinary care. Then he shook his head. "I think," he said, "we might take up the notion of his being drunk enough to fall insensible by the roadside or into a ditch. I dare say you know all the pubs round here?"

Mr Greengrave looked slightly taken aback. "I certainly know their location. But I fear that any more intimate knowledge—"

"Capital. The point is to find the fellow's route if he was returning here from one or another of them. We'll work on that."

For some fifteen minutes they cast about them and then their search was rewarded. In a dry ditch by the roadside, plainly evident in the long grass, was the impress of the body of a man. Appleby climbed down. "Not a doubt of it," he called back presently. "Here Mrs Marple's visitor lay. There's even another of those feathers."

Mr Greengrave peered down. "Dear me!" he said, "this is most dramatic. You don't by any chance see the other boot?"

"What I see is blood—quite a lot of it." Appleby hunted further. "And two distinct sets of footprints. And signs of one person being hauled out as a dead weight and with his heels trailing." He climbed back to the roadside. "Well, we'll find nothing further. And it does fit another expected piece of the puzzle into place. Let's get back to the car."

Mr Greengrave stepped back upon the road. "Am I right in thinking that this wretched man is now probably dead?"

"I am afraid there is almost no question of it."

"Yet another addition to the holocaust!" Mr Greengrave moved irresolutely forward. "And the body has been carried off?"

"Precisely so. The body has been carried off for a purpose which has probably become fairly clear to you."

"I see." Mr Greengrave, having advanced a few paces by Appleby's side, now halted again and stared before him in some perplexity. "I think I see. Only—" He hesitated. "Well, I almost hate to point it out. But in fact the body has not been carried off. I am looking at it now."

Appleby glanced ahead. In a corner of the same ditch, a few yards before them, lay the body of a man. It was clothed in rags and sprawled with its feet cocked in air. One foot was shod in a battered boot. The other was naked.

17

Mr Greengrave continued to be embarrassed. "I hope," he said, "that this does not—well, upset your view of the case?"

"It has its disconcerting side." Appleby gazed down at the body. "At least it should teach me to eschew prophecy. We were going to detect the signs of a struggle, and nothing else. I think that was it?"

"I certainly have the impression that you said something of the sort. But, of course, in so complex an affair it is understandable—"

"Help me haul him out."

They heaved up the body. The tramp was a miserable wisp of humanity. A diet of Khaki Campbells could have come his way but seldom. The ignoble discretion shown by Constable Timmins had surely been wholly unnecessary. Mr Greengrave gently closed the eyes. "I suppose," he ventured, "it could not be a matter of natural death? He scarcely looks as though he could have had much life in him, poor fellow."

"What life there was has been knocked out of him by a blow on the back of the head." Appleby was carefully examining the body. "I see!" he said suddenly. "Do you know, this criminal of ours is an uncommonly observant fellow, as well as an uncommonly able one? Look at the right hand."

Mr Greengrave looked. "Two fingers missing."

Appleby nodded grimly. "This particular body proved not up to standard. Its remains even when incinerated could not without slight risk be passed off as someone else's—the missing joints might be noticed. So it has been—well, say returned to stock."

"Good heavens!" Mr Greengrave was appalled. "Surely that does not mean that another—"

"I am afraid it does. And we may notice that there is also at work a queer instinct of tidiness. This body has been to Sherris, as the boot witnesses. It must have been there that the missing fingers were noticed and that it was consequently turned down as not good enough. It was, of course, desirable to remove it, so that it might have no appearance of connection with the Dromio affair. But why return it just here? The neurotic's exaggerated sense of orderliness is the answer. Our criminal is of the rather over-anxious type."

"Our criminal is an abominable maniac!"

"Abominable—yes. But whether he is a maniac remains to be seen. I think we'll simply put the body in the back of the car and drive back to Sherris. It's a little irregular, but time is getting on. I doubt whether the last act in the affair is timed for much after noon. I must be getting off to town."

"To town!" Mr Greengrave was quite dismayed. "I hope you have no engagement which prevents your following out these horrors to the end? Inspector Hyland is a most efficient officer, I do not doubt. But I am quite sure the only chance—"

"Will you take him under the arms? That's right. And what you were going to say is probably true. Through what was not much more than a freak of association the solution does seem to have come my way. And it may be doubted whether it would now come to anybody else.... Just let him slump down on the seat. As for my run up to town, I hope I may be back again this evening."

"With some conclusive piece of evidence?"

Appleby settled himself behind the wheel. "I have very considerable hope of it. The weather has been fine for some weeks and there should be very few common colds about."

Mr Greengrave stared blankly at Appleby. "I hardly see—"

"But it's not a question of seeing. It's a question of smelling."

Mr Greengrave sighed. "At this stage, at least, it can hardly be a matter of smelling a rat."

"A rat? Dear me, no. Say rather a hyena or a tiger."

At least, the Bentley had returned. And one of the fire-engines had departed—as had the ambulance with the dead or dying Sebastian Dromio. The ladies, too, had gone, and the huddle of helpless servants. But Hyland still sat at his little table, his constables coming and going about him. He had been provided with a telephone, and he was talking into

248

this as Appleby approached. Behind him the ruins of the great house sullenly smoked, and acrid smells mingled with the dank stench of the emptied lily pond. Firemen continued to play hoses here and there, and near the centre of the main building a group of men were working round a small crane.

Hyland put down his telephone and raised a weary head. "And how," he asked, "was the wild-goose chase after Mrs Marple's ducks?"

"Quite a successful bag." Appleby sat down. "In fact, we've brought you another body."

Hyland groaned. Then he looked hopeful. "Geoffrey Gollifer's?" he asked.

"Dear me, no. You must surely have caught Geoffrey Gollifer by this time, even if the mad baronet still eludes you."

"We have *not* caught him. It's the most damnable mess. The Chief Constable has been very decent, but I can see he's upset. I'm afraid he thinks Lord Linger may be annoyed."

"Bother Lord Linger."

"I'm afraid he thinks Lord Linger may think Mr Bottle may think it a reflection on the county as a whole." And Hyland shook his head, as if the whole weight of the English social structure were pressing on his shoulders. "But what's this body you were talking about?"

"Just a tramp's. The body of a murdered tramp. He was wearing one boot. And the other boot was found by one of your men here in a ditch."

"Then I suppose we must somehow fit him in. Probably he was snooping about, poor devil, and saw too much. So the criminal killed him, carried off the body, and dumped it—"

"Nothing like that, Hyland—nothing like that at all. He was killed over at Mrs Marple's, and brought here presumably in a car. The criminal was going to pass off his body as another's, and began to remove articles of clothing which might resist a fire. He got off one boot. Then he noticed something that made the body unsuitable for his purpose. Whereupon— either immediately or somewhat later—he took the body away again and dumped it where he found it."

"Well I'm blessed!" Hyland took refuge in naive astonishment. "It must be admitted we're up against somebody uncommonly active."

"Quite so. Ceaseless activity—that's the key to the whole thing. While you and I were sitting in there" —and Appleby waved his hand in the direction of Sir Oliver Dromio's vanished study—"while you and I were chewing over what we took to be a settled and accomplished crime, there was really a continuing process all around us. A complicated imposture was building itself up step by step. It's still doing so."

Hyland groaned. "It's a sort of nightmare. They talk of unravelling a crime. Well, here's somebody ravelling at one end far faster than we can unravel at the other. One gets the feeling that the affair may go on complicating itself indefinitely."

"Not a bit of it. The complications will stop as soon as they have gained their object. And already there are a good many questions to which we can give the answer. Who first killed whom?"

"Cain first killed Abel." Hyland roused himself to a flicker of sarcasm.

"Whose was the body you and I first saw in the study? Was it the same body that Dr Hubbard and the others saw there later? Is it the same body that is there now? Who provided us with that spectacle of satanic laughter at the crisis of the fire? What is the next spectacle proposed? Who is going to die next?"

"To die next!" Hyland rose up in consternation. "If the Chief Constable has to tell Lord Linger that he must admit to Mr Bottle that—"

"Bother Mr Bottle. But how many Dromio brothers were alive a month ago? How many were alive yesterday morning? How many are alive now? In that group of questions there still is an element of doubt, I must admit. However, I'm going up to town."

"Splendid!" An even heavier irony was now Hyland's sole resource. "And if we want to ask you anything more we'll address you care of the Brains Trust, no doubt. How many Dromio brothers will be alive next Saturday? It all depends on what you mean by Saturday, doesn't it?" Hyland threw up his hands. "Heaven preserve me from another case of homicide in this county!"

"Not at all. A beautiful murder."

"Really, my dear Appleby." Hyland switched deftly to moral indignation. "How you can allow yourself such levity with all those poor women—"

"Then I think I'll be off. Will your motorised bloodhounds have left any petrol in the Bentley? By the way, I'll give them a tip."

"A tip?"

"Yes. Let them look out for fire down below. Let them not bother with fire on the level or fire up above—not even if the whole countryside is blazing. Let them keep their noses to the ground until they find fire down below. Good-bye."

"If you really must—" Hyland stopped abruptly. "Hullo," he said, "what's that?"

A shout had been raised by the group of men working by the crane. Appleby looked across at them sharply. "Have they got at your bodies?" he asked.

Hyland shook his head. "I don't think so. They've had to give over that for a bit. Still too hot. But of course the site of the study is under observation all the time. No more possible substitutions now."

A constable came hurrying up. "They believe they've got down to it, sir."

"Got down to it! Got down to what, man?"

"The butler's room, sir. It's a bit cooler there, and they're through the charred beams to the joists and the ceiling."

"I'd clean forgotten him." Hyland turned to Appleby. "One more body, heaven help us. You'd better have a look before you go."

"Very well." And Appleby moved towards the house. "Perhaps you'd better have that dentist."

"Dentist? Oh, I see. As a matter of fact Sir Oliver's dentist is on his way here now. But I don't see what he has to do with Swindle."

"But we're not going to find Swindle—or not for certain. We're going to find a charred body in Swindle's room—just as presently you are going to find two more charred bodies in Sir Oliver's study. So it won't do to take anything for granted. Sir Oliver's dentist should be let loose on the body in Swindle's room too—if there is a body, that is to say."

"If there is a body!" Hyland was taken aback.

"Surely you haven't any reason to suppose that Swindle escaped?"

Appleby shook his head. "I'm not suggesting that he's alive. But since Sherris has seen a veritable corpses' ballet in the last twelve hours it seems almost unreasonable to expect any one body to be in its right place. Didn't I assure the vicar there would be no body at Mrs Marple's? And wasn't there?"

For the first time for a good many hours Hyland laughed. "I wish I'd been there when you were confounded in the matter. By way, you know, of learning how to carry such a situation off. But here we are. And if there's a body we shall certainly bring in the dentist. And if there isn't—well, we'll hunt for the old man elsewhere. But all the evidence suggests that he was trapped here in his room. . . . How is it going there?"

A grimy fireman paused in heaving back a blackened beam. "Just coming on it, sir. Fire swept right over these basement rooms and must have made a pretty oven of them. Some nasty gasses there now, I should say. But there would have been air of sorts for a longish time. It was slow roasting for the poor old chap if he was down there. Run round trapped and - frantic, he would, until his toes began to go."

Mr Greengrave, who had come up in time to hear this unpleasant reconstruction of Swindle's end, exclaimed in horror. "And yet," he said, "this crime would appear to have qualities of imagination. It is hard to conceive of any but the most brutalised mind contriving such abominations."

Appleby nodded. "It certainly is a grim business enough. But at least we don't know that anyone actually designed Swindle's slow roasting. . . . They've got through the ceiling. Look out!"

With dramatic suddenness a confused structure of charred wood and broken plaster had given way at their feet, and from below a blast of hot air blew over them. The fireman plied an axe and the aperture widened. Bright sunlight from above penetrated the slowly settling dust and they found that they were indeed peering down and into what had been Swindle's sanctum. It was curiously intact, like some unrifled, immemorial tomb—and, as with such a tomb, everything in it seemed ready to shrivel to a brown dust. The heat was still unbearable. On a shelf above the fireplace a row of pewter jugs had melted and spread themselves in a mess of fused metal on the floor. The curtains and carpet were seared and blackened rags. But on an intact chair in the middle of the room, and directly facing them as they gazed down, was slumped the figure of a man. A small table stood beside him, and on the table lay the remains of a decanter, split and fragmented by the heat. The man's fingers had closed round the stem of a wine-glass—and the bowl of this too the heat had destroyed. His eyes were closed.

"Well, I'm blessed!" Hyland's voice was at once horrified and relieved. "He's perfectly recognisable, praise be. It's the butler's body, all right." And Hyland turned to Appleby with no more than decently restrained glee. "So there is a corpse—just as there was at Mrs Marple's. And we don't need the dentist."

"I rather think we need the doctor. Look at him."

The figure in the chair had moved oddly—and as they gazed he lifted the stem of the wine-glass to his lips, attempted to drink from the vanished bowl, opened one sleepy and indignant eye.... "Urrr!" Swindle said. "*Urrr!*"

The fireman gave an incredulous gasp. "Gawd!" he whispered, "—if the old barstard isn't alive. It oughtn't to be possible—not even if he had an outsize in asbestos suits."

Mr Greengrave murmured what was presumably a pious ejaculation. Then he shook his head. "Alive? The place must have been as a fiery furnace. It would appear to be almost—"

"Alive?" Hyland was blankly incredulous. "The thing's impossible. It's just some queer trick of the muscles."

"He's alive, all right," said Appleby. "Miss Dromio got it quite wrong. Far from having a dangerously low flash-point and being ripe for spontaneous combustion, he was such a withered and leathery old person as to have virtually the immunities of a salamander. I suppose we ought to rejoice."

"Of course, we ought to rejoice," said Mr Greengrave. "Whatever the moral shortcomings of this old man, and indeed all the more if sin lies heavy upon him—"

"I don't mean quite that." And Appleby shook his head. "But if Swindle is alive—well, I think it means that Geoffrey Gollifer is dead. Of course, it is possible that we ought to rejoice over that too."

"Geoffrey Gollifer dead!" Mr Greengrave was bewildered. "But what possible connection—"

"It's rubbish!" Hyland's voice rose in exasperation. "Some mere hallucination. Look, he's quite still again."

But, even as he spoke, Swindle rose to his feet and spoke. "Robert!" he croaked. "Robert...." He hunched his shoulders in what appeared to be a shivering-fit. "Drat the good-for-nothink rascal. He's done it again." And Swindle shuffled towards a non-existent door. "Let my fire out...."

18

It was seven o'clock by the time that Appleby got back from town. The Bentley's bright yellow was dulled beneath a film of dust. Appleby felt that his mind was in much the same case. What chiefly occupied it was the fact that he had not shaved that day. This trivial if displeasing fact kept pushing the Dromios and their queer affairs out of consciousness. He was very tired.

The drive forked, and only just in time did he remember to swing the wheel so as to avoid the track that had led him earlier that day—for such, oddly, was the actual chronology of this interminable-seeming affair—to the slumbering Grubb and his luckless decanter. Appleby gave the accelerator a final thrust, swept rather too quickly round a curve and had the house before him.

The ruins of the house. It stood gaunt and roofless against the clear evening sky, and might to all appearance have been standing so for years. Almost one might have imagined wildflowers and grasses growing high up in the crevassed stone. During the fire the place had seemed alive with dogs; now the dogs were gone and there were cats instead—innumerable cats prowling with the automatism of displaced persons returned from desolation to desolation. At first no human being could be seen. The wide trampled lawn was untenanted. Hyland's little table was gone and in its place—product of some desperate act of salvage—stood a grand piano, a 'cello and an unstrung harp. This mute concert gave a touch of lunacy to the scene. It was as if the President of the Immortals had turned surrealist and was rummaging in His own subconscious Mind. . . .

Appleby climbed down from the car, and as he did so became aware of Hyland's Sergeant Morris broodingly on guard over the rubble. He had allowed himself a pipe, and the smoke from this rose straight in air like a tiny memorial of the morning's inferno among those blackened walls. Seeing Appleby he stuffed the pipe away and came forward. He saluted —with a sinister deference, Appleby suddenly thought.

"Good evening, sir. Glad to see you back again. And very glad that this is all over."

Appleby took out his handkerchief and wearily endeavoured to rub the sensation of dust from his stubble-covered face. "Good evening, sergeant. So it's over, is it?"

"Yes, sir. But very perplexing it was for a while."

"Ah. Well, I'm sorry I wasn't in at the death . . . I suppose there was another death?"

"Well, yes, sir—there was. Very shocking death-roll the crime has brought about. Not that the butler wasn't lucky. Although they do say his mind is gone. The heat sort of seethed it, I dare say."

"I dare say it did. Well, it's nice to know that others have remained clear-headed. And so there was another death? Well, well."

"The Inspector, sir, has gone over to dine at the vicarage. And Mr Greengrave asked me to say he would be very glad if you could join them."

Appleby looked at his watch. "I'll go over straight away . . . Hullo, who's that?"

Another figure had appeared, striding with a gloomy purposefulness among the ruins, and occasionally turning to stare resentfully towards the west.

"Press photographer, sir. No harm in it, I understand—not now that the story has broken, as you might say."

"I see. Well, I think I'll have a word with him."

The man looked up as Appleby approached. "Evening," he said perfunctorily. He was about to turn away, but paused. "You work here?" he asked with sudden interest. "Know the family?"

Appleby looked down at his crumpled clothes and felt his prickly jaw. He remembered Swindle's favourite ejaculation. "Urrr," he said firmly.

"Out-door servant?"

"Urrr."

The press-photographer glanced cautiously across at Sergeant Morris, put his hand in his trousers-pocket and contrived a loud chinking noise. "Tell me anything interesting about the family?" he asked. "Worth ten bob if it's something not generally known."

"Urrr," said Appleby—this time on an irresolute note.

259

"About the girl was mixed up in it—she's the interesting angle. Bit of allright, eeh? Had a lover, would you say?"

"Urr." The sound had the quality of a regretful and slightly salacious negative.

The press-photographer looked disappointed. "Probably you know more about the servants. Now, what about this fellow Grubb?"

Appleby considered. "Old Grubb," he said.

"Yes, that's right. What sort of a fellow was he?"

"Old Grubb."

The press-photographer swore in sudden exasperation. "Come down here for damn-all," he said. "That's about it—damn-all."

"What do you mean—damn-all?" Sergeant Morris had come up and was highly indignant. "You've photographed the scene of the crime, haven't you?"

The man swore more vigorously. "Photographed it? Just look at the sun! Couldn't have got itself into a more idiotic place." He made an extremely hostile gesture at the luminary. "And do you know I found a top-hole place not fifteen miles out of town?"

"Top-hole place for what?"

"For a scene of the crime, of course! A thoroughly sinister old house, beautifully blitzed and in a lovely light. I called up the paper at once. But news-editors have no imagination these days. They insisted on my coming right down here, all the same. And all I find is a ghastly western glare and an idiot yokel."

"If you call me an idiot yokel, young man, I'll run you in for insulting the police. I'm on duty here, I'll have you remember, and bad language to such a one is something our magistrates won't a-hear of."

"Good heavens, man, this is the yokel—not you."

And the press-photographer jerked an irritated finger at Appleby.

"And bad language to the gentry ain't no better. Now, just you clear out."

"I certainly will clear out. And blast your rotten crime."

"Don't you dare to call it a rotten crime." Sergeant Morris was suddenly very angry indeed. "It's a much better crime, young man, than you're ever likely to have your sticky nose in again."

"Do you hear that?" the man turned to Appleby. "Who's using insulting language now? And you're a witness to it—whoever you are. Good evening." And the man marched off.

But Appleby followed him. "This whole story is going to break?" he asked.

"It certainly is—right across the front page tomorrow morning."

"Sinister crime and swift, brilliant solution?"

"That sort of thing." The man was momentarily confidential. "Of course it's not a rotten crime. There's been nothing like it for years."

"That is certainly true."

"And our man has had the whole story from the big noise down here—fellow called Hyland."

"I see. Well, get your paper on the phone and tell them to hold their horses."

"What the deuce do you mean? And who do you think is going to attend to you? The story will hit the headlines all right, you may take it from me."

"Very well. But don't blame me if a number of you hit the pavement next day—that uncomfortably hard Fleet Street pavement, my dear man. Nothing worse for shoe-leather in the world."

"I think you're crazy. Who are you, anyway?"

"Appleby's my name."

"Appleby? Never heard of you." The press-photographer halted and stared. "Not John Appleby?"

"John Appleby."

"Heavens above!" The press-photographer looked first at his watch and then wildly round about him. "And I was going to give you ten bob for a good, dirty line on the affair."

"I believe there's a telephone at Hodsoll's farm. Good-night."

And Appleby climbed wearily into the Bentley. Seems like this depressed him very much. He let in the clutch, reflected, stopped again. "Morris," he called, "may I have a word with you?"

Sergeant Morris came to the side of the car. And again he saluted with that unnecessary deference—a well-satisfied, slightly smug, definitely irritating man. He knew all the answers. Indeed, he had discovered them himself. And now he was being polite to the old dug-out from Scotland Yard.

"Morris," said Appleby seriously, "you've seen your way far into this affair. Please remember that I think you did uncommonly well. Good-night."

"A safety-razor?" said Mr Greengrave. "Dear me, yes. If you will—"

Hyland appeared behind his host. He had changed his uniform and seemed to sparkle all over. "Hullo, Appleby," he called jovially, "—how are you? Our excellent friend the dentist—"

"What Appleby wants is a barber, my dear Inspector. And at least I can provide the implements, though not the man. Come upstairs. Perhaps you would care for a bath? There is ample hot water, I am glad to say—which is not always the way with us in summer. Hyland and I were about to sit down, but a bachelor meal can very well wait." Mr Greengrave was full of cheerful bustle. "Nothing but cold duck and a salad." He hesitated. "A Khaki Campbell, if the truth must be told. I hope it will not be felt to lend too macabre a touch to our meal. There are new blades in this little box. And this towel, I am thankful to find, is large, dry and warm. The fact is, I have an excellent housekeeper. Unfortunately I have discovered that she holds seances in her sitting-room. For a clergyman, it makes rather a delicate situation. I had meant to consult my friend Canon Newton on the matter last night, but it went quite out of my mind."

When Appleby came downstairs the two men were drinking sherry in the vicar's dining room. Hyland set down his glass. "Very odd," he said, "that guess of yours about fire down below. For as a matter of fact—"

"No, no—this will not do at all." Mr Greengrave urbanely interposed. "The Dromio affair has been very shocking—very shocking, indeed. It is no good concomitant of appetite. Pray, therefore, let us converse of indifferent matters as we dine. And afterwards we may talk it out. I would have you notice the little centre-piece with the roses. Connoisseurship in such matters far be it from me to claim. But I am told that it is by Claus of Innsbruck. The sea-horse is judged rather better than the Neptune."

And thus, as if he were veritably the golden-tongued Canon Newton himself, did Mr Greengrave conduct matters to the end of the meal. "And now," he said, "let us draw our chairs to the window, for the

evening is again mild. The Inspector, I believe"—
and he glanced with a faint irony from Hyland to
Appleby—"has a good deal to tell."

"Far from it." Hyland stuffed his pipe. "There is
really not a great deal to say. For, after all, we were
pretty far on the road to a solution of the matter before Appleby left us. But the queer way Sir Oliver
died in the end—well, it deserves rather more narrative skill than I can bring to it.

"We owe a great deal to Appleby." Hyland, as he
made this announcement to Mr Greengrave, nodded
his head emphatically, rather as if to give a courtesy
statement all the weight that could be contrived. "In
point of psychology, you know—the dead man's psy-
chological type."

Mr Greengrave passed a decanter of port. "You interest me," he said.

"This business of plunging down from a height into
a final sea of fire. He was compelled to do that. And
Appleby foretold it. Now, that is a remarkable
achievement—a very remarkable achievement, indeed." He paused. "Of course, a great deal of that
sort of thing is common knowledge nowadays."

"Ah," said Mr Greengrave.

"When Sir Oliver went mad certain of his dominant character-traits became massively emphasised.
One of these was ambition."

"Um," said Mr Greengrave.

Appleby poured himself port.

"The crime was ambitious—very ambitious." Hyland shook his head. "I was to be taken in."

Appleby set down the decanter and looked at his

colleague with a good deal of pleasure. "Yes," he said, "that is very true."

"In the cleverness it attempted it was a sort of megalomaniac crime, revealing Sir Oliver's desire to out-top his fellows. It revealed what you might call a wild criminal ambition. In other words he was a prey to those criminal types of ambition which cannot normally be admitted to consciousness. And what goes along with such repressed ambitions?" Hyland paused dramatically. "An obsession with, and dread of, heights. That dictated the nature of his final exhibitionistic act. That was why he made for the quarry."

"The quarry?" said Appleby. "Do you know, I thought it would be some sort of industrial plant—a blast-furnace, or something of that sort, not easy to come by in this part of the country. But a quarry was a simple solution enough."

"We don't yet know how many places he contrived to fire. But he appears to have moved in a circle, and this quarry where he was finally run to earth shortly after midday is not a dozen miles from here. It has been disused for a great many years—something like a great concave cliff of sheer stone, pointing due south. At this time of year it was a vast oven, with the base of it a jungle of parched bracken. He fired that.

"Always before this he had been off in the car he had, and so rapidly that there was no catching him. But this time he was caught—caught, I mean, by his own infernal imagination.

"I wasn't there—but I think I can pretty well see the scene. Here was his latest achievement in incendiarism—in pyromania—and above it towered this sheer face of stone. He skirted the quarry and

265

climbed to the top, so that he was looking down at this sea of fire of his own contriving. Fire down below."

Hyland paused to gulp port in a fashion that Canon Newton could not but have condemned. "And presently there was quite a crowd down below, too. For the blaze was a tremendous one, and by this time the whole countryside knew what was menacing them. He stood up there and danced, it seems, like a maniac, with the smoke beginning to rise round about him like an enveloping curtain. There was some difficulty in getting up after him—or it may have been that folk were simply a bit scared. But it was known that he was Sir Oliver Dromio, stark raving mad and with more than one murder on his hands, and some fellow who had a gun took a shot at him. Very irregular, of course, but I should be sorry to run him in, all the same. And that sent him madder than before. He danced, and he sang, and he laughed that laugh we all of us heard. The fire was terrific by this time; often he was invisible behind the smoke of it and he could have got away easily enough. But he didn't— and then it was all over in a flash. His last peal of laughter broke off in the middle, and a moment later his body was seen hurtling down the face of the cliff and into the fire. They fought the blaze for over two hours before they could get near him. He wasn't much more than bones—and most of them were broken. That was the end of Sir Oliver Dromio."

"Really Sir Oliver Dromio?" Mr Greengrave as he asked this question looked very acute.

"But of course!" Hyland was triumphant. "The moment that the body could be hauled out we had that dentist on the spot. And he made no bones about it.

The teeth were those of the man whom he had attended as Sir Oliver Dromio over a long period of years." Hyland turned to Appleby. "I hope you will admit the conclusive nature of such evidence?"

"Certainly. The body is undoubtedly Sir Oliver Dromio's. And now it only remains for you to sum up the whole story and show us how your explanation covers all the known facts. I think there was a time when you felt there were rather a lot of facts—far more than was comfortable, indeed."

"That's true enough. But it's wonderful how they all fit in. So let me begin at the beginning, and run through the whole affair as it has now discovered itself. A very nice port, if I may say so, sir." And Hyland reached for the decanter.

"The first fact is the controlling one. Sir Oliver Dromio was in a pretty tight place financially, and he had been making a desperate bid to extricate himself by marrying an American heiress. I think we must suppose that he had failed to bring this off."

Appleby set down this glass. "Isn't it a wee bit early for suppositions?" he asked. "The point, you know, is uncommonly important. For if he did have the heiress in the bag—"

"Quite so. The financial motive would vanish. But there is another which might be equally powerful. The man was a blackguard. He had been blackmailing Mrs Gollifer—and just how badly he had treated his foster-sister Lucy we don't know. Nothing is more likely than that such a bad hat was facing one or another major disaster. And it occurs to me that something of the sort may have got itself bound up with the matter of the American heiress. Suppose she had trustees or other advisors who succeeded in demanding an enquiry into Sir Oliver's financial position. And suppose that Sir Oliver, whether in conspiracy with Sebastian or otherwise, had been getting large sums of money in an improper way out of the firm. That would give us what we need—an absolute fix straight ahead of him.

"At this juncture he learnt about the existence of his brothers—and, of course, here would be the threat of further financial investigation. So he brings one of them over to England and then secretly down to Sherris, with his plan probably already forming in his mind. He will get out of his difficulties simply by vanishing—to the solace, no doubt, of some small reserve of capital which he has hidden away. But he will leave his own body behind him!

"So down these two come, and Swindle is instructed to make possible an unobtrusive entrance. Sir Oliver sees that his brother will pass very well for himself—at least for a time and in the first shock of a sensational discovery. So he kills him and changes clothes—and the effect, he sees, is excellent. And then to his horror he spots something he hadn't thought of. This long-lost brother of his, having been some sort of manual worker, has hands which nobody could mistake for those of Sir Oliver Dromio. He must find some resource, however desperate—so he lights the fire and thrusts the dead man's arms into the flames. But now there is another difficulty. Discovery must not be left too late or identification may be impossible. So he waits for what he judges to be the right moment and then attracts the attention of the household by hurling the tantalus with a crash across the room. And at that he makes his escape.

268

"His plan, however, is by no means completed, for he realises that there may still be risk of correct identification. So he collects petrol, waits his opportunity, and presently contrives to send the study—and indeed the whole house—up in flames. Now, what, we may ask ourselves, is the position at this point?

"It is really, when you come to think of it, a very pretty one. Sir Oliver Dromio is believed to have been murdered in his own study and subsequently to have been burnt to ashes. Investigation will quickly reveal him as having travelled here with an unknown man, and further investigation will almost certainly uncover the fact that this unknown man was his brother. Such a brother, newly apprised of the breeding and position of which he had been cheated, might well be a resentful and dangerous man, and there will be a strong case for supposing him the murderer. Even the fire will count here, for fire first deprived that brother of his just position, and with fire it might well have pleased him to crown his own deed. The hunt, then, will be for this brother as the murderer of Sir Oliver Dromio. But he will never be found. Because, of course, he is already dead, and it is his body that we have taken for Sir Oliver's. For Sir Oliver nobody is going to hunt, since we believe that we have nothing to do but make arrangements for his funeral."

Hyland paused for a moment, a frown of concentration on his face. Mr Greengrave leant forward. "Sir Oliver, then, in planning this diabolically clever crime, failed to think of the dentist?"

"Of course he did." Hyland was slightly impatient. "But now other events are transacting themselves in

269

such a way as enormously to increase the apparent complexity of our problem. Mrs Gollifer has confessed that she is Lucy Dromio's mother, and that she has been blackmailed by Sir Oliver. And Geoffrey Gollifer almost simultaneously discovers this and hurries to Sherris. Exactly what he witnesses we cannot, until we find him, tell. But he accepts what everybody is designed to accept—namely, that Sir Oliver Dromio has been murdered, and he knows that his mother, and perhaps Lucy whom he loves, had the strongest motives for some crime of passion against the supposed dead man. Hence the most disconcerting feature of the whole affair—Geoffrey Gollifer's attempt to shield them by taking the crime upon himself. Perhaps he meant to kill Sir Oliver, and feels that true justice requires him to accept responsibility for the actual killing. When he hears that it is not Sir Oliver who has been killed he simply loses his nerve and makes a bolt for it. . . . And now we come to the queerest fact of all. Sir Oliver heard too."

Mr Greengrave again leant forward. "Sir Oliver heard?" he asked.

"Well, I can't be quite sure. The certain fact is this —that Sir Oliver, hitherto contriving a brilliant if crazy crime of calculation, suddenly goes off his head. One gathers it is just what his father did. Of course, it may have been the mere uncontrollable excitement of the affair. But I fancy that he was still lurking near, and that he quickly learnt what had become common knowledge in the household— namely, our discovery that the body was not Sir Oliver's, and that some deception had been attempted. In fact, Sir Oliver's plan had failed, failure drove him crazy, he made his sensational appearance at the crisis of the fire, tore about the country firing things at random, and eventually made a spectacular end of it all in that quarry."

There was a short silence. Mr Greengrave turned to Appleby. "And what," he asked, "do you think of that?"

"It is very good—very good, indeed. Only it does leave one or two things out."

Hyland made an impatient gesture. "Of course it leaves things out. Grubb, for instance. But we know approximately where he came in, and precisely what prompted Sebastian Dromio to kill him."

Appleby shook his head. "I'm thinking of other things your narrative leaves out. Smaller things."

"Oh, certainly—to be sure." Hyland was relieved. "A good many details remain to be filled in."

Again Appleby shook his head. It might almost have been supposed that he was embarrassed. "That's not quite it," he said. "It's rather that your whole reconstruction needs dismantling and fresh disposition on a different basis. Some quite big things must be brought in—like the tramp. And some quite little ones—like Sir Oliver Dromio's fastidiousness in the matter of ties. . . . Still, you have got the case to one very definite point." Appleby paused. "But it's the point to which the criminal designed that you should get it."

19

Appleby paused for a moment to light his pipe. "It has to be admitted," he said, "that there are some pretty complicated passages in this Gollifer affair—"

Mr Greengrave leant forward. "Gollifer affair?" he asked.

"I think we give the matter its best emphasis by calling it that. It is on the Dromio side that much of the intricacy lies, but it was on the Gollifer side that the trigger, so to speak, was pulled. Weren't we talking about what, in the study of dreams, is called displacement? What is secondary in the dream makes up the greater part of it, and what is primary tends to be forced into some unobtrusive corner. Not that this case has been so difficult to disentangle as a dream may be. For here we had a straightforward chronology to help us. What was actually primary came first. A rose is a rose is a rose."

Hyland gave a sort of weary sigh. "For heaven's sake—" he began.

"It wasn't the study that saw the first big scene. It was the drawingroom. And what happened in the drawingroom led straight to matter so fraught with passion that it would clearly have been unwise to lose sight of it for a moment. I won't say that there weren't criminal acts anterior to, and independent of, that. One such act there certainly was, and I knew nothing of it until a few hours ago. Without it the crime would have been simpler, but there would still have been a crime. So the complex of issues touched upon in the drawingroom gives the core of the mystery. And so here is the first fact I can give you. No Dromio came to Sherris intending a crime last night.

"But somebody else came in a state of mind that might very well lead to crime. While Mrs Gollifer was revealing to Lucy that she was her mother, and that Sir Oliver Dromio had been blackmailing her, Geoffrey Gollifer was making the same discovery a few miles away. It was a shattering discovery. He was in love with Lucy, and now Lucy proved to be his half-sister. And of his knowledge of this latter fact Oliver had taken the most dastardly advantage, while at the same time he completely commanded Lucy's affections. Round this unfortunate young man everything had crashed at once: his mother's honor, the hope of gaining the girl he loved, his right to his own name and his own property. He armed himself and went straight to Sherris. Later he told us two stories. The first was plainly designed to protect his mother and his half-sister. The second was overwhelmingly probable. He had confronted the blackguard Oliver, he had been further provoked by intolerable language, he had killed him. That there were all sorts of difficulties in accepting this story, that there were almost fantastic complications seemingly impossible to relate to it, was no reason for turning it down. Our clear line was to organise everything round it.

"I got on the right lines, then, only when I made it a postulate that Geoffrey Gollifer had killed Oliver Dromio. Oliver Dromio—for the nature of the encounter was such that he could not have killed another Dromio in error. And now I could bring up the difficulties as they arose.

"The killing had been on the terrace but the body was found in the study. Somebody, therefore, upon discovering the body had acted in a very abnormal manner. Who was this somebody? Almost certainly one of the long-lost brothers. Somebody had been seen by Sebastian with Oliver earlier in the day, and later Mr Greengrave had seen something like two Olivers driving down to Sherris. It was reasonable to suppose that Oliver, having found his brothers, had brought one of them home with him, after arranging with Swindle for an unobtrusive manner of doing so. There was, of course, something odd about this secrecy. It had to be borne in mind.

"We might presume that it was the two brothers whom the footman heard talking. What happened then? Geoffrey Gollifer arrived, summoned Oliver out to the terrace, killed him, and fled. When Oliver failed to return to the room his brother would go out and find the body. And so the brother was responsible for what followed. He brought the body into the room, lit the fire and cast the body upon it so as to destroy the hands and arms. He waited for a time and then threw the tantalus, thereby summoning the household. And then he bolted. His motive for those queer proceedings was our first big problem.

"And the second big problem was the discrepant identifications of the body. We cannot express this better than by saying that it was Oliver's body and yet it wasn't! On the whole, those who denied it to be so were the better accredited witnesses. And yet it was—for that was our postulate.

"Something had happened to Oliver to make him not Oliver. It was very baffling. And for a long time I was haunted by the impression of something significant I had missed. It came back to me eventually through rather a curious association of ideas. I kept on remembering something I had seen at one particular crisis of the night's affairs. And what I eventually arrived at, with assistance that I need not detail, was the word *buttocks*. When examining the body the police-surgeon had said that it was "odd about the buttocks." And when I was able to question him again he confirmed the explanation that I had suspected. The body suggested that of a patient immobilised in bed for a considerable period of time.

"This hitched up with other facts, notably the abrupt ceasing of correspondence from Oliver while in America apart from a single request for a considerable sum or money. Had he been ill? Had he been involved in an accident? It was at this point that my mind did its one decent job of work on the affair."

There was a moment's silence in Mr Greengrave's dining room. It was punctuated by Hyland's again uttering a softly despairing noise. "Go on," he said.

"For heaven's sake, go on."

"It occurred to me that the telegram to Swindle arranging that unobtrusive return might have been sent not, so to speak, in the interest of a diffident newly discovered brother, but in the interest of Oliver himself. And with this I connected a fact of character. Oliver, it appeared, was vain. That is where his niceness in the choice of ties come in."

Mr Greengrave drained his last drop of port. "Dear me," he said. "Oh, dear me!"

"And then I saw the whole truth—or the whole truth of this particular part of the case. There had been an accident, and its physical result was such that Oliver was discomfited as to his appearance— his changed appearance. He was shy of facing those who knew him.

"And yet by the police-surgeon, as by those who had made the first identification, nothing had been remarked! What was the inference? That the accident had not been very serious, and that there had been skilful plastic surgery. It was for that that the large sum of money had been required. And so I came to the arms."

Hyland brightened. "Well I'm blessed! Was it—" He sank again into gloom. "No, I can't see it. I can't see a thing."

"It was not simply that the arms, or an arm, had been damaged in that accident in America. It was rather that an arm had subsequently been used in a particular way. I expect you know something about the technique of skin-grafts. Living tissue is required. And it can be got by bringing an arm up to the face and using a flap of skin still growing from the arm. In favorable circumstances the resulting facial repair, although changing the appearance, can be almost imperceptible, but on the arm itself a scar is left. Now, we had various theories of the fire's being lit and the arms consumed—for instance, that it was to destroy the possibility of taking finger-prints, or to destroy work-coarsened hands, or to make some sort of symbolic statement harking back to the fire at Sherris long ago. But the true explanation was this: what was being destroyed was evidence likely to draw attention to the fact that plastic surgery had been at work. In other words, when Oliver's brother found Oliver's body on the terrace he so acted as to destroy the evidence of plastic surgery. He wanted the body to pass as not Oliver's. Inevitably it would be taken for Oliver's at first, but then the changed features would be remarked and the conclusion would be that here was the body of a brother.

"Here, then, was something we were going to be invited to believe: that Sir Oliver Dromio had killed his new-found brother and fled. But why, in that case, not change the clothes? Conceivable a mere time-element had been at work. But more probably the reason was a subtle one. We were being invited to see Sir Oliver as acting with great ingenuity; as killing his brother and doing everything to suggest that the body was his own. We were to believe that Oliver had put the body into his own clothes and had then bolted. In fact, we were to believe Hyland's story: that Oliver, anxious to get clean away to a new life, had killed a brother and endeavoured to pass off the body as his own."

"Amazing!" said Mr Greengrave.

"It may be so. But what to my mind is really amazing is the fact that all this—and what followed—was pure improvisation. The brother had not himself killed Oliver. He was simply exploiting the fact of finding him suddenly murdered.

"But to what end was this intricate deception contrived? How was the brother to benefit? My first thought was simply this: that with Oliver mysteriously murdered there on the terrace he himself was in a tight spot, and that the best way out of this was to suggest that he had been killed and Oliver was fled. But as the brother in all probability closely resembled Oliver there would be only a very tenuous security in this. We should look for a Dromio, and we might find him. It was possible that further events, rightly analysed, might reveal a more intricate design. And, of course, it had to be borne in mind that the number of the Dromio brothers was three, not two. The third brother might somehow come in.

"We now pass to the point at which it appears to be discovered that the body is not Oliver's. There follows a period at which the body is not guarded, *Sergeant Morris having been called into the library*. And upon that there follows the fire.

"A stranger contrived the fire—one to whom the easiest way of getting petrol to the study was unknown. The fire, too, then, was almost certainly the brother's doing. It destroyed—or appeared to destroy—the body hard upon the decision that it was not Oliver's. But it was Oliver's—in the first instance, that is to say—and, when the fire was over, dental evidence would eventually have proved it so. Hence the necessity of a substitution before the fire. The brother had marked down the tramp. He went back to him, killed him, brought the body to Sherris.

278

And then it turned out that the tramp wouldn't do. He had fingers missing. The whole scheme was in peril. It was at this moment that he met Geoffrey Gollifer, bolting from our interview with him in the drawingroom. He leapt on him at once and killed him with a smashing blow on the back of the head. Oddly enough, it was a sort of wild justice, for it was the murderer who was killed."

Mr Greengrave put his head between his hands. "My brain reels," he said.

"He substituted Geoffrey Gollifer's body for Oliver's and fired the place. He bundled Oliver's into the car, and the tramp's too. He drove off to some hiding place nearby. Later he appeared at the crisis of the fire, behaved like a madman, and made off after giving Oliver's characteristic wave—something he had noted, maybe, when the two sailed from America together. His plan was now half-way through."

"Half-way!" Hyland was staring at Appleby, as inert as a sack.

"Just about that. And we still don't know what he is really up to."

Appleby paused to take breath. His power of exposition, he was thinking, was not what it had been. Still, he was getting through with it.

"The brother drives away with his two bodies and dumps the tramp's where he found it. He has no further use for it. But Oliver's body is vital. He has to give the impression that Oliver has committed a crime of calculation, has gone mad—and finally that he commits suicide. One fact greatly complicates his task. Oliver's body has its head smashed in and its arms burnt. It is necessary, therefore, that the apparent suicide should involve both a general smashing of bones and a complete incineration. The latter, of course, is nicely in the picture, for the mad and pyromaniac Oliver may be expected to make an end to himself this way. So he needs a height and he needs a blaze."

Hyland nodded sombrely. "Fire down below."

"Precisely. And the quarry gives it to him. He has his car and the body cached near the top; he sets the gorse ablaze; he appears and yells and prances like a madman. Then when the smoke grows thick he pitches the body down into the fire and makes his final bolt. When the body is recovered the teeth will be Oliver's—just as when the body at Sherris is recovered the teeth will not be Oliver's. He has finished his crime, and now all he has to do is to get back to America as fast as he can. Perhaps it will please him to reflect that he has carried off one of the most brilliant impostures in criminal history—and all on the spur of the moment."

Mr Greengrave looked up. "But he hasn't," he said. "You've detected him."

"I've caught him, too. He's in gaol now. They got him when he applied for a place on a plane. Didn't I say it was lucky there would be few colds in the head? You can't play with fire through a night and a day and not smell of smoke."

Hyland nodded; he was a little recovering from stupor. "But what was it all about?" he asked. "Did your information from America tell you?"

"Eked out with a little inference it told a good deal —and enough to persuade the criminal to confess. When he sees that he is really caught—as this fellow does—a man who has nearly brought off a brilliant crime generally will confess. He naturally likes you to know how smart he's been. What the American police got hold of in quick time was the plastic surgeon. And that, of course, substantiates the general lie of the affair.

"There is a number of subsidiary matters which I needn't rehearse. We have seen why Sebastian Dromio killed Grubb; it was a complication as irrelevant to the main story as is the fantasy of the incombustible Swindle. But now for the criminal's motive. It goes back to another crime—one which occurred in America some months ago.

"Oliver, it seems, did contact his brothers some time before his accident. Their names were Jaques and Orlando, and they were both struggling professional men. Just why Oliver did act on his mother's information and seek them out I don't know. But it seems clear that when he had done so he was rather inclined to amuse himself with the situation. By promising them first this and then that he contrived to set them at loggerheads. While Oliver was actually in hospital after his accident the brothers went on a fishing holiday together to talk the matter over. One day, when they were out in a boat on a lonely lake, they quarrelled. Orlando, who is a thoroughly criminal type, hit Jaques over the head with a boat-hook and killed him outright. It was a nasty situation and he made the best of it by binding the body to the anchor and dropping it in deep water. He then returned to the shore and said that his brother had got out on the other side and was walking over a range to the next valley. Later he told a similar yarn to Oliver, with whatever additions might make it more plausible. And hard upon that, and as soon as Oliver was out of hospital, he travelled with him to England. With some notion of accounting for Jaques' disappearance, and without Oliver's noticing the fact, he travelled on Jaques' passport.

"So you see that this long-lost Orlando was in a fix. He had murdered Jaques, and quite soon there would be enquiry and a lot of trouble. That was the situation when Oliver and Orlando came down here —secretly because of Oliver's shyness about his subtly changed appearance. That was the situation when Orlando stepped out on the terrace and found Oliver dead and murdered at his feet.

"It was an appalling situation. He was likely to be convicted of killing both his brothers—justly in the one case and unjustly in the other.

"I must say that each time I come back to the way he handled the matter I am compelled, in a fashion, to admire him the more. For what he instantly saw was not merely a way out of deadly peril; it was also a way into an inheritance. He would give the impression that Oliver had killed that brother who would be judged on the evidence of the immigration authorities to have travelled home with him—Jaques, to wit—and that then Oliver had committed suicide. He would then hurry back to America, resume his normal life as after a holiday, receive the news that Oliver had killed Jaques and then committed suicide, and be able as a result to claim the whole Dromio inheritance. I remember that when I worked out these comings and goings with rosebuds by a fountain's edge at Sherris this morning I added one for the heiress whom Oliver was pursuing. I have a notion that Orlando, having become a baronet, hoped to nobble her too. And I doubt whether he knew how financially embarrassed the Dromio affairs were."

There was a long silence. Then Mr Greengrave nodded. "I see," he said. "At least I think I see."

"It is certainly a very odd case. And Orlando Dromio exploited every factor in it with lightning speed to his own advantage. In another walk of life he would have made a great general. As it is, he will hang."

Hyland suddenly sat up, a man revived. His black braid glistened, his silver buttons shone. For the last word, after all, was to be his. "No," he said. "It will be the electric chair."

And Mr Greengrave rose. "It is very horrible—very horrible and very sad. With the unfortunate women who are left stricken by the calamity there will be work for which I must brace myself indeed. But now"—and he glanced at the empty decanter—"and although Appleby knows that my head is not to be trusted, I think another bottle of port would be not altogether out of the way. I am only sorry that I cannot offer you such a vintage as my friend Canon Newton might do."

Appleby looked at his watch. "Certainly the night is still young. It was a good deal less than twenty-four hours ago that Hyland and I first heard of all this."

Mr Greengrave nodded. "Do you know, I am constrained to think of our family's namesakes in Shakespeare's play? To the first appearance of those earlier Dromios there was sometimes given the title *The Night of Errors*. I think we may say that we have been through just that."